Praise for Michael Brigati's
FIRE THIEVES

"Started reading this last night and just finished via an airport stay and trip to teach in Wisconsin. Outstanding story, an easy read—the intricacies of firefighting are accessible, and those who follow the exploits of America's heroes will surely enjoy racing through the pages. It is accurate, exciting, current, and a real joy to read."

—Greg McCarraher,
Battalion Chief and paramedic,
Operations Deputy, St. Bernards Parish, LA,
(Hurricane Katrina),
National Fire Service instructor.

"If you enjoy mysteries, **Fire Thieves** serves up a cleverly constructed tale which is difficult to put down. Brigati has skillfully fused fire incidents and corruption in small town America with a healthy, and all too believable, dose of tension that seems hell-bent on exploding on the world stage. The result is a story full of twists and turns that leaves the reader guessing until the very last page."

—Mark R. Nugent,
Chief of Emergency Services,
Middlesex, Virginia,
National Fire Service spe

D1367660

"With the current tension in the Middle East, this novel shows how a catastrophic result could occur from what seems an accident in small town America. A great read for the brothers and sisters of the Fire Service and for everyone who follows the courageous men and women in this proud profession."

—**Paul Mauger,**
Chief (ret.) Chesterfield County Fire & EMS Dept.,
Adjunct instructor, Virginia Dept. of Fire Services,
Senior consultant, Prince George County, VA,
Fire & EMS Dept.

FIRE THIEVES

Michael Brigati

Trufflehouse Books

San Francisco

ISBN 978-1517573140

Copyright © 2015 by MICHAEL BRIGATI

Book & cover design by J.A. SKUTELSKY

www. firethieves.com

Fire Departments, Organizations, Foundations,
for information about special discounts for bulk purchases in fundraising efforts, please contact:
Blue Water Associates
P.O. Box 374
Chesterfield, VA23832

For 'Shooter' and 'Pickle,' my children, whose unconditional love sustains me and lives forever in my heart of hearts.

FOREWORD

I was honored when asked to write the Foreword to *Fire Thieves*, an accomplished suspense novel that immerses the reader in the harrowing world of firefighting and rescue. Retired Senior Fire Captain Michael Brigati brings to this story more than three decades as a firefighter, paramedic, and rescue diver. His knowledge and experience imbue the work with authentic and riveting detail, from political shenanigans that include cover-ups and corruption, to high-stakes personal, national, and global conflict. You'll practically smell smoke, feel the heat, and lose yourself on the fire line in Chatteron County, Virginia, the fictitious setting of this book. Insider jargon, commonly used by firefighters everywhere, combined with recognized procedures on the fire ground, provides a backdrop that resonates with authenticity. These elements, skillfully offset against tense national news events that besiege us daily, culminate in an explosive work of fiction that seems all too possible. It's a tough book to put down, with twists and turns that you won't see coming.

Borrowing a phrase firefighters use to describe a fire of consequence and intensity, *Fire Thieves* is a true 'worker' in every sense of the word. I am proud to offer my congratulations to Captain Brigati on a job well done.

Dennis L. Rubin
*Fire Chief, Consultant,
Writer and Teacher*

Prologue
Basra, Iraq

Kazem Al-Unistan chased a bead of sweat from temple to jaw with an agitated index finger. A fly buzzed past his ear. He watched it collide with the windshield and dance against the glass as the morning heat turned his faded sky-blue Mercedes into an oven.

Parked in the alleyway off Corniche al Basra Street, he adjusted his red keffiya, cocking it to one side of his head, and cracked the window. Briefly, the scent of turmeric teased his nostrils before the metallic smell of engine grease masked it. The sun struck the steel girders above the air-conditioned kiosks that were teeming with bargain hunters. Streets bustled with early morning traffic; horns honked.

Kazem's shoulders sagged. He tilted his head back, momentarily distracted. He missed the old port city of Basra, the carts filled with melons and figs, adorned with striped canvas awnings. The fragrances of sumac and sweet nutmeg once drifted on the air; now the stink of gasoline overwhelmed the more delicate spices. He grunted. Nostalgia made him soft. He relit the stub of a cigarette he had stabbed out earlier.

Sunlight slanted between the buildings, hitting him squarely in the eyes. He winced, then cupped his hand above his brow and squinted ahead. Near the intersection of the alley and the street, a young mother and two small children, a boy and a girl, crossed the thoroughfare and headed toward Pareena's Variety Store. The floor length folds of the woman's coral abaya shimmered, as though in places copper thread streaked through the fabric.

Vanity, and where would it get her? Coldly, he watched her open the door and usher her children into the shop. To his right, a double-parked delivery van, engine running, blocked traffic as the driver unloaded crates of leafy vegetables.

Kazem cranked the window down a bit further to let out more heat and smoke. A sand-colored Humvee stopped on the corner in front of him, engine idling. Saddi's Coffee Shop stood adjacent to the local police station, a squat brick building with as much character as a cardboard box. Americans, come to buy coffee on the run. What did they know? There was a proud tradition in the consumption of coffee, the first cup always intended to be shared with the host, not picked up and gulped down at some Godforsaken infidel army post. Kazem pursed his lips and spat on the pavement.

He glanced at his wristwatch. Almost eight. Flicking ash onto the sidewalk, he twisted the ignition key. The diesel sputtered to life, blue-black smoke spewing from the muffler. Kazem reached into the console for a cell phone, his thumb scrolling through the directory until he found the number he sought. He then eased the car into traffic and veered toward the highway.

In the rear view mirror, the young mother left the shop and stood framed in the shadow of the delivery truck. She scanned the street, as though unsure whether to turn left or right. The boy wrenched the handles of a yellow shopping bag away from his sister.

Kazem's gaze slid back to the windshield before taking one last look in the rearview mirror. The door to Saddi's opened and two soldiers, coffees in hand, returned to their armor-plated vehicle. Complacent fools. They imagined that soon they'd leave Basra to Iraqi security forces.

He pressed SEND just as he surged toward the onramp.

The shock wave shuddered into the rear of his car as the explosion rocked the market. A mushroom cloud of dust and splinters engulfed the stores. Shattering glass and screams tore through streets thick with falling debris.

Kazem slowed, careful to avoid a swarm of people racing away from the devastation. The remnants of a charred yellow canvas tote fluttered into the gutter. He accelerated onto Highway 6, a long strip of asphalt that ran parallel to the Shatt al Arab waterway.

Kazem Al-Unistan rolled the window down completely and tossed the cell phone. It barely made a ripple in the thick, scummy water far below.

Chapter 1
Chatterton County, Virginia

Patrick Meagher, already showered and shaved, heard the side table alarm clock vibrate. He used the darn thing as a backup, but still it grated on his nerves, even after twenty-four years and ten months as Captain at Chatterton Fire Department. Late once, a day off with no pay. Twice, suspension for two weeks. Third strike, you're out. He had never been late, not once. After all this time, he still couldn't wait to get to work. He felt lucky. He, like every other firefighter at his station, loved what he did.

Forty-four years old, the younger of two firefighter sons, Patrick continued the tradition of their father, retired Fire Marshal William 'Pops' Meagher. Patrick headed up District 14's Station and Hazardous Incident Team, routinely making life and death decisions in a split second. Wide set, gray-blue eyes, an ingenuous grin and irreverent sense of humor masked a tough veteran's pragmatism. He had the body of a thirty-year old and worked hard to keep it in shape. Less concerned with aesthetics than the functional benefits of heavy lifting, he and his crew put themselves through a strenuous conditioning routine at the start of every shift.

Still damp, he tossed the towel and reached for his faded navy job shirt. The CFD crest emblazoned on the front had seen brighter days, but the white still stood out, the letters crisp. His favorite shirt that he'd worn when called to a house fire on South Street, it still bore a stain on the label where he'd scratched his neck with bloody fingers. He'd been cradling a baby girl, born outside in the yard while her mother lay unconscious.

Patrick pulled on his fire-resistant work pants and stepped into his steel tipped boots, leaving the room without brushing his hair.

He met Kelly on the landing, and together they padded downstairs. He let her out and watched the Golden Lab stop at the willow tree before plunging into the lake. He laughed as she dashed out, shook a halo of spray onto grass that needed cutting, and galloped back toward him.

Back inside, Patrick gave her a can of beef and rice, her favorite, and made coffee while she buried her snout in her food. He scribbled the day's to-do list for his two teenage daughters, home for the weekend from James Madison University. They wouldn't stir until noon. When awake, they filled the house that otherwise stood cavernous, even with Kelly following him around.

Sometimes Patrick imagined the house was haunted. After a difficult shift, the fragrances of cinnamon and roses lingered when he withdrew his hand from the banister on his way up to bed, as though his wife, Abbey, had recently touched it. She'd used some unpronounceable perfume, and at times it still surprised him. If he opened a long shut drawer in search of something lost, or paged through the last book she'd read, a sense of her caught him off guard. Only after she died did he study the words on the bottle and make sense of them. Ylang ylang.

He almost lost the house when the insurance pricks brought in specialists to 'prove' that Abbey's cancer was a pre-existing condition. *Claim Denied.* Now, to keep his daughters in school, he worked more overtime shifts than any other officer in his district, and moonlighted as a computer geek.

After shouting goodbye up the staircase to his sleeping girls, he grabbed his keys from the peg by the front door, hopped into his pickup, and headed out on the quiet streets of Grafton Lake in the direction of Interstate 95. Getting off the ramp at Exit 8, he cruised through the intersection of Ironbound Parkway and Jefferson Davis Highway, affectionately dubbed The Pike by Chatterton's firefighters. Minutes later, he pulled into the parking lot of Fire Station 14.

The 'Big House' protected the most diverse district in Chatterton, Virginia, and as his brother, Battalion Chief Shane Meagher, supervisor of the southern district, had said a long time ago, "You just never know what to expect on The Pike." From million dollar homes to countless dilapidated doublewides, seamy strip shopping centers to high-density industrial centers; they all relied on the big engines of District 14's firehouse to watch their backs.

Dropping the bag that carried his helmet, turnout gear and mask by the front door to punch in the access code on the keypad, Patrick stopped for a moment to listen to the hum of morning rush hour and feel the sun on his face. The local citizenry, the Pike-a-nites, as they were called by emergency services personnel, were on the move. At any moment, one of them could trigger a life or death emergency call.

Just as the door swung open, the aggressive metallic buzz of the station's Klaxon Horn, anchored to the block wall, reverberated through him, shattering the morning's peace. Urgent, repetitive, it galvanized the firefighters into a collective surge of focus and energy.

Adrenalin still flooded Patrick's system every time the alarm sounded. He charged down the hall into the apparatus bay and flung his canvas gear bag alongside Engine 14, unzipping it as Tom Perrent leaped into the driver's seat, a half eaten Hardee's sausage and egg biscuit stuffed into his mouth.

"What's the matter, Tommy?" Patrick chirped. "Alarm getting in the way of breakfast?" He laughed as the driver reached for the ignition switch and grumbled something that might have been, "Fuck you, Cap."

Patrick hurried with his uniform, drawing up the bulky pants and tightening the suspenders before buckling his coat. He vaulted into the officer's seat beside the driver and caught a whiff of sulphur, the smell of burning diesel fuel as the motor roared to life. He hung his helmet on the hook behind him. Bluish gray smoke curled from the tailpipe and spiraled upwards, pulled by the giant exhaust fans anchored to the ceiling. He barely got the radio headphones in place before the dispatcher's voice filled his earpiece.

"Local alarm for Fire Engine Companies in Districts 14, 1, and 3, Truck 12, Truck 3, the Hazardous Incident Team, Battalion Chief 5, and the Mobile Command post van; respond to 712 Ironbound Parkway, Criton Chemical Plant, for a fire at the loading dock. Time of dispatch is zero eight hundred hours."

Criton was the largest employer in Chatterton County, with headquarters in Iran. The company manufactured ammonium nitrate for chemical fertilizer and cleaning products, and a fire at the plant was bad news. Three years ago, Criton had been the scene of a poisonous toxic spill. Three employees died and two firefighters had their lungs corroded, including Patrick's racquetball partner, David Carsey. With only one lung left, his days on the job had ended, and now he breathed with a respirator and tinkered with his antique VW Beetle.

Patrick turned in his seat. The two firefighters in the crew compartment behind him were strapping their self-contained breathing apparatus into place and positioning their headphones. He pressed the microphone switch to talk with them. "Simons, Horvath, you guys ready to roll?"

They both nodded as Engine 14 began to pull out of the station. With a thousand gallons of water held in a tank beneath the hose bed, each of the engines carried fifteen hundred feet of reinforced supply lines, seven hundred and fifty feet of double-jacketed attack hose, and a pair of cross laid one and a half inch diameter quick-strike lines above the engine coffin. He gave a thumbs-up to the Hazardous Material Team as their rig lumbered out beneath the station's second bay door.

Next to it, in the third bay, Truck 14 with all its gear—ventilation fans, fire ground utility lights, forcible entry equipment and one hundred foot aerial ladder—remained idle. Truck 14 usually worked alongside Engine 14, but today the three men and one woman assigned to it were nowhere in sight.

Patrick covered his mouthpiece and spoke directly to his driver. "Whoa, Tom, don't tell me the truck squad's been detailed to a different station today?"

"'Fraid so, Cap. The Fire Chief's order on that came by e-mail just before you got here."

Stanley Lowell, Chief Administrator of Fire and Emergency Medical Services, who wouldn't know a hose from a hammer if his ass were on fire, made policy decisions without considering the full implications to the men and women he was ultimately responsible for. The Meagher clan had clashed with the mayor's appointed lapdog several times, to their detriment.

Patrick turned to look out the window and swore quietly before turning back to the driver. "Okay, stay sharp, time to earn our pay."

If this was a 'shit call', a routine truck fire, they'd be back in time for Tom Perrent to have his second greasy biscuit. But Patrick had to brace for a worker, a full-blown fire, and that meant they could be heading into a deathtrap.

The engine picked up speed and barreled down Ironbound Parkway, the piercing wail of its Federal Q siren parting cars like an axe splitting a log. At every intersection, three deafening blasts of the air horn nudged traffic out of their way. Patrick turned the volume knob on his head set.

Dispatcher Lynn Lukhart's distinctive Louisiana drawl repeated the call information and acknowledged the replies of each officer in charge as they confirmed their assignments.

The radio hummed in Patrick's ear.

"Battalion Chief 5 to Chatterton Dispatch." Shane Meagher's voice, cool and composed, filled the airwaves. "I'm already on Ironbound Parkway, about five minutes from Criton. I am responding."

That's good, Patrick thought. He and his brother had worked many calls together, including the three-alarm apartment fire on Duval Street just last week. He understood how Shane would think and knew how he'd react. Patrick could almost anticipate his every move.

Shane spoke again. "Chatterton Dispatch, I will be first on location, do you have any other information regarding this alarm?"

The line crackled. "Battalion 5 and all units enroute to Ironbound Parkway, we received a call on 9-1-1 from plant personnel that a fire started near a truck at the loading dock of the ammonium plant. Criton Chemicals Emergency Response Team was unable to contain the resulting fire. They evacuated the immediate area and advise they will meet you at Gate C."

"Understood," said Shane. "Dispatch, why isn't Truck 14 responding?"

A moment of static filled the speaker, the radio transmission line open, but it took a couple of seconds for Lukhart to respond. "Uh . . . Fire Chief Lowell ordered Truck 14 out of service earlier, per his minimum staffing directive. That crew has been detailed to other stations and won't be responding to Criton Chemical."

Patrick knew Lukhart's answer would piss his brother off. Shane's silence could mean only one thing. Without the requisite manpower, he and his

18

men faced certain delays, and significantly higher danger levels had to be expected.

This alarm was starting off bad. Patrick gritted his teeth. How bad, they'd soon find out.

Chapter 2
Chatteron County, Virginia

Shane Meagher, Patrick's brother and Division Commander for the units responding to the fire at Criton, accelerated onto Highway 1. His heart rate quickened as he skirted the traffic that had pulled over to clear a path for him. *Goddamn Lowell and his service cutbacks.* He barely had enough guys to take on last month's three-alarm on Brighton Avenue, when heavy fire at a five story apartment building blew out every window on the first two floors. Child's play compared to what he now faced. If the fire had anything to do with Criton's production of the highly explosive ammonium nitrate, Shane and his men had to hit it hard and fast. If they failed, it would turn deadly, and there was every chance they could all be blown to bits.

After more than twenty-five years with the department, Shane knew fire. He could read it, understood the way it breathed, what it fed on, and what an appetite it had. This one might be the worst he'd ever faced. His shirtsleeve covered a foot long patch of burned tissue that reminded him, every time he looked at his watch or stepped in the shower, just how up close and personal a fire could get. Hell, he almost lost his arm that day, but here he was, driving to the kind of monster he knew would spare nothing and no one in its path.

Shane tightened his grip on the steering wheel. Ahead of him, less than a mile away, a pillar of black smoke billowed above the horizon, dissipating at its peak to dab a murky swathe across the sky. If the flames spread beyond the loading dock and engulfed the depot, he would need all the manpower he could get, and then some. Making matters worse, the crew from Truck 14, the team that had developed Criton Chemical's pre-fire plan that Shane would rely on to combat the blaze, was unavailable. If this alarm was as bad as he feared, those plans would be indispensable. With Truck 14 out of action, an already dangerous risk grew even higher.

After hurtling past run-down second-rate motels and abandoned businesses, Shane slowed as he drew up to the entrance of the plant and turned into the lot. Dense smoke shrouded the steel framework of the main manufacturing center alongside the facility's storage cylinders. He parked upwind on top of a gradient that overlooked the storage depots of the industrial giant. Jamming the gearshift into park, he noted Criton's flag flapping vigorously in the steady breeze, luckily heading straight toward the river and away from a nearby shopping center.

Shane grabbed the mic from the console. "This is Battalion 5 on scene at a large chemical plant with smoke showing in the area of the loading dock near the storage tanks. I will be in command of the Criton Incident." He scanned the buildings ahead of him, concrete blocks that hunkered colorless in the early morning light. An orange glow suddenly flashed above one of the warehouses and doubled in size. He keyed the mic again. "Transmit a second-alarm and dispatch our Operations Officer." He would need to delegate fire ground responsibilities, so he could focus on strategy and coordinate tactics.

21

As if in response to Shane's challenge, the hellish flicker countered. A red tongue exploded skyward and devoured a utility shed beside it, the heat wave rippling directly at Shane, who was parked over five hundred yards away. "All personnel responding to Criton Chemical, switch to Fire Radio Channel B now." He had to clear the main channel, intended for the dispatch of other alarms. Channel B would be solely dedicated to this predator.

Shane stepped out and hustled to the rear of his vehicle. He dropped the tailgate and hastily donned his protective fire gear. As he grabbed his clipboard, a similarly clad, disheveled figure scurried up the hill toward him.

"We tried to get a handle on it, fought it for about fifteen minutes," the heavily suited man huffed. "The truck was being loaded. I'm not sure exactly what went on. It happened kinda fast. Most of the guys in our Emergency Response Team were scattered at different parts of the plant and…"

An enormous groan, metal grating against metal, stopped him dead in his tracks. Both men turned abruptly. Less than a quarter of a mile away, unprotected steel I-beams, girders supporting a crane, glowed bright red from unbearable temperatures attacking from beneath. Sagging in their centers and unable to withstand the intense heat, the metal beams twisted away from their supports. The hoist thundered to the ground, consumed in a huge fireball.

The man resumed his nervous babble.

"Stop." Shane held up his hand. "Who are you, what do you do, and tell me what you do know."

"Uh . . . yeah, Sam Collier," the man wheezed. "I'm the shift leader for Criton's Fire Brigade, you know, our Emergency Response Team. I've only been doing this for two years, never had this happen, usually just small spills and some decontamination stuff. We got a truck on fire by the loading dock that stands at this end of the pier. I think its starting to burn real good, and the flames might get to heating them storage tanks if it gets outta hand." Collier shifted from one foot to the other, raking fingers through his hair. "Man, am I glad to see you."

Shane stood stone-faced and listened to the first responder's wild account. Collier paused for breath to fish a cigarette out of his breast pocket. It fell onto the tarmac as the task force of three diesel powered engines roared up, emergency lights swirling, led by Engine 14 and followed by one truck, the hazardous material truck and mobile command post van. Shane acknowledged Patrick and the officers of the other arriving apparatus and barked orders into his mic, strategically positioning the vehicles to attack the fire from every judicious tactical angle.

A firefighter from each of the engines yanked the end of a water supply line and jumped from the tailboard to screw the brass couplings onto freestanding fire hydrants. Once attached, the engines rumbled into their assigned positions, the heavy double-jacketed supply lines hitting the ground as the vehicles pulled away and the hoses stretched taut. Firefighters, each laboring with eighty pounds of gear, grabbed attack lines and prepared to do battle with the wall of flames that had consumed the remainder of the loading dock, the heat intensifying every minute. With all the noise and activity, Shane never heard the hiss of the command post van's air brakes as it came to a stop ten yards from where he stood.

The driver, Lieutenant Jerry Pruter, jumped from the open door. "What can I do, boss?"

After a busy overtime shift the night before, Shane felt like he needed to sleep for a week. But his brain had kicked into autopilot, years of experience taking control, and the fatigue retreated as Pruter awaited instruction. "Jerry, we're going to need the Hazardous Materials Safety Data Sheets for the chemicals used here. Also, get me the complex pre-plan so we have locations of everything at Criton. This here is Sam Collier."

The two shook hands. The visibly agitated fire brigade leader had trouble standing still.

"I want you to stick with the Lieutenant, Mr. Collier," Shane said, "but first, where's Hassan Muhktar? According to Criton's operating procedures, he's our liaison, supposed to meet us here in the event of an emergency." Shane and his crew relied on Criton's CEO for vital information regarding the plant and its output. Hassan Muhktar's absence would lead to inevitable delays they could ill afford.

"I don't know where he is. He's usually here by eight. It's now a quarter after that." Collier's Adam's apple bobbed several times. "I tried to raise him on the hand-held radio, but he never picked up. Usually he's the one bitching at me for not answering fast enough." He tugged at his collar as if struggling to breathe.

Shane's eyes darted between the command post van and the two men. "ASAP, Jerry . . ."

Pruter got the message. He and Collier trotted to the van and disappeared inside, just as a loud crash came from the dock. Shane whirled. The force of several roof timbers collapsing into the fire created a mushroom of angry yellow and white sparks, and rocketed a three hundred foot column of embers upward. The glow had blown up into a massive red inferno.

Pruter reappeared thirty seconds later and threw up a small folding table. "Here you go, Chief."

Collier spread out the site plans, Hazardous Materials Safety Data Sheets and colored markers before backing away.

Shane grabbed a felt tip pen and highlighted the critical structures under attack. He flashed through each section of the chemical data pages, circling the last lines in black.

> *Without question, under emergency conditions, the Criton plant is the most dangerous life and property target hazard in all of Chatterton County.*

He could feel the temperature rising with each passing moment, a time bomb with the detonator winding down to zero. The fire would soon hunger for the cylinders of explosive nitrates.

Shane looked at the task force once more. *Where the hell is Truck 3?* His eyes burned. He smeared the sweat from his brow with a dirty sleeve and checked his watch. The delay caused by the Fire Chief's staffing cancellation made the minute hand seem like a high-speed propeller. He needed protection from the master streams of the first alarm truck companies, *both* of them, and the huge volumes of water they could provide from the nozzles attached at the tips of their one hundred foot ladders.

He loosened his helmet strap. His head began to pound.

Galveston, Texas. Years ago. A ship, the *Grandcamp*, laden with ammonium nitrate and full of diesel fuel, caught fire and exploded soon after. The powerful detonation incinerated almost a thousand people instantly, and the shock wave obliterated the busy port of Texas City.

The sound of a car engine twenty feet away short-circuited the nightmare.

"What are your orders, Chief?" Captain Mike Pentino hip-checked his door shut and walked briskly over to join Shane, notepad in hand.

"Pentino, you're my Operations Officer. Take a look at this." Shane zeroed in on the complex drawings on the table. "Right now I have Engine 14 setting up dual water supply lines to feed the elevated master stream here." He jabbed the felt tip on the map between the fire and the nitrate cylinders. "The other two engine companies are on these hydrants using their attack lines. When the second-alarm units get here, I want them in a semi-circle between the fire and the ammonium nitrate. We have to get copious, and I mean *copious* amounts of water onto those storage tanks and keep them cool at all costs. Tell Captain Meagher of Engine 14 that I want a primary search of the fire area to account for all employees. And I want it done now."

Shane turned his attention to Collier. The man looked dazed, chain-smoking. Three filters already lay at his feet. "Alright, now, Mr. Collier, what else can you tell me? I need to know exactly what happened . . . Mr. Collier?" The emergency responder jerked at the mention of his name. "We don't have a lot of time."

Collier coughed spasmodically. He hacked it out as he began to speak. "We had one of the big rigs come in and park near the dock, guy said he was to receive a load of nitrate. I personally didn't talk to him, but that happens from time to time . . ."

Shane's irritated look cut him off.

Collier took another long pull on his Marlboro. "Ebi was on the forklift, and I was in the guard shack checking the invoice. I thought I heard a sharp grating sound, and then Ebi comes busting through the door shouting that he backed the forklift into the trailer and broke open a couple bags from the pallet. He said that when he repositioned the loader, he scraped the metal grate, sparking a fire on the right side of the dock. He said he pretty much emptied the water can extinguisher, but couldn't get it out."

"What material were you loading?"

Collier rooted through his pocket and produced a crumpled shipping order. "One hundred pound burlap wrapped packets of ammonium nitrate fertilizer. We tried to put the fire out, but the red ring on the hydrant in the yard showed that it was out of service. It really slowed us down; gave the fire a hell of a head start. It was weird, because I checked the maintenance log for repair items when I clocked in, and nothing was written down." Collier finished the remainder of his cigarette in one drag and threw the burnt filter onto a patch of gravel.

Shane put his hand on the man's shoulder, "Okay, calm down. No one's blaming you." He spotted Pentino. "Mike, are all employees accounted for?"

"Yes, Chief. And we're going to be cooling those storage tanks closest to the loading dock in a couple more minutes. But Chief." Pentino didn't blink. "It looks like the fire may be spreading to the rest of the storage depot and the south end of the pier. If that happens, those nearby storage tanks are going to blow because of it, and they're storing combustible fertilizer and industrial grade nitrate."

Shane pivoted away from Pentino, mic in hand. He licked dry lips. "Criton Command to Chatterton Communications Center, have the Police Department block all roads north of the intersection of Highway 1 and Willes Road."

The memory of the deadliest industrial accident in United States history, one that wiped out an entire seaport, caused the muscles in Shane's neck to spasm and lock up. *If we don't get a handle on this soon...*

Pentino adjusted his portable radio headset. "Finally! Chief, Truck 3 is on scene and reports second-alarm units are pulling in."

"Get that second master stream flowing from its ladder tip immediately. I want more water on this son of a bitch right now."

"You got it, Chief." Pentino reached for the mic coiled to his radio.

Shane stopped him. "Tell them to hustle. We have to control this soon, or I'll order those engines to pump water by themselves, leave them unattended, and evacuate everyone. Ten minutes, Mike, that's it."

Chapter 3
Criton Chemical Office, Richmond, Virginia

At the headquarters of Criton Chemical Company in downtown Richmond, Hassan Muhktar wedged the phone between his shoulder and cheek. He adjusted his starched shirtsleeves, aligned both black onyx cufflinks, and checked his watch. "It's not your concern where I am. I'll be there in about a half hour. It should be safe by then." He put the phone down and turned to the woman seated across a sprawling chestnut desk. "That was Sam Collier. A fire's raging out of control at the loading dock by the pier." He chuckled. "The fire trucks are only now putting water on it. Cancel all appointments, but take care of the delivery." He narrowed his eyes and stared across his plush office at the small figure who sat in a straight backed chair facing him. For no good reason, he wanted to pound her into the wall. Her timid manner annoyed him, the way a rodent irritates a well-fed cat.

"Have you got that, Nadia?" The businessman snatched his pack of Bahman's and clamped one of the cigarettes between his teeth. He thumbed his monogrammed silver lighter and blew a ribbon of smoke at his executive assistant. "Did you hear me? Yes? No? Earth to Nadia . . ."

His wife looked up from her notes. She covered her mouth and coughed lightly.

He glared at her. Arranged by his father, Sheik Abbas Muhktar, in Tehran years ago, the marriage had placed at Hassan's disposal a perfect

30

administrative assistant. Nadia managed his transactions with proficiency and was silently complicit in all his dealings. He had lost interest in her a couple of years ago, after repeated efforts to produce an heir failed. Now she was little more than a corporate asset.

The small woman sat ramrod straight and nodded once. "Coordinate the upcoming delivery to the Persian Gulf of ammonium nitrate fertilizer onboard the *Orient Star* with the sheik." She looked up. "And what of his request yesterday that you meet with his emissary?"

Hassan wrenched his jacket from the closet and whirled abruptly. "I'll address that personally. Go." He flicked his wrist toward the double doors and waited until she closed them softly behind her.

Crossing the room to the small bar at the far end of the office, he grabbed a bottle of Jack Daniels, poured two fingers' worth into a tumbler and swallowed it in a single gulp before following her into the reception area, where he summoned the elevator. Once inside the glass and chrome interior, he studied his reflection and admired the hand-tailored Brooks Brothers suit Cleaves Limited had delivered the previous day. Stroking a manicured finger along his chevron moustache, a habit he'd formed since hair first sprouted on his face, he smoothed the bristles over the remnants of a slight harelip, then turned away to watch the lights for each floor blink as he descended into the garage.

Hassan made his way to his car, spraying two short bursts of breath freshener onto his tongue. He accelerated when he reached the highway and leveled off once the Lincoln Navigator hit eighty. To the southeast, a column of smoke drifted in front of the sun.

His father would be pleased. Hassan would relay the news to the sheik once he'd spoken to the mayor. He tilted the visor down and again fingered his moustache, a wry smile forming.

Chapter 4
Mayor's Office. Chatterton, Virginia

In his third floor office, as the fire threatened to reduce a huge tract of his county to a dead zone and hundreds of his citizens to vaporized particles, the Honorable Jackson Stamper, Mayor of Chatterton, kept a death grip on his cell phone and delivered a blistering tirade.

Trapped on the receiving end, Shane Meagher's boss, Fire Chief Stanley Lowell listened wordlessly, muzzled by the mayor's tantrum.

"Jesus fucking Christ, you're the Fire Chief, for God's sake. Why haven't you got the fucker under control?"

Across the room, the aftermath of an explosion at some Iraqi marketplace played out on a 32-inch plasma TV. Momentarily distracted by the photo ID's of the three G.I.s killed in the bombing, the mayor flung his glasses onto his desk and rubbed his eyes. "Criton Chemical has been in business here for thirty years. Muhktar has a contract with the federal government, for crying out loud. You know that! The county gets a lot of tax revenue from Criton, and the guy's been giving a shitload of money to the community . . . hell . . . ever since you were a lieutenant at Station 8. Listen clearly, goddamn it, if Hassan Muhktar isn't happy, I'm not happy!" He pressed the phone hard against his ear. "What? Yeah, the TV's on. I'm looking right at it. Some shit storm in Iraq, a few more of our boys blown to bits. Hang

33

on." Stamper reached for the remote and thumbed through the channels until footage of Criton's chemical fire blazed across the monitor. He paused, staring at the screen as the camera cut to a still shot of Shane and two of his firefighters. "You've got that prick Meagher running the circus out there. You better get a hold of his ass and put this motherfucker out. Tell me you're on the way there?"

As his secretary knocked and put her head around the door, the mayor didn't wait for Lowell to respond. "Because I've got to tell you, if Muhktar calls me again to tell me your fire department is to blame for his plant going up in smoke, guess whose ass is on the line, Stanley?"

Janet Lester stepped into the room and looked at her wristwatch. She mouthed something at him that looked like, *only twenty minutes.* Stamper held up his hand and nodded. She crossed the room to his desk and began to gather papers, tucking them smoothly into his briefcase.

"That's right, Stanley, don't be a dumb-ass. We've got a lot riding on this, as if I have to remind you." His eyes never left the outline of his assistant's butt through her tight beige pencil skirt as she bent over, slowly, to retrieve the financial report he'd prepared for the Board of Supervisors. "I don't want to hear on Channel Six that as far as Hassan's concerned, we, as in your fire department, the one that I am ultimately responsible for, is to blame for his losses. Now take care of this shit."

Jackson Stamper jabbed the OFF icon on his phone and raised the volume on the TV.

Chapter 5
Fire District 14, Chatterton County, Virginia

On his way to the Criton fire, Stanley Lowell, Chief Administrator of Chatterton Fire & EMS Department, watched his cell go dark before tossing it on the dashboard. He turned on the emergency flashers in his staff car and swerved without glancing into the left hand lane of Route 10, almost clipping the Pontiac in front of him. He glared at its driver as he sped past, Stamper's words still reverberating.

Though he enjoyed the many perks his relationship with Jackson Stamper afforded him—the Harley Davidson, the condo up at Massanutten Ski Resort— he hated the man. Stanley had heard the whispers and caught the smirks of other department heads when he passed by, who thought of him as the mayor's bitch. He resented Stamper and his bombastic displays of self-righteousness, but Stanley had grown immune to the taunts. Without the mayor and the benefits Stanley gained as his lapdog, the good life as he knew it would dry up. Stanley was a small man in every way, and the reality of it tormented him. He needed the mayor to compensate for his shortcomings. In the end, the way Stanley rationalized it, the slights he suffered and derisive comments he absorbed were simply the price of admission he had to pay in order to play.

So, Stamper wanted a whipping boy? Fine. He'd get one, but it wasn't going to be him. Stanley was well schooled at making sure shit flowed downhill.

Shane Meagher had always been a pain in his ass. Fall guy? Yeah, he had one in mind, and he was on his way to set him up and knock him down.

A towering plume of black smoke against a pastel blue sky was all the navigation Stanley needed to guide him. He flipped the radio switch to connect with Shane and reached for the microphone. "Chief Lowell to Criton Command on Dispatch Channel."

No answer.

"This is Unit 1, Chief Lowell, to Criton Command!"

The radio buzzed for an instant before he heard Lukhart cut in on his transmission. "Chatterton Communications to Unit 1. Chief Meagher moved all radio traffic to working fire channel B to keep the main dispatch channel clear, per your departmental protocol."

Stanley offered no affirmation as he spun the knob to the designated frequency. "Unit 1 to Chief Meagher on Channel B. I'm entering the gate. Give me an updated incident report."

Shane's acknowledgment came after a pause that got Stanley to grind his teeth. "Uh, Chief, we're kind of busy up here. You're on scene, right?"

"You give me that report now." The Fire Chief slammed his mic back into its cradle as he drove toward the command post. He hit the brakes a hundred and fifty yards past the gate, his path blocked by a serpentine mass of water supply lines lacing between fire engines. The massive diesels, operating at full capacity to achieve enough water pressure to attack the blaze, roared in his ears, making it hard for him to think. Stanley pounded the wheel as he inched past them.

Engrossed in the deployment of his resources, Shane failed to acknowledge Stanley as the car pulled in behind the command post van.

"Who do you think you are, Meagher? Are you purposely ignoring me?" Stanley grabbed his helmet and turnout coat from the back seat and stormed toward Shane. "When I give an order for a report on the radio, that's what you give me. Not later, not after doing something else, but when I ask for it. Am I coming through loud and clear now?"

"Chief!" Shane spun on his heels. "I wasn't ignoring you. There are a lot of things going on that need immediate attention. Those tanks have to be cooled; I have the hazmat team in the middle of that shit to confirm no leak, and hose lines to attack the source of the fire, all at the same time. There was a delay . . ."

"You bet your ass there was a delay!" Stanley stood with hands on hips, shoulders lowered and chin set belligerently forward. "The mayor already got an earful from the plant owner blaming us because the fire's still raging. So what's the problem?" He didn't wait for an answer, whirling to grab a cup of coffee from an urn Lieutenant Pruter had set up on a folding table alongside the command post van.

"Just what are you saying, Chief?" Shane said. "That we were slow getting here? Deploying? What? The stuff at this plant is as dangerous as it gets. We followed the operating procedures to the letter, procedures you signed off on. Would you prefer we rushed in and got somebody killed?"

The coffee erupted out of the cup as Stanley slammed it on the folding table. "Just who do you think you're talking to, *pal*? Less than twenty minutes ago, the mayor got a call from Hassan Muhktar blaming my department for his losses."

"The Fire Department's responsible for his losses?" Under different circumstances, Stanley might have got a kick out of Shane's incredulity. "By Muhktar's own written insistence and part of the agreed upon pre-plan, he was the one who was supposed to meet us as liaison in the command post! We couldn't find him, and I can tell you that's one big delay we had." He stabbed his finger at the complex plan. "If he had been here, this would have been a whole lot easier to deal with." He shook his metal clipboard. "That, and the Truck Company normally assigned to District 14 was ordered out of service."

"Chief Meagher." Captain Pentino stepped between them. "I just got word. Hassan Muhktar is headed up here."

"I'll speak with him." Stanley's shoulder bumped Shane's as he muscled past him toward his car. Adjusting the side view mirror, he began to plaster stringy wisps of hair, slick with perspiration, over his ever increasing bald spot. "And Meagher, you at least try and get a handle on this fiasco of yours."

The clipboard clanged on the table. Shane took a step toward Stanley.

Pentino cut in front of him. "Shane, we're all set for the master streams to cool and protect the tanks."

"Alright, Mike." Shane unclenched his fist. "Let's drown this son of a bitch."

Stanley put his helmet back on and watched Hassan Muhktar trudging up the hill toward him.

"This is an outrage." The daggers in Hassan Muhktar's eyes were clearly aimed at Stanley. "I've been in business thirty years, and you want me to stand by as my plant burns to the ground? Why haven't you got this under control?"

The fire engine pumps cut off any further conversation, screaming as they pushed tons of water to the nozzles attached to the tips of the aerial ladders. Muhktar backed away, covering his ears.

Water poured over the tops and sides of the nitrate storage cylinders in a non-stop torrent. It was the only way to cool them and prevent an explosion that would kill them all instantly. The blast would make a hundred sticks of TNT look like a firecracker.

"Why are you pouring water on the cylinders and not the fire?" Muhktar shouted at Shane.

"Mr. Muhktar." Stanley claimed the man's attention. "We're doing all we can. The fire is secondary at the moment. We have to keep the ammonium nitrate cool. My men will soon be in position to attack the main portion of the blaze, but we must do it safely."

Down the hill, the high-speed jets continued to pound their targets.

The external loudspeakers at the command post crackled, interrupting Stanley.

"Firefighter Simons to Command. I have my crew and the one from Company 6 advancing a pair of two-and-a-half inch hose lines at the main body of fire and covering the hazmat team. Stand by, and I'll get their report to see if there's a leak."

"Okay, Firefighter Simons." Shane replied. "I've also assigned the crew from Engine 11 to you. Have Captain Patrick Meagher report to the command post with that assessment when he can. Advise if you need additional resources."

Steam hissed as the hose lines began to gouge into the seat of the dock fire.

"Who is he? Who is this man?" Muhktar flicked his hand at Shane as if swatting an annoying insect. "Is he the one responsible for the loss I'm taking here?" He straightened his tie. "You'll suitably discipline him for his incompetence, is that not correct, Chief Lowell?" The plant owner jerked his head in Shane's direction. "You're in charge of him, aren't you, or should I speak to someone higher up?"

The barb and veiled threat were not lost on Stanley. He cleared his throat. "You need go no higher than me, Mr. Muhktar. As commanding officer of Chatterton Fire & EMS, I personally assure you, I'll see to it." Though Stanley silently acknowledged Shane's strategy and tactics as sensible and judicious, his feral sense of self-preservation demanded Shane be thrown to the wolves. He was aware that the rank and file believed his career was built on blind loyalty to the mayor and what they considered the gutless sacrifice of others. What did they know? He understood the game and how to play it. "I've noted the actions taken here, and all will be addressed accordingly. You can take that to the bank."

Muhktar smiled. "Yes. To the bank, as you Americans like to say." With a grimace of distaste, he brushed at the dust on his suit.

"Pentino." Stanley snapped his fingers. "Give me those pre-plans and then bring a bottle of water over here for Mr. Muhktar."

Shane could only shake his head as the Operations Officer, engrossed in carrying out the crucial assignments he had given him, dropped his jaw and fumbled for a response.

"It's okay, Mike," Shane said, "we're making good headway here." The fire's dark smoke had begun to lighten, a sign that the necessary steam to extinguish the conflagration was being produced. He grabbed Pentino's clipboard. "Just do as he asks, and don't make things hard on yourself. He's already pissed."

"Command, the fire has been knocked down." Again, the voice of Master Firefighter Simons, supervising the crews attacking the body of the fire on the loading dock, reverberated through the speakers on Fire Channel B. "Damage is contained to the loading dock, depot and it's contents and a good part of the pier. The forklift and truck are absolute toast. We're keeping our lines in on the heat and will continue to cool and monitor the nitrate cylinders. Go ahead and mark the situation under control."

Shane keyed the mic and patched through to Lukhart. "Criton Command to Chatterton Dispatch; mark the situation under control. We'll be remaining on scene for quite some time."

"Ten-four, Chief Meagher." Lukhart confirmed. "The incident at Criton Chemical is under control at eleven fifteen hours."

"It's about time." Hassan stalked toward Shane. "But under whose control, might I ask?" Failing to elicit a response, he turned to easier prey. "Chief Lowell, I've already spoken with Mayor Stamper. This shutdown will cost my company a great deal of time and a large sum of money. Criton has important contractual obligations with your government, as well as many others."

"I assure you, Mr. Muhktar, I'll have a full report on Mr. Stamper's desk within twenty four hours."

"Most considerate of you." Muhktar pivoted abruptly and moved toward Stanley's sedan. "There's much to be done. Perhaps you would be so kind as to take me to my office near the main gate?" He stood by the passenger door, hands clasped in front of him.

"Yes, of course, I'll be right with you." Stanley turned away from Muhktar, his obsequious mask transforming into a very real snarl of hostility as he growled at Shane. "As for you, Meagher." He crushed one of the empty Styrofoam coffee cups. "You have your ass in my office first thing tomorrow morning, got it?" He tossed the container on the ground at Shane's feet. "And clean up this mess of yours."

The two glared angrily at one another for an instant before Stanley completed a quick about face, smile in place once more, and hurried over to open the car door for the waiting plant owner.

A moment later, they were gone.

Chapter 6
Shane Meagher's home, Chatterton County, Virginia

Patrick shielded his eyes as he looked up at the sun. Clouds were moving in, and now it issued a feeble yellow light that seemed to match the mood of the men gathered in the backyard of Shane's house on Mulden Lane. Patrick fished a beer from an old metal washtub filled with ice that sat on the picnic table he'd helped his older brother build last Memorial Day weekend. A jagged half-moon scar crested the base of his thumb, a souvenir from his clumsy handling of a power drill during a Budweiser-fueled day of construction.

Patrick drifted over to his two daughters. "You two are officially in charge of the meat. Don't let the steaks burn and make me call the fire department to this party."

Colleen, his eighteen year old, grinned as she reached for the tongs.

Her older sister, Shannon murmured, "Whatever."

He knew she was teasing him, the elfish half-smile giving her away. She was so much like Abbey. Shannon, recently turned twenty-one, had high cheekbones and a tangled mass of dark brown hair that tumbled below her shoulder blades. Colleen had cut hers short, although he'd asked her not to. Her red mane was now a close-cropped rainbow cap of pink, green and purple, and she had more piercings in her ears that Patrick cared to count. The impossible-to-define love he had for them and the weight of

Abbey's memory snuck up on him. He tore open the ring tab of his beer with more force than necessary, spilling some of the can's contents onto the patio slate.

"Whoa!" Colleen said. "Careful there, Dad. You don't want to be wasting any."

Patrick caught a quick flash of sadness in her eyes before she turned toward the grill. He left them to join his father and Shane beneath the mottled shade of a maple tree.

William Meagher could easily be mistaken for the grandfatherly cover model of last month's *L.L. Bean* catalog. The man was elegant in his plaid sweater vest, stonewashed khakis, and Rockport Walkers. The big Irishman eased his six foot two inch frame into a nylon webbed lawn chair. Patrick watched his father deliberately reposition a pair of tortoiseshell bifocals on a nose broken decades ago in a barroom fight in Dublin. His father had started the brawl to impress their mom, Kathleen, the girl he'd married and was still in love with. She'd left for Boston two days ago to take care of her sister, who had just had back surgery.

Behind those spectacles, his father's steel gray eyes missed nothing. After a career as Fire Marshal, the lead officer of Chatterton's Fire Prevention and Investigation Division, his mind was as sharp and calculating as ever. It continued to serve him well in the private arson investigative service he ran for insurance companies.

Now those eyes and that mind were hard at work, observing and listening as Shane paced back and forth, raving.

44

"That spineless weasel." Shane stopped in mid-stride and banged his own beer down on the wooden picnic table. "I walk into Lowell's office, and he says our meeting is going to be a critique of the Criton incident, a chance to review procedures. What a bunch of crap. Less than ten minutes later he hands me a letter of reprimand and two weeks suspension without pay. All that nimrod talked about was a complaint lodged by Muhktar to the mayor."

"And did you get a chance to explain your strategy, why you attacked the fire the way you did?"

"I got railroaded, Dad. He wouldn't listen to a thing I said, and I don't have any recourse to appeal, according to the county's grievance procedure. I did what had to be done, by the numbers. Come on, two weeks with no pay and a letter of reprimand? There's Maggie's part-time job, but the bills from Colin's accident just keep coming . . . friggin' lawyers still arguing about who's at fault." Shane glanced over his shoulder as his injured son, leg splinted from ankle to hip and propped on a bench, threw a bully stick to Toto, their feisty Jack Russell.

"He's right, Dad," Patrick said. "I was there. Those chemicals could have gone off like a bomb. Lowell must have been smoking something to imagine that anyone could have handled that fire better. It's not right. Reminded me of the shit storm when you were intentionally passed over for promotion to Fire Chief when Stamper got elected. The job should have been yours."

"Maybe so." William flicked several ice shavings from the rim of his can. "But county policy stipulates the mayor can choose who he wants, and it doesn't

45

take a genius to figure I'd be the last man he'd pick. I was never a political beast. And that's what Shane's dealing with—politics." Patrick's father loathed Jackson Stamper. He would never have toed the line the way Lowell did.

Patrick shook his head. "Nah, it's more than that. This whole thing stinks."

William cocked his head toward him and purposefully removed his glasses. "Stinks how?"

"Look." Patrick's tone took on a sharp edge. "You heard what Shane said; the fire crews followed procedure exactly. And this delay Lowell pinned on him, along with the complaint from Stamper—it's bogus. Lowell himself cancelled some of the manpower needed for the initial response, and even the plant foreman was surprised the hydrant at Criton wasn't working. Something isn't adding up."

William's brow furrowed, the lines on either side of his eyes deepening. "What are you implying, Pat, that this was some kind of cover-up? For what? An insurance scam?"

The sound of a car pulling up in front of the house caused Toto to sit up and trot over to the fence. His clipped tail wagged like a high-speed metronome even before the gate opened.

"Hey Dad, Vincent's here!" Colleen brandished the tongs and poked her sister with an elbow. "And look who's blushing."

Shannon curled a lock of hair behind an ear. "Shut up, Colleen."

Maggie, Shane's wife, came out of the house carrying a bowl of potato salad and placed it on the table. On her way back in, she rested a hand on

46

Patrick's arm and murmured, "You know she's not a little girl anymore, don't you?"

Patrick noted the subtle change in the way Shannon looked up at Vincent Rigardo, the young fire inspector she'd known all her life. He'd have to keep a closer eye on the two of them.

"Did you potato eatin' Irishmen save a burger or two for me? I'm starving!" Vincent opened his arms to give Colleen a quick hug and winked at Shannon.

"Three things, you greasy guinea." Patrick said, grinning. "One, get your hands off my daughter. Two, we saved you a meatball, and three, drinks are on ice, help yourself."

"Oh, yeah? Watch this." Vincent grasped Shannon's waist with both hands and pulled her close. "You can try pulling rank, with me being a lowly Fire Inspector, but I haven't listened to you since we were kids. I'm damn sure not gonna pay attention now!"

Hollywood smile, dark auburn hair in his trademark buzz cut and always ready with a joke, Vincent Charles Rigardo was part of the family. Thirteen years younger than Patrick, he grew up around the Meagher boys and came to live with them when his own parents were killed on the way to the airport just after his fifteenth birthday. Vincent, as William and Kathleen always referred to him, was as much a brother to Patrick as Shane. And Vince loved them all in return. With his irrepressible sense of humor and deep loyalty, he was the one who bestowed the nickname 'Pops' on William.

Vince plunged his hand into the tub and took out a beer. "I saw your five minutes of fame on the TV news clip about the fire, Shane." The clack of the pull top punctuated the comment. "I'm still wondering what Lowell was doing there at Criton anyway. He doesn't normally show up at a call. He's an office man." He gulped half the can before turning toward William. "I know you always said to respect the position, Pops—that's one thing—but that guy? No can do."

"You boys in the Fire Marshal's office finish your investigation report on Criton?" Patrick asked as Vince shoved a fistful of Cheetos into his mouth. Several fell to the ground, and Toto pounced on them. "It's in the district you're assigned to, right?"

"It is," Vince said, "but the Chief had my boss, Eddie Tammerlin, do it by himself. I had no say in the matter, even though Criton is one of the businesses I'm responsible for. I thought it was kind of strange, Lowell telling the head honcho of the division to do it solo."

Patrick's gaze landed squarely on his father. "Well? You held that position, and now you're a private investigator. Did you ever probe a huge fire like this on your own when you were in charge of Chatterton's Inspection Division? You can't say you did one this big all by yourself."

"That's not how I would do things." William folded his arms across his chest. "But to suggest there's something criminal?"

"Listen," Shane said, "it's a done deal. Dad's right, its politics. Lowell was just looking for a scapegoat. I don't like it one bit, but I have no choice other than to sit out my suspension and get back to work. I guess what really got me going was Lowell's comment before I left his office. 'Have a nice weekend, *pal.*'"

Maggie joined them and smiled up at Vince, who kissed her on the cheek. "It's two weeks, hon," she said to Shane. "We'll manage."

"Food's ready!" Shannon shouted across the yard.

William got up. As he, Maggie and Shane distributed plates and passed around the salads, Patrick drew Vince to one side. "We need to talk," he said. "Too many things aren't adding up."

William looked back at him. "Let it go, Patrick. You're on the hazardous materials team now, not in the Fire Marshal's office. The Criton incident is closed, and the last thing Shane needs, or you for that matter, is to stir things up." He handed Patrick a plate. "Get some potato salad."

Patrick glanced at Vince, who nodded almost imperceptibly. "Later," he murmured.

Chapter 7
City Hall, Chatterton, Virginia

"Want another cup?" Mayor Jackson Stamper turned his back on Stanley Lowell and refilled his own mug from the glass carafe that sat on the corner table. "I hate Mondays, Stanley, and it's late in the day. I'm expecting your report to improve my mood before I head home." Without waiting for the Fire Chief to answer, he walked over to his desk and sat down. "This Criton thing . . . I want it to go away as soon as possible."

Stanley glanced into his cup and swirled the remnants of lukewarm coffee. "Uh, no, thanks, I'm good."

"I got a call from the Feds earlier, wanting to know what happened at Criton. 'Concerned' was the word they used. Hope you appreciate that, Stanley?" Stamper leaned back, pursed his lips, and blew across the rim of his mug. Twenty years of wary career manipulation had taught him to pose just the right questions in just the right way to keep his underlings off balance. They toed the line, and he stayed in control.

"The federal government?" Stanley sat bolt upright. "Today? What's their beef?"

Stamper put his cup down. "Need a translation, Stan?" He wheeled his leather swivel around the corner of his desk and stopped directly in front of the Fire Chief. "What it means is Muhktar has already spoken with them and given his account. He's their

50

industrial grade chemical supplier, and he knows they want their product. Incidents involving ammonium nitrate always get their attention." He rolled his chair back in place and tightened the line. "I imagine a visit by a government agent will soon follow to ensure all is in order and terrorism wasn't a factor."

"Terrorism?" Stanley blustered. "But . . . but we got the fertilizer fire out. They buy fertilizer from him too?"

The mayor made a show of positioning his mug on the corner of the desk blotter. "Listen close, Stan, this is important." He began counting points off on his fingers. "One. Criton is a large supplier of industrial grade nitrate, so of *course* they'll be more than interested. Two. We stopped the fire, but the damage to the plant suspends their upcoming shipments. And three, Hassan Muhktar has contributed heavily to this office, and you personally have benefitted from his generosity. Catch my drift?"

Lowell's right eye started twitching. "Hey, if you're talking about the use of his corporate jet that time, I was on vacation, had to come back on official county business. He offered the jet, I accepted. We've been through this."

"Jesus H. Christ, Stanley, that's only part of it! And by the way, as you better recall, *we*, as in the *county*," Stamper clarified irritably, "ended up paying for that flight. You were *skiing* at Vail, and don't play that shit on me, I know who you were with out there, and she's married." He eased back against the cushion and watched Stanley slacken his tie as if it were a noose.

"My return was business related—part of Councilwoman Taylor's estate burned up." Stanley rubbed his eye. "And I just happened to run into Kay in Colorado."

Lowell's nervous squeak set Stamper's teeth on edge. "Go sell that lame story to someone else. The councilwoman's utility shed caught fire, not her estate." Stamper cocked and aimed his finger at Lowell's head. "A lot of people grumbled. Do I have to remind you the heat we took for using that jet, the numerous favors I exchanged to get that expense approved and to keep things quiet? A lot of people thought you should've been canned for not taking your scheduled flight. At the very least, it called your judgment into question; at worst, that kind of crap will always come back to haunt you. We don't need that kind of publicity, considering our relationship with Criton and the other big businesses in Chatterton." He shook his head dismissively. "Okay, let's move on. What can you tell me about the incident at the chemical plant and your investigation?" Arms folded across his chest, he watched as Lowell steadily gouged at his eye.

The Fire Chief reached into his briefcase and removed a folder. "Well, to begin with, after I went to the scene following the phone conversation I had with you, I called my Fire Marshal, Edward Tammerlin, and instructed him to handle the investigation. I made sure he understood that the circumstances warranted his personal involvement."

"That's an unusual demand." Stamper twirled a fountain pen between his fingers. "A bit like me having to personally inspect a commercial structure when I was the one in charge of the county's entire Building and Inspection Department way back when. How did your Chief Inspector respond to that order? Was he suspicious? Did he ask a lot of questions?"

"I thought of that. I made sure he understood that government contracts were at stake with Criton and convinced him Chatterton County's reputation was largely in his hands."

"Good, good, and that satisfied him?"

"I told him a swift conclusion would please me, and of course the mayor's office, and would be viewed by all parties concerned as being efficient and highly professional. Tammerlin salivates when I throw a bone like that at him."

Stamper spun toward the window and watched several clouds slowly float by. "Tammerlin, though somewhat lacking as far as I'm concerned, isn't a complete fool. What did he say about Meagher's handling of the incident? After all, on a strictly strategic level, he did a credible job controlling that fire and keeping it from those tanks."

"You told me to fix it, didn't you?" Lowell grumbled. "Eddie wasn't there . . . I was. He knows only what I told him, that there was a delay and that Meagher *admitted* there was a delay." The Fire Chief's beady eyes narrowed as he scanned the room from side to side, another quirky habit that got on Stamper's nerves. "Besides, Eddie has spent most of his career out of the Operations Division; he'll do what I say, always has. I emphasized he'd do the most good for all involved, especially himself, by pinpointing the cause of the fire quickly. Period."

Stamper clapped his hands together. "And that's why I chose you to become Fire Chief, Stan. Beautiful! So, where does that leave us? You've spoken to him again, haven't you?"

Stanley sifted through the stack of papers he had brought and produced a second sheaf. "We met earlier today. This is his report." He began reading excerpts aloud. *"Fire appears to have been started by a diesel forklift scraping a metal deck plate, a part of the loading dock. The collision put a tear in the fuel tank, the diesel from it helping the fire to spread. The operator was out there by himself readying wooden pallets of combustible fertilizer to be put on a truck owned by Forceful Freight Express."* Lowell licked his thumb and flipped to the next page. "Let's see, Tammerlin writes that in his interview with the lift operator, the man says he inadvertently knocked over a couple bags, and they busted open. When he repositioned his machine to prevent other stacks from falling, that's when it happened. The scrape ignited some sparks."

"So." Stamper began drumming his fingers on the desktop. "These sparks caused that stuff to go up?"

The Fire Chief slid his reading glasses down to the tip of his nose and looked over the top. "Combined with Class A combustibles—materials like burlap and wood pallets—fertilizer burns rapidly. It's not to be taken lightly." He repositioned the frames and continued. "The worker, a guy named, uhh, here it is—Ebi Rostum—initially tried to put the fire out by himself with an extinguisher. What's unfortunate is he's even a member of Criton's Fire Brigade and still couldn't douse it. Also admits he started loading too soon; Criton guidelines require two men on the dock at all times. When Rostum couldn't contain it, that's when he ran for help."

Stamper pushed away from his desk. "Okay. I got this part, some flunky screws up, starts a fire, not our problem. You said they have an on-site fire department, so I'm sure Muhktar will deal with him." The mayor rapped his knuckles on the desktop. "My biggest concern is the image this office projects. Then there's our relationship with the business community and our own association with Muhktar and Criton. What else does Tammerlin have to say?"

Lowell dropped the commentary back in the attaché case and rummaged for another file. "Their fire brigade team leader, Sam Collier, stated that the hydrant dedicated to the dock was out of service and slowed Criton's initial response. That lapse helped the fire gain strength. Eddie Tammerlin says when he got there, it was back on line and probably fixed. Mr. Muhktar will be pissed at the poor preparation and lack of maintenance by his own people. It's going to cost him a lot of money."

Lowell handed the fire report to Stamper. "Take a look yourself; it's all there. As you can see, the loss is sizable but not complete. And here," he stabbed at a highlighted paragraph, "this is the damage assessment. It might change some, but Tammerlin doesn't think so. Forklift. Tractor trailer. Loading dock. Storage depot."

Stamper held up his hand. "Wait a minute, I thought we prevented that from burning up?"

"What you're thinking of is the tank storage farm. That was four hundred and fifty, maybe five hundred feet away. The storage depot is the big building that contains bags of inventory and other material stockpiled for delivery. It's where the trucks are headed when they go to the loading dock, and it's the back end of the depot that opens up to the Criton pier."

Stamper made a note on his copy.

"Muhktar also lost a good portion of that pier and one of two overhead cranes used to load vessels. Oh yeah, there was a ship at the end of the dock, but it wasn't involved at all. I'm sure some more mechanized equipment in the building was destroyed as well. Like I mentioned, Tammerlin will get back to me on that. He said he was headed out there one more time to finish up. We should have the final word today."

"This looks good, Stan." Stamper rocked back and forth in his swivel chair. "We have the cause, the mistakes made by Criton's own people, and for those screaming for our heads, we have the guy who's supposedly responsible on our end, right?"

"Yes." Lowell resembled an enthusiastic bobble head doll. "I've dealt with Meagher—reprimand and two weeks suspended from the department with loss of salary. That should satisfy any detractors, quiet the press and Mr. Muhktar as well. Wanna laugh? Quite a few of those tanks Meagher was so worried about? They had nothing in them."

Stamper stood up abruptly. "You know what I get a real kick out of? That Meagher's the son of that fucking know-it-all William. Excellent job, Stanley." He walked toward the door.

Lowell gleefully collected his papers and followed him.

The mayor hesitated before opening the door. "I'll be meeting with Muhktar to make sure this has been resolved to our mutual satisfaction. Some may not like Criton Chemical, or Muhktar for that matter, but he and his business are important to us. You realize it's in everybody's best interest to keep things just the way they are, don't you?"

Lowell bobbed his head. "Of course."

Chapter 8
Criton Chemical Headquarters. Richmond, Virginia

Lounging comfortably on a plush sofa in his office at Criton Chemical's headquarters in Richmond's high-rise business district, Hassan Muhktar withdrew a cigarette from an engraved silver case. He lit it before lifting the phone and dialing Tehran, where Sheik Abbas Muhktar, his father and CEO of Criton Industries worldwide, awaited his call.

The sheik had built Criton over thirty-five years ago during the reign of the Shah, and had labored for decades to provide the kind of affluence Hassan now took for granted. More impressive than the establishment of Criton in the U.S. was the sheik's cunning political maneuvering away from Reza Pahlavi's government to a warily crafted allegiance with the loyalists of the 1979 Iranian revolution. The move facilitated the growth and sustainability of what had become a global empire.

The phone rang only once before the sheik answered. "*As-salamu alaykum.*"

"*Wa alaykumu s-salam*, Father."

"Hassan!" The sheik's voice boomed, and Hassan flinched. His father's hearing wasn't what it used to be. "You are well?"

"Yes, thank you, Father, better than well. I'm pleased to tell you that everything has gone according to plan. Operations at the Virginia plant have been suspended, and all the necessary reports of losses from the fire have been drawn up and handed over to the authorities. We followed your instructions to the letter."

"With production suspended, what about the *Orient Star*?"

The *Orient Star* was a worn freighter with rusted decks and cranes that had seen better days. Docked at Criton's plant in Chatterton, she routinely ferried ammonium nitrate fertilizer to users in several countries, including legitimate clients like the Iranian government, and more recently, an Iraqi warlord in the crumbling Iranian port of Khorromshahr, where under cover of night, black market money changed hands.

"The ship will sail on time. It wasn't affected." Hassan pulled the ashtray closer and tapped his cigarette. "We need to discuss a few things. I've spoken to Jackson Stamper, who as you know is amenable to working with us."

"Of course," the sheik said. "We made sizable contributions to his election campaign, and being so compromised, he should have our best interests at heart."

"Yes. He's found a way to bypass code regulations regarding storage requirements, so we can overstock the warehouse on Mandarin Turnpike. Now moving some of the packaging materials and shipping containers for storage won't be a problem. It's the perfect fire hazard we want to set up."

"And what of the rezoning of your home and estate property to industrial land use so it fetches a higher profit when you sell it?"

Hassan held the phone an inch away from his ear and got up to pour himself a drink. The sheik would

59

not approve, but that was the beauty of living on the other side of the world. "I made it clear that the rezoning was a priority. The mayor is not a complete fool, so he asked that we be reasonable. Changing residential property to industrial in that area of Chatterton County is not commonplace, but he reassured me he'd do everything he could to meet our needs." Hassan poured himself a glass of Manzanilla and swirled the Spanish sherry in the intricately etched crystal wine glass before lifting it to his lips. He took a surreptitious sip, then added, "He reiterated his personal guarantee that his office is more than willing to cooperate with us."

"Good." Sheik Abbas coughed, and Hassan winced as his father wheezed. He was showing his age, but the old man's mind was as sharp as ever. "What about the lead fire officer of their emergency services, Lowell? You say the investigation and report have been finalized? I don't have a copy."

Hassan put the wineglass down and pressed a call button beneath the bar. "No. I haven't sent it. Just a moment, I'll get Nadia."

Moments later he heard a knock on the door. "Come," he called, and turned to face his wife. Today she wore a discreetly embroidered caftan and matching blue headscarf. The cloth fell in folds to her feet, effectively camouflaging the petite frame underneath.

Hassan nodded curtly at her, and she made her way over to the straight-backed chair opposite his desk, where she sat down with her laptop and waited.

"Just a minute, I have her here." He mouthed the words, *The Criton fire file,* and she quickly pulled up the electronic folder. "Print it out and email it to my father," he said. He found it easier to work off a hard copy. Within seconds, the laser printer hummed and began stacking documents neatly in its tray. Hassan leaned over Nadia's shoulder to retrieve the pile.

"We just sent it across now."

"That's fine, but while I have you on the phone, let's go through it. I may have questions."

Hassan ran his finger down the report. "The statement substantiates the preliminary findings of their investigator, Fire Marshal Edward Tammerlin. I'll read his initial conclusions to you." Hassan unfolded his glasses and perched them on his nose. *"A probable series of sparks were created when the driver of a forklift struck the metal grid of the loading dock. This followed his accidental tearing of a product bag. The identified material in the one hundred pound sacks, ammonium nitrate, is an oxidizing agent which warrants a class 9 hazards label."* Hassan peered over his spectacles at Nadia, who sat with her eyes downcast, awaiting instruction. "That's defined as a product that might not readily burn, but will accelerate the burning of combustible materials it contaminates, and . . ."

"Wait," Abbas interrupted. "Did this Tammerlin determine what the combustible material was?"

Hassan's eyes ran over the page. "Yes—here it is—*A leak of diesel fuel from the forklift, combined with the ammonium nitrate based fertilizer product created the initial combustible mixture.*"

"And? Anything else?"

"His commentary is critical of some of our procedures. I'll have the second document forwarded to you." Hassan gestured at Nadia. "Do you have it?" Without waiting for an answer, he plunged into the list of causative factors. *"One: regarding the forklift and hydrant, inadequate and faulty maintenance contributed to the fire. Two: Criton's loading dock operating procedure is excessively vague. Three: an open container of oily rags found adjacent to the metal grid was required by fire code to be in an explosion-proof canister, lid closed.* It needs to be relocated as well. Lastly, he suggests regularly scheduled and documented fire extinguisher training. The report ends with his conclusion citing the fire as accidental." Chain-smoking, Hassan popped another cigarette from his pack of Bahman's and tapped the filtered end on the edge of the box.

"And our man, the forklift operator, you fired him?"

"Yes. Ebi Rostum took the fall, and I made sure his foreman, Sam Collier, witnessed the dismissal and subsequent threats Rostum made. He's out of the picture, for now of course, at least as far as the authorities are concerned; according to plan."

"That's good," the sheik replied. "Rest assured, Hassan, the federal government will be interested in the results of Fire Marshal Tammerlin's report. Our plant and products are closely monitored, for obvious reasons. They may profit from our business, but that doesn't mean they like us." Again he coughed, and Hassan felt a tug of alarm. For a moment, his father's voice sounded frail. "I would expect, and you should prepare for a follow up visit from federal officials, perhaps from the Department of Homeland Security. I'm not certain of their bureaucratic jurisdictions.

They'll want to be sure this was just an accidental fire and nothing more."

"What is it you suggest I do? What should I say to ensure they suspect nothing?"

"They've just provided you the framework for answering any questions. It's in that report. Tammerlin's comments are official. Respond courteously, use them as guidelines, and under no circumstances give a personal opinion or disagree with his findings. Allow the federal regulator open access to Criton's files should he request them. He's long since reviewed all documents, and interviewing you is probably just a part of procedure. There's an American saying that applies here. Do not upset the apple cart."

"I understand."

"Good. They'll recognize this was simply an unfortunate fire and nothing else, just as I told you from the start. No one will suspect it as a ruse to hide the transfer of inventory to the *Orient Star*."

Hassan refilled his glass with the pale sherry. "Shall I wait until I meet with the authorities before having our claim forwarded to our insurance carrier?"

"No. One has nothing to do with the other. The government bureaucrat will care nothing of that. Whoever is sent will be concerned with only two things: that the fire was an accident, and when business will resume. Have Nadia complete the appropriate forms and submit them as soon as possible to the insurance company."

"As you wish." Hassan heard the phone click. He turned to his wife.

"Insurance claim. Get moving. We need to have the forms out by this afternoon.

Nadia said nothing and left the room.

Chapter 9
Criton Chemical Office. Richmond, Virginia

Nadia closed her office door and took a deep breath, bracing for the added workload. These ten-by-twelve walls imprisoned her, made her gasp for air like an asthmatic. Some day she'd simply choke on her husband's curt demands.

A decade in the United States had not liberated her. If anything, the years had highlighted her conflict between the deeply embedded customs of her culture and the freedom American women took for granted. She could only press her nose against the glass and yearn for a different life. As much as Hassan made his contempt for her plain, she kept her eyes downcast, less in deference than a need to hide her hatred of him.

A streak of lightning lit up the sky to the southwest. Moving over to the window beside the filing cabinet, Nadia peered out at the plum colored clouds angling in swiftly along the James River valley. Rain had already begun to fall, creating erratic patterns on the windowpane. Captivated by the rivulets, she let her mind drift away from Hassan to days she'd spent with her mother, Amira, at the bazaar in Qom. The rich, heady smell of myrrh incense had filled her senses, and the streets had hummed with chatter as bargains were made and goods traded.

Nadia's mother held her hand as they crossed Wahir Street to buy a piece of *sohan ghom* from the confectionary. Amira carved the Persian pistachio brittle into pieces for Nadia to share with her younger half-brother, Farid, a rare treat in a childhood dominated by Malik Al-Qahar, their father, a man who made Hassan seem like a prince. Acne-scarred and perpetually scowling, the shopkeeper beat his daughter whenever the mood took him: a bad day at work, a meal not quite to his liking. Sometimes just her presence was enough to send him into a rage. He'd wanted a son.

A second streak of lightning, closer this time, bisected the Richmond city skyline. Trembling now as much as she had when storms swept through Qom, Nadia recalled her mother's sense of isolation when Malik had taken another wife, Behi.

Behi did bear him a son, and Malik tolerated the unshakeable bond between the children until Farid was diagnosed with palsy, and Malik discovered that the delicate boy would never be the son he'd wanted. His loathing for Farid grew, and eventually the boy and his mother were cast out, abandoned in a small apartment in Aliabad.

As for Nadia, after her mother died, Malik saw value only in his daughter's potential to attract a husband. Determined to marry her off well, he sent her to the university, and soon after she graduated, arranged for her to marry Hassan. Farid and his mother were never spoken of again, to the extent that Hassan had no knowledge of Nadia's half-brother. However, the siblings remained close across the geographical distance that separated them, a secret Nadia relished keeping from her husband.

"My education." The windowpane fogged as she whispered the words. "All it gave you, dear father, was a chance to redeem your sullied reputation and salvage the name of Al-Qahar. And look where it's gotten me. The only good thing you ever made possible was the love two forgotten children still have for one another."

Her office door burst open. "I'm leaving," Hassan said. "Make sure those reports get done."

Nadia sat at her desk, the door ajar, as his footsteps faded on the tiled floor of the outer hallway. She listened for the elevator, and when she heard the doors close, smiled. "The reports can wait. I have something more important to attend to."

Chapter 10
Sharq News Agency, Tehran

Late in the afternoon, with the heat of the day at its peak, Farid Barmeen sat at his desk at Sharq News in Tehran, typing feverishly. Today his long, pale fingers cooperated with his sense of urgency, and he was pleased with the speed at which they tapped the keys. Fewer typos too—good news to a man who took no physical accomplishment for granted. Everything, from walking to turning the page of a book, challenged him. Some people jotted down their thoughts, but 'jotting' was a foreign concept to Farid, his body to his mind as the tortoise to the hare. But he comforted himself with the outcome of the race between them. The tortoise always came in first.

A short while ago, his editor had hovered over his desk and pushed him to meet a looming deadline, but right now, incoming emails took priority. Farid would have his article reporting another bombing in Iran near the Pakistan border done in a few minutes. He tapped the SAVE icon and thought about his informant, an anonymous, gravelly voice on the phone and clipped email correspondent who had begun feeding him specifics about seemingly random acts of terrorism that had recently escalated.

Farid pushed aside his crutches and rolled his chair across the office to shutter the blinds. At thirty-six, seventeen years of them in journalism when he'd started as a copy boy, he had his own office and could shut out the afternoon light without having to ask a dozen other reporters if they objected. Just as well. He wasn't a fan of the blazing sun and relentless heat, an irony that didn't escape him. Maybe there was still time to move to Greenland or Iceland or some place where it rained continuously . . . the UK even; maybe Seattle in the US. He suspected his small office had more to do with accommodating his physicality than his sharp reporting skills, but Farid Barmeen was good at what he did, and he no longer cared when others underestimated him because of his gaunt features and slender, awkward body.

Back at his desk, he opened an email from his sister, Nadia, whose unhappy marriage to a man he loathed caused Farid no end of regret.

Farid,

I have news. As you know, Hassan keeps me busy at the office, and something has come to my attention that will be of interest to you. I'm in the process of transcribing testimony and filling out insurance reports regarding a fire at Criton Chemical here in Chatterton. You also know that I'm privy to all correspondence between Hassan and his father, and many times I've felt uneasy about the content of files and memoranda that pass between them. It is all highly confidential, of course, but recently your newspaper came up in a note from the sheik, and I became concerned. He referred to various articles that you've written for Sharq and hints at trouble brewing for Criton Industries in Tehran. He speaks of political turbulence and retribution against those

69

involved in challenging the status quo. I worry that you're in the middle of something bigger than all of us. I love and cherish you and fear for your safety. You know I couldn't bear it if anything happened to you.

Your loving sister,
Nadia.

Farid took off his reading glasses. His hand trembled. Sometimes it shook or went into spasm, leaving him exhausted and groaning with frustration. The small tremors he could handle. He massaged the soft skin at his temples where a headache lurked, and his gaze drifted to the aluminum crutches that leaned against his desk. Whatever his plight, he was better off than his gentle sister, who led a life of unrelenting servitude to a vain, strutting peacock of a man who treated her like chattel. That she was obliged to keep the secrets of the corrupt house of Muhktar grated on his nerves and reinforced his contempt for their father.

A fire at Criton. Puzzled, Farid was torn between the need to protect Nadia and his wish to question her. He wrote instead:

Nadia,
You have always worried so about me, but there's no need. Try to think of my work as a puzzle needing to be solved, and I'm merely stringing the pieces together. Cold comfort I know, but I am not in any danger. Be careful, and keep our communication a secret. I don't

*want you to do anything to compromise your
position at Criton or anger your husband.
Promise me you'll be cautious!*

With fond affection,
Farid

Sharq was one of the last remaining newspapers
not yet controlled by the government. It had been shut
down for several months after security forces arrested
Ahmed Bahir, Editor in Chief, for his support of
opposition leaders who rallied against Iran's
president, Hassan Rouhani, and his policies. Since
reopening, the bulletin had been less inclined to
agitate the political leaders of the Republic, and Farid
and his colleagues were more circumspect about their
reporting. Many people, after being 'interviewed' by
the Revolutionary Guard, had been known to
disappear. He hadn't seen or heard any news of
Danush, the copy editor, or the man's wife, for three
weeks.

The window air conditioner, rattling on its last
legs, knocked the room temperature down a few
degrees, but Farid stifled in the heat. He'd been on
edge for the last two months, documenting not only
the ongoing Shi'ite terror attacks against the
Americans in Iraq, but also the chaotic events in Iran
as well. Some days he could swear the papers in his
basket were not as he'd left them.

The day was almost over, and he still hadn't heard
from his informer. He went back to his article.

TEHRAN, Iran. A car laden with explosives was detonated in the crowded business district of Zahedan early this morning, killing nine and injuring twenty-four. No one has yet claimed responsibility, but officials issued a statement accusing groups financed by foreign interests intent on crippling the government.

The FARS news agency reported the attack took place at 7:15 when a vehicle, parked in front of a large mercantile building, blew up moments after its occupants were seen running from the scene. The office of the provincial governor reports two of the attackers have been arrested and a cache of materials used to make bombs has been located. Hossein Ali Shahriyari, a deputy administrator of Zahedan has pledged, "Not only will we eliminate the cowards who commit such a vile atrocity, but we will bring final justice to those who support and provide the means to attack our nation."

The cell on his desk vibrated, and Farid flipped it open. *Unknown.* Heart thumping in his chest, hands cold and clammy and beginning to shake, he rolled his chair over to the door and closed it before uttering a faint, "Yes?" and clearing his throat.

"It's the same as the bombing of last week. You'll meet us where I told you, exactly when I told you. Don't be late, journalist."

Chapter 11
Criton Headquarters. Richmond, Virginia

The woman behind the desk adjacent to Hassan Muhktar's office lifted her gaze as Marcus Delorme stepped through the door. She looked startled, and Marcus smiled inwardly. His size often had that effect on strangers. Wearing the traditional headscarf of devout Muslim women, Muhktar's assistant, petite and timid, might suspect he could swallow her in one gulp.

"Special Agent Marcus Delorme, FBI, to see Mr. Muhktar," he said gently.

The woman smiled, and, distracted for a moment by the warmth in her dark brown eyes, Marcus caught himself staring.

"Please take a seat, Special Agent Delorme."

He nodded and moved away as the woman buzzed Hassan Muhktar over the intercom.

Special Agent of the FBI assigned to the Department of Homeland Security and former linebacker for Penn State University, Marcus sank all two hundred and five muscular pounds into one of the chairs in the waiting room of Criton Chemical. He reached for the latest edition of *TIME* and began flipping through its pages.

Mounted on the far wall, the television, a familiar voice emanating from it, caught his attention. He knew Jason Emora, the CNN anchor that was reporting on bombings in the Middle East wrought by improvised explosive devices. One had struck a marketplace in Basra, Iraq, while another demolished the Iranian business district of Zahedan.

Marcus was familiar with both incidents. Just that morning he had re-read the official brief while still at his office in the J. Edgar Hoover building in D.C. He made a mental note to take a second look at the surge of IED's and the attacks striking the hated rivals almost simultaneously. Someone was trying to send a special message to both governments.

Marcus put the magazine down on the glass side table and scanned the room. He had been in a number of offices very similar to this one over the past twenty plus years and had met with many foreign nationals. The profile he'd been studying indicated that Hassan Muhktar's father, Abbas, an influential Iranian national during the reign of Shah Reza Pahlavi, had established Criton Chemical in 1975 and turned it over to his son years later. Hassan Muhktar was not considered nearly as competent as his father. His penchant for alcohol and displays of ill temper certainly did not mirror his father's adroit social and business skills.

Iran was once a friend to America. Things must have changed for this company and the man who ran it now. Marcus was used to being on high alert in all things Middle Eastern, and the Criton fire had taken his radar up a notch. Investigators had found no evidence of arson, but for some reason, he felt uncomfortable about the speedily delivered report that neatly stitched up an incident with dangerous implications. Timothy McVeigh, the American born terrorist who used ammonium nitrate to build his bomb, had vaulted the products manufactured at

Criton into the public eye. The Federal government took an interest in any incident involving nitrates, and Marcus had to be certain terrorism was not a factor here.

The door swung open, and he took in the form of Hassan Muhktar, impeccably dressed in a dark brown pinstriped suit, cream shirt and ocher silk tie.

The plant owner extended his palm and gestured for Marcus to precede him into the office. "Special Agent Delorme, please come in. It's a pleasure to meet you."

Marcus stood, picked up his briefcase and extended his hand, all the while sizing up the man. *Manicured fingernails. Black onyx cufflinks, Rolex Cosmograph.* Even with a soft Iranian lilt in his voice, the man's pronunciation of English was precise. *Oxford? Cambridge?*

"Thank you for your time, Mr. Muhktar."

They shook hands, and Marcus glanced back at the woman who sat quietly behind her desk, watching them. His eyes met hers briefly, and she quickly looked away.

Muhktar pointed to a comfortable chair opposite his desk. "Please have a seat. Would you like a drink, water or coffee, perhaps?"

"No thank you." Marcus said. "I don't wish to take up any more of your time than necessary." He lifted the leather case onto his lap, unclasped the locks and removed a manila folder. "You know why I'm here, Mr. Muhktar."

"Yes, of course. The fire. How can I help you?"

"Let's begin by going through the report. I have a few questions, a few things we need to clear up.

Firstly, can you confirm that this wasn't industrial grade ammonium nitrate?"

Muhktar folded his hands in front of him on his desk. "No, it wasn't. The material in question was packaged fertilizer."

"I see the local fire authorities have determined the fire was an accident. Quite impressive, finalizing the report so quickly, don't you think?"

Muhktar stared at him coldly. "We leave nothing to chance in such matters."

"And what 'matters' would those be?"

The man opened a desk drawer and shut it, a nervous gesture that failed to distract Marcus. If anything, he caught Muhktar's growing tension and sat forward, noting a bead of sweat break out on the plant owner's forehead.

"Accidents, of course. What else?"

Marcus shook his head. "So you lost upwards of fifteen thousand tons of packaged fertilizer that was stored in the depot destroyed by the fire? No industrial grade ammonium nitrate?"

Muhktar huffed, "It's in the report to the Department of Transportation. The nitrate for the mining industry had already shipped." He pointed to a copy of the freight bill. "We've conducted our own internal evaluation too. There's no doubt it was an accident."

"Fair enough. We'll need to talk to your dockworkers too. The incipient fire couldn't be contained by your emergency fire team?"

"The hydrant at the dock was out of service that morning; there was a delay. The Fire Department successfully connected to other yard hydrants at the plant."

Marcus made a quick note and skimmed over to the section of the file detailing past incidents at the chemical company. "And you've never had an event like this?"

Hassan shook his head vigorously. "Not such as this in the thirty five years since my father built this facility. There was an incident, several years ago, but it was merely a spill. There was no fire."

Marcus looked up from his dossier, barely managing to keep his expression neutral. *Three of your workers died of respiratory failure, two firefighters had severe chemical burns, and you consider that a mere spill?* He underlined the event and scribbled a quick reminder to take a second look. For the next half hour, he asked probing questions about storage, delivery, and product contracts. Muhktar's answers were short and precise, and Marcus sensed they'd been rehearsed.

At last he looked up from his notes and sat back. "I have one more question. You've accounted for *all* the materials, as required by federal law?"

"Absolutely." Muhktar exhaled forcefully and sat up straight. "Special Agent Delorme, what are you driving at? Criton's records are in order. I have them right here."

Marcus noted the stiff change in body language. Years of interviews had taught him that one way to get below the surface, to find any revealing or contradictory evidence in such meetings was to get the subject to feel comfortable, get him to think he had the upper hand. If there were anything out of the ordinary, it would show up when the man's guard was down. "No doubt," he said. "Before we wrap up, can we go over one more time how the fire started?"

Muhktar again opened the top drawer. "You won't mind if I refer to a few of my own notes, to be accurate, of course?" He withdrew a few handwritten sheets of paper. "My personnel had just begun loading pallets of fertilizer onto a tractor-trailer. The forklift operator, Ebi Rostum, claimed to have misunderstood our standard operating procedure, which requires two men on the dock while loading."

"Oh?" Marcus studied him. "He was the only one there?"

Muhktar frowned and scanned his notes. "A second man, the supervisor, Sam Collier, was still in the guard shack checking the loading invoice. Our forklifts are not supposed to operate on that dock until two men are out there. Statistics have shown backing maneuvers are the biggest cause of accidents on loading docks. One of the primary tasks of the second worker is to prevent that. Had he been there, this would have been avoided."

"Mr. Collier, the foreman." Marcus placed a check next to their names. "Is he still with you?"

"I'm sorry." Muhktar pressed his fingertips together and flexed them. "Was I vague? I don't hold Mr. Collier responsible. He's still with Criton. However, I personally dismissed Mr. Rostum. He's no longer an employee. Clearly he was incompetent, violated our most basic operating procedures. He had to go."

"We'll need to locate him. Do you know where we can find him?"

"How would I know? I fired him. He could be holed up in some motel for all I know, binge drinking. It's no longer my concern."

"How did he take the news, Mr. Muhktar? With the recession we're in, losing one's job can be devastating."

Muhktar scowled. "He was angry, swore at me. So what? This isn't the first time I've dismissed an employee, and no one has ever been happy about it."

Marcus capped his pen and clipped it to the pad. "Is there anything else you care to add, Mr. Muhktar? Do you have a time frame for when Criton will be up and running again?"

"No, not at this moment. We're still busy with clean up and inspection." Muhktar stood. "Now if we're done here…"

Marcus closed his briefcase and got up. "Thanks, Mr. Muhktar. I'll let you know if I need anything else." He handed over his business card. "I'll need an address for Ebi Rostum, which you must have on record. We need to speak with him."

"Of course. Nadia will look it up." He ushered Marcus through the door and followed him over to his assistant's desk. "Special Agent Delorme needs an address for Ebi Rostum," he said curtly. Then he turned, shook hands with Marcus, and returned to his office.

Chapter 12
Rosie Connolly's Pub, Richmond, Virginia

Seated in his car outside Hassan Muhktar's office, Marcus hit a number on his speed dial and waited.

"Uh, hang on, yeah . . . Meagher Investigative Services."

"Is that how you answer your office line, you old goat? Just another reason why Stamper put you out to pasture when he took over." Marcus laughed. "And when are we playing golf again, give me a chance to win some of my money back?"

"Hey, Marcus! You caught me looking for my damn cell phone charger."

The FBI agent could hear the springs in William's seat squeak, followed by a dull thud, and pictured his old friend landing his shoes on the desk. He'd seen him do it countless times.

"I'd love to take some more of your pay any time you'd like. Where in the world are you?"

"Like you could sink that eighteen footer on the last hole again. Jut a lucky putt, that's all it was. And as a matter of fact, I'm in Richmond, following up on that fire at Criton Chemical. Any chance you're working on that? I just finished up an appointment with the CEO and have the rest of the afternoon off, thought we might grab some lunch, maybe compare notes?"

"Sounds great. For a change, your timing couldn't be better. Look, I'm meeting up with the boys in ten minutes at Rosie Connolly's Pub. I know they'll be happy to see you. As for Criton, their insurance company hasn't called me, so I haven't anything to tell you, nothing official anyway. Shane was in charge though, and Patrick's crew was there as well. He's a little suspicious about it being an accident. But you know Patrick, always been a bit of a skeptic."

"He may have a point," Marcus said. "I think I will join you. I have a few questions of my own. Some about Criton's head man, Hassan Muhktar. I'm sure you know him after all your years in the Fire Department."

"That I do." William said. "So, meet us at one?"

"Sure thing. And since you're bragging about our last golf match, you can pick up the tab."

Marcus didn't give William a chance to argue. He ended the call, tossed his phone onto the passenger seat and headed down the hill on Broad Street. The conversation made him wish he had thrown his clubs in the trunk, maybe get nine holes in. He loved the game and was proud of his sixteen over handicap. Not bad for a hacker who was only getting on the course once a month. He knew he was working too many hours; eighteen holes at Yankee Trace Country Club would have suited him fine, a chance for a couple of beers and to blow off some steam, even if William usually got the better of him.

Turning left onto East Main Street, he squeezed the Chevrolet into a parking spot in front of the Farmer's Market and trotted across the street to Rosie Connolly's Pub. He pushed open the door and flung his jacket onto the brass coat rack. "My man! Tommy, how the heck are you?"

"Marcus!" The cheerful Englishman from Liverpool called out from behind the bar. "Good to see you."

"I see you're still your own hardest working bartender. How's the wife?"

"Doing fine, mate, thanks. She'll be in later. Have a seat. What'll you have?"

"I'll take a club soda with a wedge of lime while I'm waiting for the Meaghers, and we'll all be grabbing something to eat. I'll sit in our usual booth in the corner."

"Make yourself comfortable. I'll bring it to you."

Marcus sat down, arched his back and stretched his legs. Through the years, he and William had tipped a few pints together in this very spot, taking turns as sounding board to one another regarding the incidents they had run. It had been a while since he'd seen Patrick and Shane. It would be good to see them again as well. He'd known William for twenty years, ever since a crystal meth lab the Outlaws had operated off of Centralia Avenue had burned up. The Chatterton police had called in the FBI after discovering the Maryland based gang had crossed the state line and partially dismembered two members of a rival group in the east end of town. They'd left them with their throats slit, after being shot in the balls. That was some night. The flash-bang grenade Marcus had tossed prematurely caught the curtains in the kitchen on fire and ruptured the eardrum of the special agent in charge. It earned him an ass chewing he'd never forgotten and the nickname 'Mad Bomber' by the Fire Department Investigator called to the scene, William Meagher.

The entrance door bounced against its stop, and Marcus turned when he heard William's voice at his shoulder.

"You know, it's a shame that you only work half the day, and my taxes are paying your salary." William held up two fingers, his sign to the bartender for two pints.

Marcus sprang to his feet. "Don't mess with the FBI, you fire hose jockey!" They slapped each other on the back. "Always good to see you, William."

"Same here." The old wooden bench groaned as they sat. "You sticking with that?" William gestured to Marcus's drink. "I ordered you a pint—you're done for the day, aren't you?"

"Sure am. A beer with lunch is fine. It's the company I'm with that is a concern, though." The agent grinned.

"So," William said once Tommy had brought over their mugs, "you're here to check on Criton, eh?"

"Yes, if anything happens at one of these plants, we have to make sure it doesn't constitute a terrorist threat."

They toasted each other and took a sip.

"So, what do you think of Muhktar?" William said. "I met him a few times while still at the department. All business, and not very cordial. I'm curious to know your opinion, besides what happened at the plant."

Marcus drummed his fingers on the tabletop for a couple of seconds as William spun his glass between both hands, waiting for a reply. "Interesting background. Heads the operation his father started many years ago when ties with our government were

83

a lot more hospitable. Very direct, very prepared. I expected that. He's the controlling type. He didn't seem to enjoy my visit, but he had all the needed documents and the Fire Department's report as well. You ever meet his father, the sheik, Abbas Muhktar?"

"Oh, I've seen the man." William continued to palm his schooner. "Many years ago at some big to-do at the plant. All polite smiles and flash with Mayor Berkline and the other Chatterton big wigs at the time. I was there with a couple of my fire engines. We were told to stand by at Criton during the event. A real political dog and pony show for the public it was."

Marcus sipped his beer. "Well, his son sure as hell inherited that cagey smile and lofty disposition you're talking about. But you know, with the political climate in this country the way it is now, I have to take that into consideration as regards his behavior. Coupled with this lengthy downturn in the economy, a more complete picture of Muhktar and Criton comes into focus. You wouldn't believe what crosses my desk regarding Iranians living and working in this country. Lots of hate directed at them, guilt by association, if you know what I mean. I'm sure that factors into his defensive attitude as well."

William nodded. "I do." He edged forward. "What about the fire itself, what are your thoughts on that?"

"It's funny, I got the sense he wasn't really all that upset about the fire. Hell, he barely blinked talking about three of his people dying a few years ago at the plant. But I'm not seeing any discrepancies in the processing, storage, and distribution of nitrates, nothing missing, and all domestic shipments

84

accounted for. Criton is a worldwide company, so we're unable to track all its accounts. At this point, it appears the fire on the loading dock was just that—an accident—caused by one of the employees. I found no irregularities in their records, and the report indicates no evidence of arson. I intend to interview the guy who started it, Ebi Rostum. From what I can tell, he's pissed about being fired."

A commotion at the door distracted them as Vince, Shane and Patrick burst into the pub.

"You're out of your mind, Rigardo. No way will the Yankees beat Boston this season. It's a . . ." Patrick broke off and grinned when he spotted Marcus. "Look who the wind blew in. Marcus, what are you doing here?"

The three men joined them in the corner, squeezing onto the bench across the table.

"Special Agent Marcus Delorme, no less." Vince extended his hand, and Marcus noted the *Firefighter of the Year* ring he wore since he'd won the award two years ago. A sapphire nestled in a block the size of a nickel on a band of gold engraved with the Chatterton Fire and EMS logo. "Finally escaped from the DC beltway crowd, huh?" He snickered, his grip dwarfed by Marcus's grasp.

"We weren't expecting you," Shane said. "What brings you to town?"

"What do you think? I came to arrest you for gross incompetence at a hazardous materials fire."

"So you heard I got suspended?"

"Suspended?" Marcus shook his head. "Your strategy and tactics were sound. The entire industrial park and part of Chatterton could've been wiped out."

"You lot eating or what?" Tommy called from behind the bar.

They ordered shepherd's pie, fish and chips, and three portions of bangers and mash before Shane continued. "The Chief got a bug by the name of Stamper up his ass, because the plant owner complained about our response. I got two weeks on the street with no pay for a delay Lowell claims compounded the loss at the facility. The funny thing is, part of the holdup was due to Lowell's own staffing cutbacks."

Patrick chimed in. "The real delay had nothing to do with us either. Procedure on the loading dock wasn't followed. The fire never should've started, or at least they should have handled it."

"Sorry to have touched a nerve." Marcus said. "For what it's worth, Hassan Muhktar fired the forklift operator. The rest of what happened is in the Fire Inspector's report."

"The report. You mean the one Lowell had the top dog of investigations do *personally*?" Vincent's sarcasm wasn't lost on Marcus. "Criton is in my jurisdiction. I'm responsible for all the things that go on out there, but I was never involved. My boss, Eddie Tammerlin, told me he was handling it. I know that facility a whole lot better than he does, yet I never saw any paperwork or had any input. What a bunch of crap. No wonder Shane was railroaded."

"The Fire Marshal compiled the report by himself?" Marcus's interest ratcheted up a notch. "That's not typical, is it?"

Patrick exchanged a telling look with Vince and said, "You got that right. There's nothing typical about this fire."

Tommy brought over three more pints, giving Marcus and William a chance to reconnect as the younger men bantered with the bartender.

"You smell a rat?" Marcus said softly.

William raised his eyebrows and grimaced. "Hard to say. Nothing we can do though without making a rough deal a lot worse."

Marcus caught Patrick watching them, and William wagged a finger at his son. "I'm telling you, Pat, let it rest."

Torrents of rain began to fall and knocked against the windows. Thunder rumbled. Subdued, they waited for their food.

Marcus kept an eye on Patrick and Vince as he tucked into his mashed potatoes. He'd have to take a much closer look at Hassan Muhktar and the Criton fire. Starting with Ebi Rostum.

Chapter 13
The Port of Khorromshahr, Iran

It was a long, nerve-wracking drive from Tehran to the decaying Iranian port city of Khorromshahr. Balancing on his crutches, Farid got out of the car and pressed his hip against the door to shut it, all the while wondering why the dark voice with the cryptic message had demanded they meet here. He stood still on the bank of the Shatt al Arab, the muddy river separating Iran from Iraq, and allowed his senses to synchronize. It was the only way he could envision the seaport as it was before the war. Farid's palms were wet, and he wiped them dry on his trousers. A brackish taste lodged at the back of his throat as he made his way along the embankment. Now and again he stopped and leaned on his crutches, furtively looking around.

Fifteen feet below him, the rainbow colored sheen of bilge oil leaking from a Panamanian freighter floated on the water and lapped against the rusted bulwarks of the dock. The putrid smell of rotting fish bobbing in the slick, their pale, dead eyes matching the weak light of the low lying moon, mixed with the stench of diesel fumes and seemed to choke the life from the deserted harbor front.

Farid moved forward to the tick-tick cadence of his crutches' metal tips on the steel deck plates of the pier. He hobbled past the abandoned waterfront storehouses that once were filled to capacity and paused. The pockmarked scars of Iraqi automatic weapons fire, left years ago on the smoke stained concrete walls, added to his growing anxiety and heightened his vigilance.

He moved cautiously, as if unseen eyes had already targeted him. With every step, he recalled stories he had written about Khorromshahr, how it was once Iran's largest non-oil port city. Now, it was all but abandoned, and his words, and what was left of the place, haunted him. The destruction wrought by Saddam Hussein's forces years ago remained starkly evident, and the once bustling seaport resembled a ghost town.

In its place, Bandar Abbass, along the Strait of Hormuz, bustled and had been developed to become the major harbor and shining new face of Iran. Khorromshahr and its residents were forgotten, lost in the shadows, and left to fend for themselves.

Farid stopped and squinted at his watch. He dared not be late. He heard scurrying amongst the piles of garbage at the end of the litter-strewn alley ahead of him. Sweat began to stain his linen shirt as he struggled to control his thoughts and emotions. Why here, in this Godforsaken place?

A crumpled wad of newspaper landed at his feet.

"Journalist."

Farid froze.

"Don't look up. Don't even move."

A can tumbled from a trash heap to his left, and he looked down as it settled against his shoe. Hard arms shoved him, banging his face against a stone wall. Pain blinded him momentarily, and he felt a trickle of blood drip from his nose. Then a dark hood was thrown over his head and cinched as a second pair of rough hands roved deftly over his body, searching. Farid could smell them: men who bore the stench of lives left to fester in the decay of Khorromshahr.

"You ´ will not speak, journalist," The voice commanded. "We have nothing to lose. But you, well?"

Farid's crutches clattered onto the sidewalk. He stumbled before groping and picking them up. Men on either side steadied him and hauled him forward. He estimated they covered roughly one hundred feet before he was guided over a threshold. Behind him, hinges creaked; wood scraped the floor. A strong grip forced him down into a stiff backed chair.

"You take great risks with your life, journalist," said the voice from the alley. "We do it gladly; it is Allah's will. Is it so for you?"

Farid clasped his hands together in an effort to still his shaking. "I do what I do for love of my country," he croaked. "Is that not considered guidance by the will of God?"

A thick hand slapped him on the back.

"Fear not, Farid Barmeen, you would not be here if Allah, and the great Sheik Kazem Al-Unistan did not wish it."

The hood was yanked off his head.

Farid squinted and rubbed his eyes. An oil lamp hanging from a chain above a plastic table cast dirty light over the room. A man draped in an ankle length robe materialized from beyond the dingy glow of the lantern.

"There's no need for you to strain your vision. It matters more that you hear me." The man swooped on

Farid and grabbed his jaw in a tight grip that forced his head upward.

Farid immediately recognized the intense black eyes and craggy features. "Kazem Al-Unistan!" His body quivered. What was an Iraqi Shi'ite tribal chief doing in Iran? Farid's knuckles turned white as he clung to the seat of his chair.

The warlord released him. "We've been following your reports." He spoke softly, his voice deceptively amiable. "I'm the one who's been supplying you with information. You're making powerful enemies, Farid Barmeen. There are corrupt men in Iran. Powerful businessmen who profit from death and conflict. Abbas Muhktar is such a man. You smoke, yes?"

Farid nodded.

A match flared behind his ear, and the smell of burning sulfur filled his nostrils. A cigarette was coaxed between his lips.

Farid sucked hard and coughed, losing the cigarette. No one picked it up off the floor. He caught his breath and said, "The bombing in Zahaden and the attack at the marketplace in Basra, that was Muhktar's work? In both countries?"

"Yes and no. On the surface, I take credit for that."

"I don't understand. You're connected with the Muhktars through terrorism? Why? You're wanting to destabilize both your own country and Iran?"

The sheik placed his hands on the plastic table and leaned in close. "I want America and its puppet government in Iraq to choke on their own blood. I want Iran to be a distant memory, obliterated from the map of a new Middle East, united under one righteous leader, a man who will walk in the footsteps of the

Prophet Muhammad and claim the allegiance of all Muslims across the world."

Farid stared at him. "I'm a journalist."

"You are a journalist, and you will expose Criton Chemical for what it is—an Iranian company that profits from the death of Iranians."

"At your hands."

"It is the first piece of a puzzle that you will eventually understand. The first step toward the Awakening."

Farid's hands shook uncontrollably. "How can I possibly be of use?"

The lantern above the table flickered as Al-Unistan glided silently past him. "Your newspaper is critical of the government, a government I wish to destroy myself. I intend to use Sharq to my advantage. You will help me discredit one of the foremost Iranian businessmen, a man the government and the people of Iran look up to."

Farid's mind raced as he grappled with the implications of a link between Criton and the bombings. Then it dawned on him. "Criton is supplying you with industrial grade fertilizer for use in the bombings."

Al-Unistan's face, cast in shadow, gave nothing away.

Caught up in the enormity of his discovery, Farid abandoned caution. "But that would make the Muhktars complicit. Why would you want to expose Criton?" It made no sense. Then slowly it came to him. This wasn't just about Iran. It had everything to do with the Americans. Criton had a branch in the United States. If the company were implicated in acts of terrorism, that would place enormous strain on American/Iranian relations. The Iranians would blame the bombings on America's ties to Criton, and the US would blame Iran for producing industrial grade ammonium nitrate on American soil. He felt sick.

Al-Unistan spoke softly. "You should know the Iranian government has no interest in Khorromshahr. The city rots, its people starve. What little commerce finds its way to the harbor is poorly regulated. In such places where laws are few and need is great, deals are made. A man can't enjoy the sunrise when hunger is all he knows. Don't you agree, Farid Barmeen? The people here in Khorromshahr, they know only hunger."

"But I still don't understand." Farid rasped, his mouth parched.

Al-Unistan swept his arm in a wide arc. "Along the waters of the Shatt al Arab, the black market flourishes. The impoverished suffer from the imposed restrictions of those who lust for power. Forgotten and abandoned by the corrupt, the people fashion a meager existence, loyal only to their own survival."

Again the tribal chief placed his hands on the table and leaned in. "I'll put it in simple language. The bombs for the attacks in Iraq and Iran, they were all assembled using materials unloaded from ships moored at the docks of Khorromshahr. And yes, the ships belong to Abbas Muhktar."

Events that once seemed unrelated now intersected. The anonymous phone tips at Farid's office regarding Criton. Nadia's last email alluding to messages between Hassan and Abbas. The explosions and killings in Iran and Iraq. "Does Sheik Muhktar *know* his ships are being offloaded in Khorromshahr?"

Al-Unistan threw him a humorless smile. "At this point you have all you need. Hear me, Farid Barmeen, for your life means nothing to me—the media is as fraudulent as Abbas Muhktar and the regime he deceives. I'll take this information, that you *will* write and publish for us, to the Arat Council members in Iraq and persuade our leaders to increase their efforts against Iran." He handed a folded piece of paper to Farid. "Read this, and memorize the instructions precisely regarding your return to Khorromshahr when Muhktar's ship arrives."

Farid unfolded and read the note, then wordlessly handed it back to Al-Unistan.

"Your cooperation will make Behi most proud of her only son, do you not think?" The warlord clapped his hands. "Cover his head and return him to the dock, so he may find his way to that apartment above the market. The one he shares with his mother."

Farid had to be helped to his feet.

Chapter 14
Criton Chemical Office. Richmond, Virginia

Hassan Muhktar fiddled with the diamond encrusted pinkie ring on his left hand, enjoying the way the stones caught the sunlight streaming in through his office window. He spun the band and turned his attention to Nadia, who sat opposite him. "North American Insurance Company has contacted us regarding our claim?"

Nadia handed him the newly arrived letter from the insurance giant.

"The letter opener." He held his hand out, getting a kick out of the exasperated look on her face as she shot up and gingerly placed the blade in his hand before retreating. He ran his index finger down its dull edge, inserted it under the gummed flap and sliced meticulously. Turning to face the window, he unfolded and read it before speaking. "Excellent. It's settled. Six million plus."

"Shall I deposit it to Criton and transfer the money to your account or to the account you share with the sheik?"

Hassan stood and circled Nadia before backing against the front of his desk to face her, arms folded. "Create a separate interest bearing business account for the claim, and leave the funds for now." He tossed the letter of settlement on the edge of the desk. "Take it. I need to speak with the sheik." Reaching for his phone and a pack of Bahman's, he lit the last one before pressing the number on speed dial.

"Yes? Hassan?"

Hassan heard the sound of passing traffic. His father must be navigating Tehran's busy streets.

"Hassan?"

"Hello? Yes . . . Father, how are you?" Hassan jabbed at the volume control on his phone.

"It's difficult to hear you. I'm standing at the bottom of the hill on Avenue Valiesr. My meeting with the Minister of Commerce is in ten minutes."

"I've received the settlement for our damages at Criton. You told me to call. We were going to review it."

"I can't be late for this, Hassan. The Minister and I plan to discuss the next, and last, shipment of nitrates to the Iranian government."

Hassan squeezed the bridge of his nose, frustration overcoming his usual formality. "Father, this *is* about the shipment." The annoyance in his voice grew. "I've heard from Jalal regarding the *Orient Star.*"

Jalal Hamadi, known to Hassan and Abbas as none other than Ebi Rostum, was his father's closest aide. As far as Hassan was concerned, the man was an inconvenient thug who couldn't be trusted and now, with the FBI sniffing around, he was a danger to the entire operation.

"You're breaking up, but I heard you mention something about the *Star*. Send the details to me in an email, and I'll read it when I get back to the office."

"I'll have it sent right . . ." Hassan's cell went blank in mid-sentence. Flushed, he focused his anger on Nadia as she worked on her laptop. "What are you doing?"

"I'm checking the accounts."

"That can wait. I want this taken care of now. You're making sure all our correspondence is encrypted, right?"

She nodded. "Of course. The algorithm I am using turns everything to cipher text. It's impossible to read without the code and only you and I, your father, and of course, Jalal Hamadi, have that."

Hassan soured at hearing Jalal's name. He turned his attention to the bar and thought for a moment before beginning to dictate. Seizing the Jack Daniels, he said, "The *Orient Star* will arrive in the Persian Gulf Friday and dock at Pier 6 in Khorromshahr at midnight. It's carrying 15,000 tons of ammonium nitrate fertilizer. The captain will hand over control of the vessel to Jalal, who'll manage the sale and transfer of the ship and remaining nitrates to Kazem Al-Unistan, as planned. Jalal will then return to Virginia."

Nadia typed as he spoke, and Hassan looked over her shoulder. He grunted and downed the whiskey left in his tumbler. "Add this: I must once again relay my continued unease that Jalal has direct access to our Khorromshahr account with such large sums changing hands. He could easily steal from us. Please contact me after your meeting."

Nadia's fingers flew over the keys. That much he had to give her. She was efficient.

"Encrypt it, send it, and contact Sam Collier at Criton. Tell him I've received Fire Department authorization allowing transfer of the remaining shipping containers, pallets of burlap sacks, and stacks of cardboard boxes from the plant to our warehouse on Mandarin Turnpike."

"Is there anything else?"

"Advise him I'll be there this afternoon. He's to start immediately. I don't want any of this to wait any longer than necessary."

Chapter 15
Criton Chemical Plant

Without warning, the oncoming truck sliced across the centerline of the entrance road at Criton Chemical and barreled straight toward Vince Rigardo. He pounded the horn and flashed his headlights in repeated bursts, but the son of a bitch didn't seem to give a rat's ass and kept coming. Vince swerved, braking hard, and veered onto the gravel shoulder before sliding to a stop, the dust forming a gritty cloud that surrounded the Fire Department van.

"Hey!" Vince yelled as the truck sped by. "You wanna get that thing onto your side of the road?"

With a sudden flash of brake lights, the truck screeched to a halt, giving off a noxious smell of burnt rubber as its tires dug into the asphalt. The driver careened his pick-up truck in reverse toward Vince, almost crashing into his door.

"You got something to say, asshole?" The angry round face looked like it belonged to a boxer: deep-set eyes; thick, bony forehead; nose that appeared to have been used as a punching bag; and a patchy four day growth sprouting from his lower jaw. "You want something? Well I'll tell you what *I* want—I want you to go *fuck* yourself!"

Startled by the excessive verbal barrage, Vince said nothing and could only blink at the man.

The driver fired his middle finger before mashing his pickup into first gear, accelerating, and disappearing through the gates of the plant into the traffic on Ironbound Parkway.

"Heck of a welcome, and a hell of a place for the Fire Marshal to do his first solo investigation," Vince mused quietly as he pulled back onto the blacktop. He shook his head at the thought of his boss handling the incident from A to Z. The last couple of years, Vince had been the one to do the site work. It was time to get back to normal, see what he could find out, and do some snooping. Something was up. He nosed the vehicle into a slot by the guard shack and cut the engine.

"Hey, Inspector Rigardo!" The foreman, Sam Collier, waved as he jumped off the tailboard of his brown Ford F-250 parked near what remained of the beams that supported the loading dock. "Wondered when I was gonna see you again. Figured you were supposed to head up the Fire Departments looking into this mess. Where you been?"

"Hello, Sam."

They shook hands while Vince observed the tangled steel trusses of the large storage building that had collapsed into a pile of twisted burnt metal strands. "Good to see you, must have been quite a morning?"

"You ain't kidding." Collier grinned. "Scared the shit outta me. But I'm sure you know all about that, huh? What can I do for you?"

"Well, I just thought I'd take a look around, maybe even get you to be my tour guide."

"No problem. I was just taking a break from loading these pallets anyway. Mr. Muhktar says we've got to move them, you know, to our warehouse off of Mandarin Turnpike?"

Vince balanced a notepad on the van's fender, opened the rear door, and stepped into a pair of dark blue, fire resistant Nomex overalls. Craning his neck, he surveyed the heaps of burlap sacks used to package fertilizer and columns of folded cardboard boxes that were piled in the lot near the depot. "This all has to go?" He yanked on a pair of knee-length rubber boots and grabbed a canvas satchel with Chatterton Fire Investigation stenciled on the side.

"Yup." Collier grabbed his hard hat. "You all set, Inspector?"

The two men walked toward the misshapen truss work, the skeletal remains of the depot that had stood attached to the loading dock, its blackened bones projecting grotesquely at all angles from its charred body.

"Sam, where did the fire start exactly?" Vince unzipped his bag to remove a camera and an oblong shaped leather carry case.

"Over here. I'm pretty sure anyway." Collier pointed to a smoke stain at the base of the loading dock and then at the object Vince had tugged from its protective covering. "What's that you got there?"

"It's a hazardous material chemical identifier—it analyzes the burn. Sort of figures out what was involved." The fire inspector made his way over to a metal canister about the size of a small kitchen trash can, lying on its side near the twisted grid deck. He poked the wand of the device inside to check for the presence of accelerants. "Our first look will be right here where the heaviest alligator hide pattern is located."

Collier's eyebrows arched. "Say what?"

Vince got up from his crouch. "See this charring on the wood joists, sort of like an alligator's skin?" He tapped the remains of the destroyed beams. "The depth of the char, as compared to the unburned portions, helps figure out the length of time of the burn itself, and this V-shaped pattern above it tells me it started right here. But these blisters on the wood, this alligatoring?" Vince scraped one of the crusty, bubble shaped cells. "They seem much bigger than I would have imagined. That size tells me it went up kind of quick and moved away from this point real fast. There would have to be a reason for that." He lifted the can he'd just examined. Coarse, colorless granules mixed with the gravel in a small circle beneath it. "And you say this is where your operator scraped the grid?" He returned the infrared spectrographic device to its case and grabbed his legal pad.

"I suppose so." Collier shrugged. "I was inside checking the papers. Like I told your Fire Chief in charge that night, I didn't see it happen. I didn't know nothing till my guy comes in yelling at me to call you guys."

Vince squatted by the metal can once more, and sifting through bits of charred cloth, found what appeared to be the melted remains of a cigarette filter. "Hand me that bag, will you?"

"Here you go." Collier watched as Vince dropped the butt into a plastic evidence bag and wrote on the tag.

"So, this forklift driver, he's out here by himself loading nitrate fertilizer, even though he knows there are supposed to be two plant workers?"

"Yeah, he's been here long enough." Collier tilted his hard hat. "That's a standard operating procedure. He should've known better, must have been in a hurry. You just missed him, in fact."

"Toss me that Stanley measuring tape, please." Vince cupped his hands. "Does he have a scraggly beard, drive a mid-sized, light brown pick-up truck?"

"Yeah, that's him, Ebi Rostum, he's on our ERT. And he's got a Dodge Dakota that color." The tape arched through the air. "Why, did you see him?"

"Thanks." Vince hooked the end on the warped deck beneath a *No Smoking* sign, measuring the distance from the can to the scorched forklift. "There are too many faces in those occasional fire training classes I teach here to recognize most of your crew. I did almost get run off the road by one pissed off driver though, right by the gate. The guy looked like someone busted his nose real good, sort of like yours."

Collier laughed. "This?" He pinched the crooked mound. "Chalk that up to some drunken pike-a-nite. Some loser, I think his name was Wayne, but everyone knew him as Boss Hog. Son of a bitch blindsided me with his pool stick a few years ago at Sylvester's Bar on Jeff Davis Highway after I took him for five *costly* games in a row, double or nothing." Collier grinned. "Get it, Inspector? Chalk it up?"

103

"Hard to miss, Sam." Vince smirked. "But I got a newsflash for you, you're not Jimmy Kimmel. If I were you, I'd keep the day job here at Criton."

"I hear you, but no doubt though, that was Ebi for sure." The plant foreman lit up a Marlboro Red. "He was still bitching about Muhktar when he got here to clean out his locker. Anyway, while he was here we went into the guard shack over there, and I asked him for his turnout gear. The guy starts cursing, bounces his lit cigarette off me and tells me to fuck off, like it's my fault he got canned. He can shove them fancy cigarettes of his up his ass, some kind of funky foreign brand. I think they taste like shit anyway."

Vince watched Collier's cigarette smoke spiral upwards. He cut his eyes toward the *No Smoking* sign.

"Oh, sorry Inspector." Collier toed it out.

"So he was a member of your Emergency Response Team and he smoked, too? What's with you guys?" Vince fingered a small puncture in the fuel tank of the burnt forklift that Ebi Rostum had crunched into the dock, starting the fire. The 35 mm Canon flashed. "He tried to put the fire out using an extinguisher, right?"

"He got on the team about two, maybe two and a half months ago. Muhktar okayed it. Guess he's kicking himself in the ass for that decision," Collier laughed. "And yeah, he used the extinguisher attached to the forklift. I showed it to your guy Eddie, Eddie Tammerlin. He wanted to see it when he came to investigate the fire."

Vince stepped back, and the digital camera flashed again. "Mind if I take a look at the extinguisher too?"

"Got it in there." Collier jerked his head toward the guard shack. "Tammerlin checked that out, too."

Vince scribbled some more notes before climbing down off the dock and made his way toward a fire hydrant to his left. He rapped his pen on the five-inch water discharge cap and looked over his shoulder at Collier. "Is this the one that was out of service?"

"Yeah, that's it."

"And you're sure it wasn't working during the fire?"

"It had the metal ring on top. Like your department, that's how we show if it can't be used, you know, maintenance and stuff. Told that to your Fire Marshal when he was here. Maybe I missed it on the clipboard, the one that has daily reports and tracks work orders. I only took a quick look."

Vince's eyes shifted back and forth between Collier and the cinder block guard shack. "You still keep your records in there, right?"

Collier chomped nervously on a fingernail. "The maintenance log is hanging by the door. Hasn't been much need to go in there since the fire. C'mon, and you can see that extinguisher also."

Vince wedged the notepad under his arm, picked up his workbag and trudged after Collier. Behind them, the nitrate storage silos closest to the depot stood like giant metal tombstones, the surface paint on each blistered and burned, scorched inscriptions stark reminders of the narrowly avoided incineration and massive explosion that might have sent hundreds to their grave in the blink of an eye. "What's with all the packaging materials you said you were moving to the warehouse at Mandarin Turnpike?"

"The man doesn't confide in me, you know." Collier waved his arm at the pallets. "He tells me to do something, I just do it."

Vince recalled the last time he'd been to the three-story brick warehouse, conducting a sprinkler inspection of the place. Every square inch of floor space in the dark old building set in the back of the industrial park was loaded with the containers used to ship the plant's products.

"Correct me if I'm wrong, that warehouse, even though it's got sprinklers, it's darn near full, isn't it? Where are you supposed to be putting all of this, in the yard? Or maybe it's been emptied? I haven't been there in a while."

"All I know is I got a call from headquarters saying Mr. Muhktar got the okay from you guys in the Fire Department to haul it. I'm headed over there in a little while with a truckload after I get the gate key from him. He's been keeping it with him lately. But I'll tell you this, last I was there, it was like ten pounds of shit was squeezed in a five pound bag."

Reaching the guard shack, Collier climbed the steps and shoved the door. "Damn thing gets stuck." He shouldered it a second time, and it clanged loudly against a metal filing cabinet just inside. "I'll get the maintenance log for you, and there's Ebi Rostum's cigarette butt, the one he nailed me with. That's the water extinguisher right there."

"You don't mind if I take that?" Vince tweezered and sealed the half-burned cigarette in another ziplock evidence bag and lifted the brass-cylindered extinguisher, the contents sloshing around as he hefted it. "This is a standard two and a half gallon pressurized water can. Seems at least half full? You guys also keep two twenty-pound Class-ABC extinguishers on the loading dock, right, the required size and type to tackle ordinary combustibles, flammable liquid and electrical fires? Your guy didn't think to try them when the diesel fuel in the forklift started burning from the puncture in its tank?"

"Guess not, can't tell you why," Collier replied. He handed the maintenance clipboard to Vince.

Vince placed his open notebook on the counter and studied the worksheet, his finger tracking the entries listed around the date of the fire. "Hey, Sam, the hydrant being out of service, I don't see a word on this page."

The sudden loud clank of the door rebounding off the file cabinet surprised them.

"What's the meaning of this?"

"Mr. Muhktar!" Collier's eyes lit up. "Oh, hey, you remember Inspector Rigardo, don't you? He's the Fire Department's usual inspector at Criton. He's taught some of our emergency training classes."

Vince put the extinguisher down and extended his hand.

Muhktar grabbed the doorknob instead, sweeping the door shut behind him, staring icily as Vince retracted his greeting.

"Uh, it's okay," Collier sputtered. "Inspector Rigardo has always worked with us, and . . ."

His boss held up his hand. He squinted at Vince's breast pocket name badge and then the open notes on the counter. "Rigardo, is it?"

"Yes, Mr. Muhktar, Criton Chemical is in my district. I thought I'd come and see what damage you have, offer some suggestions to keep any remaining fertilizer secure, or review storage needs at your warehouse. Just want to ensure we've done our job and limit your losses. We don't want anything to happen now that you're shut down."

"You're assigned to Chief Tammerlin, aren't you?"

"Yes, sir, I am and . . ."

"And your Chief has finished his investigation and filed the necessary reports. The matter is closed, isn't it?"

"Yes, but . . ."

"Then at this time, there is nothing more you can add to his completed effort."

"I'm not trying to add to the report Mr. Muhktar, I just . . ."

"Thank you, Inspector," Hassan interrupted. "I'm sure your intentions are professionally motivated. However, we're busy, and Mr. Collier and I have important business." He snatched the knob and wrenched the door open. "I'm certain you understand that I must ask you to leave so we may conduct it. Right now."

Vince inclined his head. "Good afternoon, Mr. Muhktar." He picked up his notes from the counter where Muhktar stood glaring down at them. Grabbing his satchel, he descended the steps, walked over to his vehicle, and drove off.

Chapter 17
Sharq News Agency, Tehran

The return trip from Farid's jarring encounter at the seedy docks of Khorromshahr to Sharq News in Tehran took what was left of the night and all of the following morning. It also took what little restraint Farid had left. His hands shook and sweated on the wheel, and he fought the urge to speed as he put as much distance as he could between Kazem Al-Unistan's ultimatum and the relative safety of his office. How on earth would he find a way to articulate anything in print without getting killed by the factions involved?

He caught a glimpse of his haggard face in the rearview mirror. His eyes were red, his hair matted, cheeks sunken and pale. And it wasn't just his face. His body was achy and argumentative. The twenty-hour round trip had long since taken its toll. But nothing was as draining as his thoughts. He felt as if he were onboard an overloaded freight train going way too fast on a bad curve, with no way to get it under control.

Finally arriving at Sharq, Farid pulled into the back lot and grimaced as he lifted his withered leg onto the tarmac. He had to use both hands; the leg felt like a lead anchor. It was all he could do to hobble into his office, lock the door behind him, and collapse into the chair. There might have been other noises out in the corridor, but the only sound he heard was the echo of Kazem Al-Unistan's voice, playing over and over in his head. *Your cooperation will make Behi most proud of her only son, do you not think?*

To disobey the fanatical, murderous zealot, to ignore his warning, would guarantee his mother's death. Yet if he revealed Sheik Muhktar's subterfuge based on the maniacal rant of the terrorist chieftain, the very least Farid could expect was imprisonment.

More probable would be his disappearance at the hands of the Revolutionary Guard, or Muhktar's hired thugs. Farid had met the sheik at a news conference, had even been roughed up by one of his henchmen— Jalal Hamadi, a cruel man with cold, soulless eyes— for getting too close.

His dismal options raged in his head. The deadline for the morning's news report was less than an hour off. He had to warn his mother.

Farid lunged for the phone.

One ring. Two. Three. He checked his watch. *She wouldn't be at the market now?* Four rings. Five. Six. His stomach began to churn. *Maybe she's gone next door to see Lelah.* Seven. Eight.

The phone stopped ringing. Frantic, he crushed the receiver to his ear. All he heard on the other end of the line was faint, measured breathing. About to challenge whoever had picked up, Farid paused when he heard his mother's voice.

"Hello?" She sounded tired, but not afraid. "Hello?"

He opened his mouth. No words formed. There was no sense in warning her. He was terrified enough for the both of them. Only slightly relieved, Farid broke the connection and silently settled the phone in its cradle.

"I'm finished, no matter the outcome," he murmured to himself. "Even if Abbas Muhktar is innocent, the Guard trusts no one. His reputation and financial empire will be ruined, his wealth, gone." The acid in his gut surged. Abbas was one thing, Hassan another. Nadia had told Farid about the alcohol fueled beating the man had given her after he had botched the negotiations in a Canadian deal that cost him millions. Muhktar blamed her for misplacing a critical spreadsheet, one that he had left behind, forgotten on his desk.

The complexity of the situation defied comprehension. At this point, any choice Farid made, any decision, would be a gamble. He had to find a way to protect Behi and warn his sister without unduly worrying her. He opened his laptop and started typing.

Nadia,

An extraordinary claim has been made that Sheik Abbas Muhktar is involved in a scheme to sell ammonium nitrate fertilizer here in Iran on the black market. He's allegedly involved in a plot that could have international implications. I've been compromised and tasked with exposing a scheme involving a freighter owned by the sheik that sails from America to the Persian Gulf. On board it carries materials manufactured at Hassan's chemical plant, allegedly for sale on the black market to be used for evil purposes.

I don't know the extent of the Muhktars' complicity, if indeed there is any, however I have been instructed to secretly document the ship's arrival at Khorromshahr and write an article supporting this accusation. I tell you this, dear sister, so you are aware and may protect yourself as best you can, for I recall all too well Hassan's cruelty and cowardice. If in some way fate has permitted me the smallest of opportunities to prepare you by warning you of these things, I'll gladly follow this difficult path.

Please, delete these messages, and keep them only in your heart.

Farid read over his email and swallowed hard as he tapped SEND.

Chapter 18
Chatterton County Fire Marshal's Office

Vince checked both side view mirrors before backing the van into one of the spots reserved for employees in front of the Fire Inspection Division. It wasn't an arbitrary decision. Driving rule number one *was* carved in stone, chiseled in place a long time ago. You drive any of Chatterton County's emergency vehicles, you better have it facing out, ready to go, or be prepared to have your ass handed to you. Vince never forgot it, or the time he lost a cheek by learning the lesson directly from the Fire Chief up in his office when he was still a rookie.

He turned the ignition off, the familiar rattle shaking the van as the diesel gasped and coughed one last time before giving up the ghost with a final belch. Vince pocketed his keys and stuffed the notes he'd collected at Criton into his knapsack. He slid his sleeve back: 4:47 p.m., time for his co-workers to start packing it in for the day. He hoped so anyway, he wanted to check the building codes for storage requirements at warehouses, not get into a conversation about his trip to Criton. He grabbed his bag and jogged toward the door.

"Hi, Inspector." The division secretary looked up from her word processor. "I thought you were gone for the day?"

Vince tore the wrapper off one of the miniature Snickers bars she kept in a bowl on the counter. "Just came back to see you." He took a bite and grinned. "What are you working on?"

"Oh, just some new inspection guidelines Chief Tammerlin wanted me to finish by the end of the day."

"Is he still here? I didn't see his car out front."

"He's here somewhere." She adjusted the notes on the tilted copy board and kept typing. "Do you need him? I can go look for him."

Vince licked dots of chocolate from his fingers. "Nah, just going to review a few things and take advantage of the quiet. By the way, we need some more of these." He winked and returned her smile, then rifled through the candy dish one more time before heading down the hall to his cube.

Tossing the bag on the floor, he pulled his notes out and began searching for the codebook he'd left in his briefcase on the desk. He plucked the National Fire Protection Agency Manual, #230, the NFPA bible regarding the standards for protection and storage, from inside.

The manual was explicit, stating that if there was a change in what or how much was being stored, a warehouse had to be evaluated to make sure the sprinkler system could handle the additional load, and all stored materials had to be below the truss work in the ceiling. He flipped the page. The regulation was clear—there had to be less weight on each floor if the material was water absorbent. He thought of what Collier had said: *like ten pounds of shit in a five pound bag.*

"I didn't hear you come in, Rigardo." Chief of the Division, Edward Tammerlin, poked his head past the opening in the partition wall. "What are you doing? It's almost five o'clock. Thought for sure you weren't coming back today."

"Oh, hey, Chief. I had to bring the van back."

"I saw on the message board by Esther's desk that you went to Criton. What gives?"

Vince bookmarked and closed the manual, then returned the notepad to his backpack under the desk. "Yeah, I was out there for a while this afternoon. I talked with Sam Collier, the foreman—he showed me around."

"What for? There's nothing for us to do out there unless the owner submits plans to rebuild." Spotting a scrap of paper sticking out from between the pages of the NFPA codebook, Tammerlin stepped all the way into the room and spun it toward him. "Is this about Criton?" He frowned, and his voice turned irritated and suspicious. "Storage arrangements. Piling procedures and precautions. Commodity clearance in aisles." The Fire Marshal dropped his briefcase and sat down. "What are you up to, Rigardo?"

Vince sat forward with his elbows on the desk. "Collier mentioned to me the Fire Department gave permission to store quite a bit of additional materials inside their warehouse near Mandarin Turnpike. I saw a good amount of pallets holding ordinary Class A combustibles loaded on a truck, ready to go."

Tammerlin crossed his arms defensively. "And?"

"And last I talked to Captain Digman—that warehouse is in his jurisdiction—he told me the place was full. Now we're letting Hassan Muhktar move tons more in there? I wanted to check the codebook."

Tammerlin bunched his chin, looked down, and scratched the remnants of lunch from his clip-on tie. "Not that it's any of your concern, but Muhktar made the request to the Fire Chief, and then he and I discussed it. And I don't care what you and Ken Digman talked about. He doesn't make the decisions. I do."

"Whoa, Eddie." Vince surrendered, hands up. "I got it. You administrate the division. All we're trying to do is our jobs, what we get paid for. If we didn't look into this kind of situation, you'd be crawling all over us for that."

"Pay attention, Rigardo, there's nothing else to discuss about Criton. I finished that. Got it? The incident is closed."

"Damn *right* it's closed!" A beet red Stanley Lowell charged into the cubicle. "Get up!"

Vince stifled a laugh as Tammerlin started to stand, knocking the desk lamp over.

"Not you, Eddie, for crying out loud. You!" Lowell glared at Vince. "Just what were you doing at the chemical plant today?"

Vince remained seated, arms defiantly folded across his chest. "It's in my district. I went out there to take a look."

"You listen to me, pal, I'm sick and tired of getting phone calls from Hassan Muhktar like the one I just got, and you better watch that sarcastic tone of yours, or you'll be driving a logistics truck delivering toilet paper to the stations by morning, got it? That investigation is finished. Period."

"Uhh," Tammerlin stammered, "that's what I just told him when you walked in."

116

Lowell's scorching gaze silenced Tammerlin. Mission accomplished, the chief turned and zeroed in on Vince. "And Rigardo," he snarled. "Not one more word from you. You don't say anything; you don't *do* anything. It's done. Now get the hell out of here. As for you," he snapped at the beleaguered Fire Marshal, "your office. Now."

The two men left the cubicle, and Vince waited for their footsteps to recede before picking up the phone and punching in the number to the Battalion Chief's office at Station 14. "Patrick, it's me. Glad I got you. You going to be there for a while?"

"Hey Vince, what's up? Yeah, it's almost time for dinner—homemade lasagna. I'm sure there'll be enough, come on and have some; the crew would like to see you. You know the fire house rules for meals though—you've got to bring dessert."

"Absolutely. Ice cream and pie on me. Maybe we can talk after?"

"Sure. Everything okay, Vince?"

"I need to run some thoughts by you, that's all, maybe get your opinion."

"Sounds good. Bring your appetite. And I'll see you in twenty minutes?"

Wedging one of the NFPA booklets in with his notes, Vince slung the backpack onto his shoulder and closed his fire department brief case, leaving it on the desk. After elbowing the light switch, he headed for the side exit at the end of the corridor adjacent to Tammerlin's office. He couldn't help but hear Lowell's scathing, one-sided, expletive-laced tirade about Criton being over and done with.

Vince bumped the door open and snickered. "Way to stand up for yourself, Eddie."

Chapter 19
Fire Station 14

Vince pulled into Fire Station 14 just as Medic 14 rolled out from the apparatus bay, lights flashing. Ever since being assigned there, it seemed to run non-stop. For many of the inhabitants crammed into the trailer parks lining both sides of the Pike, that yellow and white vehicle was their entire health care system rolled into one. No need for Obamacare, all you had to do was call 9-1-1 and you'd get on-the-spot, top-notch treatment for whatever ailed you, no questions asked. From hangnails to gunshot wounds, it made no difference, the gut box, as it was called on the sly, responded twenty-four hours a day, three hundred and sixty five days a year. For emergency services personnel, there was no such thing as closed for the holidays.

Recognizing the crew, Vince returned a wave to the driver and paramedic as they hit the street, Federal Q siren splitting the air wide open. He watched as they turned north on Jeff Davis Highway before walking past the SUV's and pickup trucks in the parking lot.

Reaching the alcove in front, he pressed the buttons for the entry code and twisted the door handle. Nothing happened. He stabbed at the keypad a second time. *Nada*. Suddenly, the door swung open from within.

"Can I help you, sir? Do you have an emergency?"

"When did you guys change the combination?" Vince complained when he saw the deadpan expression on Firefighter Bryce Pullen's face.

"We have to change it now and again to keep riff-raff like you from getting in." Pullen busted out laughing. "How the heck are you, Vinnie-boy? Good timing, table's being set, come on in."

Vince stepped into the foyer, closed his eyes and inhaled. "Oh, man, does that smell good."

"It better," said Truck 14 Captain Greg McCarron. "Labante has dodged work all day making Grandma Rosa's secret tomato sauce. So much easier and better tasting would be some cabbage, red potatoes and corned beef."

"Geez, Cap, there you go with that famine food of Ireland again." Vince dropped his pack on the floor of the radio room. "Isn't all them potatoes why you leprechauns fled the Emerald Isle in the first place?" The two shook hands. "Good to see you, Greg. Hope you aren't still mad for my almost dropping that extension ladder on your head at that room and contents fire last month."

"Y'all white folks are crazy." Raymond Harkness, his distinctive gap-toothed grin plastered in place, joined the group. "Can't be nothing better than my mama's chicken and dumplings." He slapped Vince on the back. "Damn glad you got to see me, Cuz."

This was a firehouse, and every soul in the place was family. It wasn't an arena for the weak or those with thin skin. Everyone here would put their life on the line, had in some cases, for the firefighter next to him.

As their banter continued, the door to the office flew open. Patrick leaned against its frame. "Hey you Sicilian meatball, I see you're empty handed. Where's the ice cream? Don't tell me you forgot it already? Something must really be on your mind."

Vince winced. In the short time it had taken him to drive to the station, he'd forgotten dessert.

"Whaaaat?" The sharks smelled blood, and Pullen took another bite out of Vince's hide. "You come here expecting to eat, without a reservation no less, and don't plan on paying your way? What a lump."

"Hey, are you guys gonna bust balls all night, or do you wanna eat?" Carmine Labante stuck his head out of the kitchen, large dented saucepan in hand. "C'mon. I ain't sayin' it again."

A second announcement was never necessary. Ask any firefighter anywhere, and the response will always be the same; when the dinner bell goes off, better get out the way.

Only Patrick lagged behind as the group charged down the corridor. "Do you miss the station life, Vince?" he asked.

The young inspector surveyed the numerous citations displayed on the walls, awards he and his friends had earned through the years. "More than I could ever tell you."

***

"Hey Labante!" Harkness patted his gut. "Not bad for a ginzo. Too bad we don't have any dessert."

"Alright, alright!" Vince gave up. "I'll go get it."

Patrick took the bowl of leftover salad to the refrigerator. "Tell you what, Inspector Rigardo, even though it's only a mile away, and we should make you walk as punishment, I'll personally drive you over to Friendly's Ice Cream Shop. We can talk on the way. Come on."

The two men walked out into the apparatus bay and hopped into a Chatterton Fire Department staff car.

"So, what gives?" Patrick started the engine and eased out onto the ramp.

"Shit." Vince grabbed the door handle. "I got some notes inside, can we go back a second?"

"Notes, just to talk to me? You're kidding." Patrick accelerated away from the station. "Come on, what's bugging you?"

"Look, a couple weeks back you said you smelled a rat around the Criton fire."

Patrick shot him a sharp look before turning his eyes to the road, all trace of humor gone.

Vince continued. "You know Criton is one of my assigned target hazards, so after what you said, I went over there to check it out. It's my job, bad enough I was never part of the investigation to begin with."

"What did you find out?" Patrick ignored the turn lane into the ice cream store.

"Some of the things I saw made me think this wasn't an accident."

Patrick nodded. "It doesn't surprise me. Like what?"

"For one thing, the level of the hole in the forklift was lower than the grid—it couldn't have been caused by backing into the loading dock."

Patrick had been an investigator. He knew how to play devil's advocate to cover all the angles. "Well, how about this; the forklift driver was working near the end of a tractor-trailer, and maybe he clipped the tailgate? It's not uncommon. Collier reported the guy was in a hurry. He'd already proved he wasn't paying attention when he disregarded the procedure to have a man backing him up on the loading dock. Shit like that happens when you're not concentrating."

"It's possible, I suppose." Vince twisted in his seat and looked straight at Pat. "But I'm not buying it. I also didn't see any comments on their maintenance clipboard for the broken hydrant."

"Maybe it was on a separate work order? We do that here."

Vince threw his hands up. "Come on, I know you're covering options, but there's more to it. Muhktar got the go ahead from Lowell to move additional packaging materials to his warehouse near Mandarin Turnpike." His voice rose. "If the place is full like I think it is, that would be flat out against the code. When I brought it to Tammerlin's attention, he told me it wasn't my business. It *is* my business, for God's sake, and you know it!"

Patrick had unconsciously picked up speed. A quick glance at the speedometer told him he was doing eighty. He slowed down. "Where are you going with this, Vince?"

"The place is called Standard Cold Storage. It's not in my jurisdiction, so I think I'll go and check it out on my own time, see if this storage situation is kosher."

Patrick hit the turn signal for the upcoming cloverleaf. "I don't like the sound of this. You shouldn't go alone, Vince. I'll come with you. We don't know what we're dealing with here."

"We'll see. Look, maybe we're just being paranoid."

"Maybe, maybe not. Don't go alone." Patrick merged into the northbound lane of the interstate.

They drove in silence as they headed back to Friendly's Ice Cream Store.

Chapter 20
Khorromshahr Harbor, Iran

The chunk of moon that hung above the deserted harbor was the color of raw bone, pinned in place by a thick, still night. The impenetrable heat and humidity hung in the air along a sluggish Shatt al Arab as it flowed past Khorromshahr.

Farid parked behind a rundown, abandoned warehouse and, already sweating, hauled himself out of the car. He hitched a pack of outdated audio and visual equipment onto his back and tightened the band securing the small headlamp to his forehead. Making his way carefully along a concrete verge toward a set of double doors, he did his best to move quietly. But every sound he made echoed through the dark, empty building as his single beam of light illuminated a path to an iron staircase leading to the roof. At first he thought they'd made a mistake, forgotten to unlock the door for him, and for seconds, a clash of relief and terror almost sent him hurrying back to his car. However, the consequences of leaving would be fatal, so he threw his weight behind a shoulder and pushed until the heavy door opened with a groan.

Grunting with effort after climbing the steps, the smell of his own fear and agitation increasing his discomfort, Farid moved over the concrete to a vantage point where he had a clear view of Pier Six and the freighter tied up beside it. He settled down and caught his breath. Feeling a little steadier, he opened his bag to haul out the equipment, and mounted the DVR on a small tripod, not ideal but good enough to do the job.

Earlier that day, on his way home from work, he'd received a text message with instructions from Kazem Al-Unistan mapping out the location of the warehouse and ordering him to document the unloading of Muhktar's ship: chemical nitrate intended for the government of Iran, diverted to Khorromshahr. Al-Unistan planned to use the cargo to create explosives. Farid's article, with proof of the Muhktars' complicity, must be published before the end of the week.

Even in the oppressive heat, Farid felt a chill run through him. Although he'd dressed in dark clothes, he pressed tight against an abutment to avoid being detected.

The muscles in his shoulders and lower back began to stiffen. He reached for the thermos he had brought with him and unscrewed the top. Suddenly, the loud grinding of gears splintered the eerie quiet suffocating the harbor. Lukewarm coffee splattered onto his lap as the plastic cup slipped from his grasp. Farid lunged for the switch that was paired to the portable parabolic microphone, turned it on and grabbed his camera.

Lights on the vertical steel girders of the shipboard crane came on and flooded a section of the wharf as the derrick rolled on its tracks to take up position over the cargo hold. Farid cradled the lens and zeroed in on the nameplate affixed to the bow of the vessel. The shutter clicked. The *Orient Star*. Movement on the bridge caught his attention. He aimed and captured several figures descending the rusted steps on the starboard side gangway adjacent to the dock. Panning ahead of them, focusing near the bottom of a giant land based hoist, he spotted a second group of men suddenly appear from the gloom. Each was armed with an AK-47 and stood in a protective semi-circle around a man who wore a robe and keffiya. Farid twisted the telephoto lens to magnify the image.

Al-Unistan.

Farid pulled back and leaned against the parapet wall. He took a moment to steady his head in both hands as the camera dangled from his neck, breathing deep to calm himself. When muffled voices from the dockyard below drifted upwards, he adjusted the headphones that were synchronized to the parabolic mic, and inched forward to peer over the edge of the rooftop.

Less than a hundred meters away, the group of men from the ship, also heavily armed, assembled by the bulkhead in a tight cluster. One of them, a powerfully built, bald man dressed in pleated slacks and a crisp oxford shirt, wielding a sidearm, stood in the center, his back toward Farid. He began directing the men to different locations on the dock. They moved off as he holstered his gun and approached Al-Unistan.

Farid took a couple of photos and laid the camera down. The red recording light on the DVR glowed, and he squinted through the viewfinder. Although the two men were well framed, the scene remained blurry as the shutter shifted, trying to hold focus. Farid cursed. The newer version would certainly have captured clearer images and sharper sound, but the old equipment was all he had.

Physically less imposing than the man from the freighter and cloaked in an ankle length kandura, a traditional Persian robe, Al-Unistan stood a good four inches shorter.

"The voyage went smoothly?" The warlord's voice sounded in Farid's headphones.

"Not a single glitch and right on time, as always. You want to tell me why you're unloading some here and keeping the rest on board?"

Although he couldn't see the man's expression, Farid could detect the probing nature of his question.

A chilly note crept into Al-Unistan's voice. "You receive a fortune for your services. Be satisfied with that. You're not paid to ask questions."

Scarcely breathing, Farid watched as Al-Unistan motioned toward a faded blue Mercedes parked thirty meters away. The two men walked toward the car, the brawny figure facing away from Farid's lens.

"We ... care about what you do ... ship ... only that we ... paid." The still faceless man laughed. "Will ... keep it ... Khorromshahr?" The conversation filtered through in sporadic bursts as they strode past some ironworks.

"Not now!" Farid fidgeted desperately with the audio controls.

The men stopped alongside the sedan as one of Al-Unistan's men opened the trunk and removed one of three large suitcases, which he placed on the hood.

Farid could just make out the warlord's voice. "Iraq depot security ... pipeline ... Basra, not ... explode ... there. The Amer ... ship ... Faw ... blame each oth ... and I will watch ... comp ... annihilation."

Farid rapped the headphones several times. Frustrated, he grabbed the camera and zoomed in on the banded stacks of one hundred dollar bills that filled the open suitcase. The man picked one of them up and fanned the edges with his thumb before tossing it back and closing the case. As he turned and signaled to the wheelhouse of the *Orient Star*, Farid caught a glimpse of his face.

The man was Abbas Muhktar's bodyguard, the same one who had shoved Farid aside at a press conference months ago for getting too close to his boss. Jalal Hamadi removed a cell phone from his pocket and handed it to Al-Unistan before returning the suitcase to the trunk. Then he got into the front seat of the Mercedes, started the engine, and drove away. His men filed off the dock and disappeared into the night, leaving Al-Unistan and his cohorts alone on the wharf.

Al-Unistan watched as the car drove off. He grabbed a Kalashnikov assault rifle from one of his men and swung the muzzle in the direction of the warehouse. Farid pointed his viewfinder just as the warlord raised the barrel of his automatic rifle and aimed at the parapet wall, precisely where Farid was sitting. He was dead in his sights. Farid froze, recalling his instructions.

You will remain until the ship has left, then go back to your office to write your article. Need I remind you of the consequences for you and Behi should you deviate from this plan?

Without warning, Farid's stomach heaved, and he vomited. Coughing, wiping his mouth, he watched as heavy machinery began to remove cargo from the ship's hold. Printed in block letters on each of the one hundred pound burlap bags that were lowered onto the pier was Criton Chemicals' company logo.

Farid took a few more shots, then replaced the lens cap and packed the camera, DVR, headphones and small parabolic dish into his well-worn knapsack. He secured the disassembled aluminum tripod to the bag's webbing.

At last, he leaned against the abutment and stared into the blackness with nothing to do but wait. Exhausted, he closed his eyes.

***

Farid lurched awake to silence, hands instinctively raised to protect his face, a legacy from his father's beatings. He gulped the remnants of his thermos and peeked over the edge of the roof. All he could see of the *Orient Star* was the barely visible navigational lights high atop its superstructure as it sailed away.

A vague hint of pastel light began to emerge far to the east. Farid checked the time. The sun would be up in an hour and bring its sweltering heat to the inhospitable seaport and those who eked out their existence along the almost barren waterway. He hitched the nylon rucksack onto his back, thrust his forearms into his crutches and agonizingly clambered down the stairs back to his car, where he collapsed into the driver's seat.

He'd have to drive a long way to get back to Tehran. He would need that time to think. He had observed an ominous transaction, but had no real evidence of conspiracy and treason. His article would raise more questions than he had answers for, and place him firmly in the center of the vicious storm that would rage once it was printed. He'd become everyone's target, most notably the Muhktars.

Adrenalin fueled his racing thoughts, and he couldn't help but smile grimly at the irony. He had stumbled onto the scoop of the century, one that could earn him awards for his investigative journalism, assuming he was able to see it through and that his editor agreed to print his inflammatory story. And if he could persuade Sharq to publish his findings, the Muhktars would put a price on his head. If Sharq refused, Al-Unistan would simply have his head.

Farid was as good as dead, whichever road he traveled. For now he focused on crossing the desert lowlands to the north and east of Khorromshahr, into the forbidding topography of the Zagros Mountains. He murmured into a digital voice recorder as he drove. "Headline to read: Insurgents divert chemicals destined for Tehran to Khorromshahr. Lead with: A freighter laden with ammonium nitrate fertilizer, reportedly bound for the seaport of Bandar Abbaas, was diverted and offloaded in the harbor of Khorromshahr under cover of darkness on Thursday night. (Insert pic with label.) Iraqi tribal chieftain Kazem Al-Unistan and an unidentified man oversee the offloading of the *Orient Star*. Khorromshahr, which lies across from Iraq, separated only by the Shatt al Arab, was one of the focal points in the war between the two nations and remains bitterly contested. Stricken by poverty, the port is a known hotbed for black market activities. Al-Unistan, who claims responsibility for recent bombings in Iran and Iraq, posted on a website frequently used by the insurgent leader—check the link for the quote—something to the effect that, 'There are no walls to protect the illegitimate government in Tehran. Soon it will be revealed the bombings spreading throughout Iran are in fact nurtured by the deceitful head of one of its largest businesses, Abbas Muhktar.' The mid-sized twenty five thousand ton dry bulk carrier, which is owned by Sheik Abbas Muhktar, executive officer of Criton Industries based in Tehran, is frequently used because its size allows entry to smaller ports. The material transported, ammonium nitrate fertilizer, produced by Criton Chemical in the United States and used in agriculture, is also a component of Improvised Explosive Devices (IEDs) manufactured by insurgents. It is undetermined if the ship was hijacked."

Chapter 21
Tohid Square, Tehran, Iran

Two days passed without a word from Al-Unistan. Sharq's editor had chosen to back Farid, even encouraged deeper investigation, and the newspaper had published the article.

Driving home from work, Farid turned left at the corner nearest the Anshan Market. He maneuvered around a week's worth of rotting vegetables and squeezed into a spot past the seeping cardboard boxes the vendors had left piled at the curb. The rancid smell had attracted voracious black flies that hummed at his head as he got out of the car. He swatted at them.

Above him an array of towels, robes and sheets fluttered like colorful flags on the clothes lines anchored to the rutted walls of the apartments on either side of the alley. He watched them flap for a moment, then squeezed his eyes shut. Sleep hadn't come easily lately, and Farid was bone tired.

He lumbered toward the stairway door leading to the second story apartment he shared with Behi and pushed against it. It was strangely reluctant to open. Farid put his weight into it and shoved. Small traces of dust had collected inside, and he looked down at fresh shoe prints, too large and too many to belong to his mother or the neighbor. He felt as if a cold hand grabbed his throat from behind, making it difficult to breathe.

The passageway was barely adequate and painfully steep. In a panic, he wrestled with his crutches, holding both in his right hand. Clutching the banister with his left, he hauled himself up the stairs.

Usually his mother opened the door when she heard him approach, but today it remained shut.

Alarmed, Farid pounded on the wood. "Mother?" he called, his voice hoarse. Fumbling for his keys, he dropped them from shaking fingers. "Mother!" He hammered on the door again until suddenly it was wrenched open from within.

"Farid!" Behi, catching the panicked look on her son's face, stepped to the side. "I was in the kitchen. What's wrong?"

"Nuh . . . nothing," Farid stammered. "I thought maybe you had fallen, that's all."

Behi, her back bent from too many years hunched over a machine as a seamstress, reached up and cradled his chin. "You worry needlessly. Come and sit. I'll bring you some tea." She moved past him and pushed aside the frayed curtain separating the living area from the kitchen. "How was your day? I've made your favorite by the way, kofta kabobs. I had to barter for half an hour with that greedy butcher. Time well spent." She chuckled. "He said I made him crazy."

"But you've been ill. Did Lelah help with the shopping?" Farid placed his crutches against a recliner that had seen better days, and eased himself into it.

"No, I'm fine. I managed. I don't like to call on her too often."

"She's our neighbor, and she offered. She's happy to do it." Farid jerked the lever on the side of the chair and eased his leg onto the footrest. "How did you bring the groceries upstairs? Did the butcher's son help?"

Returning, she handed him a glass of warm amber liquid. "No, your friends were waiting downstairs when I got back. They were kind enough to carry my parcels up here. Nice men."

"My friends?" Farid sat up quickly, spilling tea onto his pants. "What friends?"

"I don't know. I didn't recognize them, but they knew who I was and offered to help." She eased herself onto the shabby sofa opposite her son and reconfigured the pin holding the meticulous weave of her gray hair.

"Mother, what were their names?"

"I didn't ask." Arthritic fingers brushed the hem of her apron. "They spoke of your work at the newspaper. I thought perhaps they worked with you."

"And they said nothing else? They *did* nothing else?"

"They were kind, pleasant, you know. Why?" The lines above Behi's brow and at the corners of her eyes deepened. "Farid, what's the matter?"

"It's nothing." He flipped his hand indifferently, trying to make the lie more convincing. "Just long days at work. I'm tired. What did they look like, my friends?"

"You're worrying me, Farid. I don't know; the young one had curly hair, too long if you ask me. The other two looked like they spend too much time in the gym." She sniffed and coughed, a rasping hack that had plagued her for a week. "So much fuss. They know you work; they should have come later in the

135

afternoon." She got up to return to the kitchen. "Now come to the table and eat."

Farid raised his voice over the clatter of the oven door. "But what did they want? Did they leave a message?"

"They said they'd call you after dinner. Come, come Farid, it's ready."

Farid's gaze jumped uneasily between the door and the couch. The room felt different. He felt different. Violated. Outraged. Petrified. He felt the way they'd meant him to. *They came into our home, stood right there, next to my mother.* His head began to throb as he headed for the table.

***

"You barely ate a thing." Behi patted his wrist. "Aren't you hungry?"

Farid covered her thin hand with both of his. "Mother, I couldn't have gotten a better meal at a restaurant." He took a few more bites to make her happy, knowing he did the food, fragrant with ginger and mint, a huge disservice by failing to savor every taste. He edged away from the table. "Now, I'm going back out for some cigarettes and dessert, some *sohan ghom* for us. Karim makes the best. I should have thought to get some on the way home."

His mother smiled. "Don't be long, Farid. You smoke too much."

He kissed her forehead. "Lock the door behind me."

Once outside in the alley, he made his way to the edge of Tohid Square and sat on a cast iron bench.

136

The plaza was almost empty. He stretched his legs and lit a cigarette, then felt for his phone. This was not a conversation he wanted his mother to hear.

When it rang, Farid stared at it before answering. He wanted to toss it into the dumpster. Swallowing a sudden surge of rage, at last he took the call.

"Journalist, the lamb, it was good?"

"I did as you requested."

"No, you didn't. I wanted Muhktar implicated, but you gave him an out by insinuating the ship may have been hijacked. And you reported what you saw, not what I told you. I asked you a question, Farid Barmeen. The lamb, how was it?"

Farid couldn't respond.

A soft laugh purred against his ear. "You'll implicate Muhktar *directly*. You have a day to redeem yourself."

Chapter 22
Criton Chemical Office. Richmond, Virginia

Hassan paced back and forth, swatting a rolled up copy of Sharq News against his thigh as he spoke to Abbas Muhktar two continents away. He needed a drink.

"Don't panic, Hassan. I've already called the Minister of Commerce and voiced my concern. We're meeting later today."

"What about? What will you say to him?" Hassan tore at his cuticles. No longer smooth and even, the flesh was rough and curled along the nail bed.

"We're prepared for this type of thing. I'll confirm an act of piracy and express outrage. And of course, support an independent investigation as we implement our own." His father's voice revealed no trace of anxiety. If anything, he sounded amused.

"Yes, but . . ."

"And the records that very efficient wife of yours keeps for our dealings with Tehran, they appear legitimate?"

"Of course."

"So as long as the numbers match, we won't have a problem."

Hassan splashed a finger of Jack Daniels into a glass. "Yes, but how do we explain the photos?" He considered for a moment how much he'd enjoy throttling the journalist, one Farid Barmeen.

"The photos. Can you see who it is?"

"His back's to the camera, but it shouldn't take too long for them to find out."

"I wouldn't worry. Who on the dock that night would ever consider assisting the authorities? During my discussion with the minister, I'll raise the prospect of a large reward for information leading to this unidentified thief's arrest. I'll promise to scour all of Iran for a traitorous criminal who steals from our beloved regime and defames the honored name of Muhktar." He chuckled. "Given the choice to believe either their sworn enemy, Al-Unistan, or me, I doubt the holy imams will choose him."

Abbas's lack of concern caught Hassan off guard. "This will convince them? The Revolutionary Guard is wary of everyone."

"I'm counting on that. Sharq is a hated newspaper. Remember, it's been shut down before for upsetting the government. Protected by opposition leader Karroubi, whose own days are numbered, Sharq could well be facing its demise." There was a pause before he added, "And remember, Hassan, Criton Industries has well paid friends employed at the Islamic Republic News Agency."

"Of course. I'd forgotten Anwar Hadid at IRNA. He'd enjoy turning this around for us."

"Exactly. He'll make a liar of that rag, accuse it of spreading stories for its European and American masters."

Hassan finished his drink and poured another. If his father heard the splash, he refrained from comment.

Hassan exhaled with a gust. "Now that Jalal Hamadi is back in the States, any search for him in

139

Iran will be a waste of time. They wouldn't think to look for him here, would they?"

"So, he's arrived safely?"

"Yes, on the corporate jet. American security is an afterthought when it comes to private flights."

"And the money?"

Hassan renewed his pacing. "His fee for this last deal—it's exorbitant. You know I don't trust him having direct access to our money."

His father's voice sharpened. "Do not concern yourself with his fee, and do not interfere with payments for any of his work, or his methods. Just ensure the funds are always available."

"Of course." Hassan dug into his vest pocket and pulled out a cigarette. He bounced the filtered end firmly on the back of his hand.

"Let me know when it's done and when you and he have concluded your business. Remind him I'll contact him in Qom when he returns to Iran. He has the details." The sheik murmured goodbye and ended the call without waiting for a response.

Hassan finished the last of his whiskey and lit his cigarette before pressing the intercom button. "Come in here."

Within seconds, Nadia stepped through the door with her laptop.

"The money in that account for Khorromshahr, it's available?"

"Yes."

Hassan pulled the window curtain back as far as it would go and gazed down at the rapids of the James River that gushed under the I-95 bridge. "Pull it up. In fact, pull all the accounts up."

140

Nadia flipped the cover open and entered her private password to unlock the PC.

Hassan wandered over as she typed in the URL address and watched as the graphics loaded.

Welcome to Credit Suisse.

"Move." Hassan, impatient to see his money, elbowed her aside and typed in the combination of letters and numbers that would give him access to the account. He tapped the ENTER key.

"Now, let's start with my money for Khorromshahr."

Nadia watched as Hassan traced his finger down the listing of deposits and withdrawals. The greedy gleam in his eye dissipated when he saw the final tally.

Client: 04011979 : Balance: $2,019,000.14.

"Only two million, and this includes all the other deliveries as well?" Hassan scowled. "My father's lackey has taken a hefty cut. He'd better deposit the proceeds from the sale of our ship soon. You'll track this constantly. I *warned* the sheik about him. Alright, now bring up the North American Insurance balance."

Nadia's fingers flew over the keys. "Here. This is the separate account the sheik wanted for the insurance claim paid for the fire loss at Criton. $6,400,000. Do you wish to see the one for Criton Chemical Company as well?"

"No. This will do." Hassan squared himself to the mirror behind the bar and sucked in his stomach. "I've done well." He adjusted his tie before turning once more toward Nadia. "Make a reservation. Dinner for two at Morton's on Virginia Street. Make it for 6.30, and forward the dinner invitation to the sheik's lapdog. He's staying at the Marriot."

Nadia touched the keyboard to close out the account. Trusting no one, Hassan stood over her, watching as the computer screen cleared.

Chapter 23
The home of William Meagher

"Come on Patrick, leave your queen open like that, she's mine. It'll all be over, and we only just started." William stuffed his pipe and reached for the butane lighter. "You're happy to disgrace yourself so early in the game?"

Patrick scratched the back of his head and cricked his neck. "Sorry, guess I'm just tired. Anxious, you know?" He moved a knight into position to protect his queen. "There. Better?"

William puffed and watched distorted smoke haloes drift toward the ceiling. "I think it's more than that. You want to tell me what's really going on?"

Patrick got up and reached for the black and white photograph he'd been staring at on the mantle above the fireplace. "I don't know, Dad." He traced his late wife's face with a fingertip. She'd been grappling with a smallmouth bass from Smith Mountain Lake, grinning at him as he'd captured the moment. "At times, since Abbey died, I feel like it's all a bad dream." He replaced the photo and reached for a second.

"I know, son. And I know there's nothing I can say to lessen the pain."

William had loved Abbey, and Patrick easily read the sadness in his father's eyes every time her name was mentioned. More than sadness; something like despair rested there, or perhaps frustration. His father, invincible and afraid of nothing, had been powerless in the face of Abbey's illness, and now had no impact on the grief that refused to rest in Patrick since her death.

Patrick showed him the photo he held of his two girls splashing in the surf. "You remember this? We were at that house we rented from the Twiddy company on the Outer Banks of North Carolina, and a minute later some wild horses trotted over the dunes."

William nodded. "Of course I remember."

"But college for Shannon and Colleen; I don't know if I can make enough for them to finish. Overtime on the job has just about dried up, and the computer business is slow. I'm not bringing in enough."

"Things will get better," William said. "We'll find a way. I'm more than happy to help my granddaughters."

"Look, Dad." Patrick replaced the photograph of the girls beside their mother. "Your pension covers you and Mom, but there's no way it's meant for costs like that."

"Well, what of my investigation business? You could help me. You were a fine arson investigator all those years before you requested that transfer to the hazardous material team at the station house."

"Come on, you've got a pretty decent one man show going. The clients have been small, and your take is only five to ten percent of what you recover anyway." Patrick sat down again and moved his castle halfway across the board. "Thanks, though, it's a good offer." Maybe he should consider it. The two of them could expand the business, land a few lucrative contracts, and pull in bigger clients.

The phone rang, and William tipped his pipe into the ashtray as he picked up the receiver. "Meagher residence. Hello Vincent! I'm giving Patrick a lesson in the gentlemen's game of chess. Here, I'll put the phone on speaker."

Patrick grinned when he heard Vince say, "So, you're wearing him out again, huh?"

"What are you up to?" Patrick leaned closer to the phone.

"I'm at Fire Headquarters; figure I'll work for a while tonight. I want to go over some notes I took about Criton that I've got in my backpack. I'm also staring at the blueprints of the mall being built, and the info regarding its water requirements. The Fire Marshal's been pushing to get it done."

Patrick tapped his father on the arm and spoke quietly. "I need to get going." He flexed his wrist and pointed at his watch. "I'm supposed to bring pizza— Shannon's orders." He raised his voice. "Hey Vince, you still coming over tomorrow? The girls are expecting you at seven, so don't be late. You been to the Red Box video rental yet?"

Vince laughed. "Yeah, I got the flick in the Jeep, the one Colleen wanted. There's nothing I wouldn't do for you and the girls. Movie night will be fun. Now, go get that pizza and let me talk to Pops. Take it easy, Pat."

Patrick mouthed his goodbye and zipped up his raincoat as he headed down the hallway.

Chapter 24
Fire Marshal's Office, Chatterton, Virginia

Finishing his phone call to William, Vince went back to wrestling with the unruly velum, eventually securing the stiff architectural paper with cellophane tape. He put the dispenser down, eyes and thoughts ping-ponging between the blueprints Tammerlin had assigned him and his backpack that lay on the floor.

"Oh, who am I kidding, Criton Chemical is a heck of a lot more interesting." The bag landed on top of the blueprints. He yanked his Criton notes from inside and turned the desk lamp to its brightest setting. "The mall can wait."

Vince hadn't paid much attention to the rain until he hung up the phone with William. A steady, rhythmic drumming on the air conditioner casing, it now seemed to be picking up. He opened the blinds and peered through the window. "Oh, yeah, here it comes." A huge bank of clouds hurtled toward Chatterton County. Several miles away, the knife-edge of a lightning bolt cut the southwestern sky into irregular pieces. Rivulets streamed onto the sill from the eaves of Fire Headquarters, and the puddles in the parking lot were beginning to resemble small lakes.

The worst storms usually came in from Amelia County, and if he were going to miss this one, he'd have to get moving. Finding the remote partly covered by the county street map book lying on his locker, he directed it at the TV. The screen blinked to life.

". . . and the radar shows the storm is tracking in from the west, following the Appomattox River. There are reports of swollen streams in Prince Edward County and some localized flooding in low lying areas around Farmville." The weather reporter skidded the green dot of her laser pointer over a map. "Power crews are being recalled to restore electricity to customers in Buckingham and Cumberland counties. The line of squalls are expected to dump upwards of three inches and arrive in the greater Richmond metropolitan within the hour or so . . ."

"Ok, I'm out of here." Vince stapled his notes from Criton together and stuffed them back into the yellow inter-office envelope. He threw a final glance at the bright red bands representing the line of severe thunderstorms on the TV as they marched easterly toward Chatterton County.

After hoisting his backpack and adjusting the strap, he surveyed his cubicle one last time before hitting the light switch. One of the fluorescent tubes darkened, but continued to emit its peculiar purplish light, a sure sign the connection socket was on its last legs. For a moment he stood bathed in its eerie glow as a low roll of thunder heralded the coming storm. Yanking the collar of his denim jacket high around his neck, he bolted through pools of rainwater toward his Wrangler. The rain was increasing by the minute, the wind pushing it past the rubber door seals. He snatched a towel from the back, doubled it, and threw it on his seat before jumping in.

Vince jammed the key in the ignition and pumped the gas pedal. The engine started sluggishly. He allowed it to warm up before leaving the lot and turning onto the main road. Though a bit out of his way considering the bad weather, he decided again on Applebee's Grill and Bar. Sandy, a friend and bartender, would be working, and he hadn't seen her in a while. The place was also close to Criton Chemicals' warehouse on Mandarin Turnpike.

***

"Welcome stranger, wet enough for you?" Sandy, all curves and happy to see him, reached for the toggle on the blender anchored at the far end of the bar. "What can I get you?"

"Hey, Sandy, how about a Sam Adams?" Vince dropped his bag on the floor in the entranceway and shed the soaking wet jacket. Droplets flew everywhere as he shook it out and hung it on a hook before brushing rainwater from his hair. He had only limited success.

"Lager okay? Tall or short?" The blender roared to life.

"A short will do, and a menu when you get a chance." He chose the bar stool closest to her. "Damn, I'll say it every time. You even make that uniform look good, you know that?"

The whirring stopped. "Don't ever stop saying it."

Vince lost himself in the warm gaze of emerald green eyes.

"But why are you out on a night like this?" She slung a glass under the tap and handed him a menu. "What have you been doing, and where have you been? It's been a while."

"Working late. Staying busy. Got a lot of things going on in the Fire Department."

"Like what?" She bent toward him, very much in slow motion, knowing it provided an unobstructed view of her jaw dropping cleavage. She slid the glass onto a coaster. "Too busy for me, too?" She flipped a dripping lock of hair away from his forehead.

Vince lifted the schooner and peered over the rim. The maneuver was doubly rewarding. The beer was tasty, and it allowed him to indulge in the incredible view she offered of her breasts easily straining the one-size-too-small red polo shirt.

"Never too busy for you, but the Inspection Division was under the gun for the mall project." Vince began skating the beer glass back and forth between his hands. "That, and I've been checking a few things regarding a fire we had not too long ago, might even stop by at the industrial park near here after I eat. There's a warehouse that may have something to do with the fire at Criton Chemical." He pushed the tri-fold plastic menu card toward the drink rail. "How about the Cajun sampler platter?"

Sandy scrawled the request on a pad and took the menu from him, her fingers tickling his wrist. "No appetizer?" The smile was wicked. She turned and swayed toward the kitchen with the order. "One sampler comin' up!"

The swinging doors closed behind her as a loud clap of thunder crashed directly overhead. The restaurant vibrated and lights flickered. Vince twisted in his seat, back turned to the bar, practiced eyes sizing up the room. Over by the table beneath the front windows, a tall, skinny waiter pocketed his tip and began stacking dinner dishes onto an already crowded tray. A young couple seated in a dimly lit booth, convinced no one was watching, or caring, shared a kiss. They were the only ones left in the place.

Vince shifted his gaze, the wobbling, unbalanced fan blades above the empty hostess stand capturing his attention. *Why was that rag canister at Criton so close to the loading dock grid, and what were those nitrate granules doing beneath it? And that cigarette butt: why would an employee smoke in a restricted area?* He drummed his fingers on the bar. The whirling fan became a blur.

"Miss me?" Sandy leaned over the rinse sink. "Your order will be right up. Want another while you tell me what's troubling you? I saw from the kitchen. You look like a zombie."

Vince's tongue poked the inside of his cheek. "Did you ever have something bother you to the point you can't shake it, even when you're not certain where it's coming from?"

"Of course, who doesn't?" She started organizing several tulip shaped cocktail glasses in a plastic rack and stacked it on a stand near the dishwasher. "What's bugging you?"

"We had a fire, a pretty close call. The guys did a really good job, and no one was hurt."

"And?"

"And it's been investigated, signed, sealed, and delivered. Everyone, including Shane, and he was in charge, is satisfied it was an accident."

The kitchen doors swung open, and a petite, freckled waitress put a steaming plate of beef and crawfish on the bar by the cash register.

"Thanks, Patsy." Sandy passed the meal on to Vince. "But you don't think it was that simple?"

"I don't know. I went out there where it happened, took a look around. Something doesn't add up."

"Look, if you want to talk about it, I mean if you can, I'd be happy to listen, give you an unbiased opinion. I open here early tomorrow morning, but I'll be off by two. Come on by my place, and I'll cook dinner."

"You know, I think I would like that, a lot."

"Me, too. Now, you go ahead and eat. If you need something, holler. It's getting late; this weather is keeping everyone home. I'm going to start inventory, maybe even get out of here early. Enjoy your dinner." Sandy squeezed his hand and disappeared into the back.

***

Vince dipped a slice of bread in the spicy sauce. "That hit the spot." He pushed the empty plate aside and finished the last of his Sam Adams. "What do I owe you?" A long roll of thunder was immediately followed by back-to-back streaks of lightning. He caught a glimpse of the trees out front. They looked more like bending reeds.

"Glad you liked it. What time will you be at the apartment tomorrow? Anything in particular you'd like me to make?" Sandy removed the dish, swiped the bar and handed him the receipt.

"Surprise me. I'll be by around six." He set the beer mug down on top of two twenties. "You just make sure you drive home safe. I've got to get going myself. I'll see you tomorrow night. I'll bring the wine."

"Well, since you *are* a duly sworn Fire Inspector and have the same authority as any policeman, I suppose I must obey your every order?"

Vince grinned and headed for the foyer to retrieve his still-wet jacket. He pulled it up over his head with both hands, bumped the brass exit bar and ran out into the storm. The rain pelted him as he snatched open the door to his car and jumped inside.

Leaving the lot, he turned right onto Mandarin Turnpike and drove cautiously. He went about a mile before approaching the traffic signal at the intersection with Commercial Boulevard, when he realized he'd left his bag at Applebee's. He down shifted, pumped the brakes and coasted to a stop.

Vince grabbed the steering wheel with both hands as a blast of wind rocked the Jeep. He decided against turning back. Sandy would take care of the backpack, and he'd pick it up tomorrow. Above him, the overhead stoplight, its thin cable tether undulating wildly, pitched violently from side to side. Without warning, a bolt of lightning exploded into the side of a large power company transformer box alongside the roadway. He looked up as the top lens of the signal light surged a brilliant red, and then went out. An instant later the entire stretch of roadway and businesses on both sides were plunged into darkness. In the distance, sirens began to wail.

Sheets of rain pummeled his vehicle. His eyes strained, adjusting to the liquid blue-black sky. Another flash. A branch rocketed past him and thumped into a sign on his left.

Standard Cold Storage
Criton Yard
Trucks use second entrance.

Vince reached for the shift knob and slowly backed off on the clutch as he turned onto Commercial Boulevard. It twisted like a serpent, leaves and debris sliding across its wet back. One third of a mile later, behind a stand of large oak trees, a three story brick building ghosted into view.

The Jeep crept onto the service road. He let the engine idle for a moment and looked around. Near the corner he observed a pair of light colored stake-body Chevrolets, each emblazoned with the Criton logo and parked beneath an unlit halogen lamppost. On the closest side of the warehouse, razor wire topped the ten-foot high chain link fence he had driven past on the way in.

Vince shifted into second and approached the enclosed protected storage yard, the heavy rain compounding the gloom. He tapped the high beam lever. There were no pallets anywhere. The yard was empty except for the outline of three Kenworth tractors coupled to flatbed trailers like the one he saw Sam Collier loading at Criton.

Vince revved the engine and headed toward the exit. Accelerating back onto the service road, he caught a glimpse of the fence line as a burst of lightning accompanied a loud crack of thunder. He stomped on the brakes, and the Jeep fishtailed to a stop. He put it in reverse. A sturdy galvanized padlock dangled from the end of a thick chain fastened to the gate. The chain was severed and the gate left partly open. He left the engine running and got out.

The large rusted wheels at the bottom of the track screeched every half turn as Vince pushed. He scanned the north side of the building before clambering back into his car. The Jeep skimmed along the base of the warehouse, and he studied the double hung windows spaced along the brickwork on the first floor. The glass panes were intact. He looped around to the west side and drove along the rear loading docks. The wind sounded like a freight train. Vince reached into the glove compartment, rummaging for the powerful mini-mag light buried inside. He twisted it, targeting the beam at each of the locks at the base of the corrugated steel roll up doors. None were tampered with.

The rain was coming in sideways now, the wipers, slapping loudly, barely keeping up with the torrent. Vince wheeled around the southwest corner, staying close to the brick façade. A series of industrial grade, wire meshed, casement windows ran from one end of the warehouse to the other. They were undisturbed.

At the far end, he spied an awning covering a set of steps. He raised the flashlight and rested it on the car's doorframe. The compact cylinder of high energy LED light searched the door under the canopy. Vince zipped the canvas clad Jeep window down and squinted for a better look. The metal frame of the entrance door was scarred, deep scratches cutting across the area surrounding the strike plate. He jerked the lever to engage the parking brake.

Vince looked up the side of the wall. A faint light bounced erratically from an open window of a corner room on the third floor. He unlocked the metal console compartment between the seats and removed a leather holster. He didn't bother to take off his jacket as he climbed the concrete steps and looked around, his flashlight's thin beam spearing the area around him. On the far side of a utility shed he saw it, a brown pick-up truck, the Criton parking decal reflecting from the windshield.

Vince chambered a round in his Glock 22 and pushed the door inward.

Chapter 25
Standard Cold Storage Warehouse.

Even with the storm roaring outside and the latch ticking against the strike plate, Vince thought he heard a door close. He crouched low, back against the wall of the dark, cavernous interior and killed the flashlight, hoping his eyes would adjust. He rotated his head a few degrees at a time; listening, but the high winds and torrential rains battering the building were the only sounds he could confirm. Palming the semi-automatic in his right hand, he switched the pen light back on with his left and fanned its pencil shaped beam in a slow circle.

Pallets of empty cardboard containers, each stamped with the Criton Chemical logo, were stacked on the rough concrete floor. He followed the LED light upward. The piles rested against webbed metal trusses supporting the floor above. Vince flashed his light between the rows, each barely fifteen inches wide instead of the required twenty-four, and squeezed past the piles of merchandise. Probing deeper into the room, he sniffed the air. A faint but familiar odor stopped him cold.

Diesel fuel.

With his hand against the block wall, firefighter training took over, and Vince retraced his steps to the entranceway. Squatting, he directed the light to his left. Fifteen yards away, the black metal framework of the steps leading to the other floors came into view. His heart was pounding. He had no backup and there wouldn't be any. This section of Chatterton County merged with the drug infested apartment complexes of South Richmond. Combined with the many storm related incidents certain to occur, emergency personnel from both jurisdictions would have their hands full dealing with the chaos that was sure to ensue in those neighborhoods.

Seizing the step railing, Vince took a deep breath. His footfalls were deathly quiet as he settled on each tread plate. Pausing at the second floor landing, he laid his fingertips against the steel door and felt for any vibration that might tell him someone was behind it. Sensing none, he braced his body against the cold slab and inched it open just wide enough to slide by. Once through, he feathered the door closed and pressed his back against it.

A staccato blast of thunder echoed through the building. Vince squatted behind a fifty-five gallon steel drum until the rumble faded. He tightened his grip on the Glock, flattened against the wall and moved slowly into the room. The smell of diesel grew stronger. The area in front of him was crammed full of merchandise layered well above the pendent heads of the automatic sprinkler system laced throughout the old structure. Vince recalled Collier's words when they met at Criton: *like ten pounds of shit in a five pound bag*. Sweat dripped into his eyes. He swiped at the sting and backed out of the room toward the stairwell.

A muffled, grating noise came from the farthest corner of the floor above. Every muscle in his body tensed as a furious wind buffeted the window, rain

157

thudding heavily against the glass. Vince clutched the gun against his chest, his heart beating wildly. He ascended the last flight of stairs, leaden legs barely able to lift his feet. White knuckled, he clutched the iron railing surrounding the landing and stepped onto the deck plate. Something grain-like crunched beneath his feet. He stooped to pick up a couple of gritty, colorless granules and rolled them slowly between his fingers.

Ammonium nitrate . . . from Criton's loading dock?

Vince doused his light, eyes straining. He clamped the barrel of the mini-mag flashlight between his teeth and traced his trembling hand around the doorframe to the third floor storage area. A hint of light filtered above the threshold, moving. He cracked the door open and poked the .40 caliber past the edge, his head following deliberately behind it. He froze as he heard footsteps, followed by the sound of liquid splattering on concrete.

Vince waited for the splashing to stop and the footfalls behind the door to move on. He nudged the door, reaching behind the frame as he heard it tap against what sounded like metal. A can. He moved it out of the way and crept inside. He needed both hands to steady the Glock as he ducked behind a mound of burlap sacks. The smell of diesel filled the room. More granules. The dim light inside had stopped moving.

Suddenly, a flash of lightning blistered the skylights, and a snapshot of the room materialized into searing visibility.

Vince spotted a burst of movement from the corner of his eye. He spun, losing balance. Frozen in the strobe, a wide-eyed, angry face glared at him like an apparition from a nightmare. He caught the fleeting impression of raised hands with something in them, targeting his head. The object swung toward his face.

Vince lifted the gun and fired without aiming. The bullet slammed into the roof as he fell.

***

The bloodied pipe dropped to the floor, its loud clang reverberating. Kneeling, the ghostly figure pressed two fingers against Vince's carotid artery and felt for a pulse.

"You picked a bad night to be out, Inspector."

Using his sleeve, he wiped the blood off the metal rod. After removing his shirt, he reached into a green Nike sports bag stashed near the gas can, and pulled on a black hooded sweatshirt. He stuffed the blood smeared flannel into a plastic bag and picked up Vincent's Glock, quickly ejecting the magazine and tossing all of it into the bag.

Cutting a length of wire from a spool near the piled burlap sacks, the man cinched it tightly around Vince's wrists as he lay unconscious. "I wish you hadn't shown up. Now I've got to be certain you don't go anywhere while I finish, and since you've seen me again..." He dragged Vince face down into a corner and continued to distribute diesel fuel, nitrates and combustible material.

Once done, he yanked a coil of industrial grade detonation cord from his supplies and stepped back onto the metal drum he'd been balancing on. Grasping the steel alloy beams above his head with one hand, he attached the chemical laden flexible strand to wooden boxes loaded with diesel soaked nitrate fertilizer. These he'd secured above the sprinkler heads. Jumping from the barrel, his feet made a dull sound on the hard floor. He pulled the cord as he walked, careful to string the high-speed fuse around the periphery of the room.

As he went about his work, he pushed on each windowpane. The inspector wouldn't approve of the mix of fertilizer and fuel, but it was crudely efficient, and as Vince had taught him in Criton's fire training classes, the extra air from the open windows would get things going quickly.

The man snatched up his flashlight and repacked the nylon bag alongside Vince, who lay crumpled in a heap, his chest rising and falling as he breathed. He dug a pack of cigarettes from his pocket. A match flared as he scraped it against the concrete wall. "You don't care if I smoke now, do you?" He smirked as he lit two.

After a couple of leisurely puffs, he meticulously secured one cigarette to the terminal end of the primer cord, and then hefted his bag. "Pardon my leaving so quickly, but this only gives me about seven minutes." He carefully laid the makeshift triggering device on the floor of the landing, grabbed the diesel can, and bounded down the steps.

The exit door on the ground floor banged against the wall as he pushed it open. The rain was cascading off the steps like a waterfall. He spotted Vince's vehicle immediately; right where it shouldn't be. The can toppled on its side as he dropped it and jerked his sleeve back. Six and a half minutes until the cigarette hit the primer. Seeing the Jeep, the Fire Department would assume there was someone inside and work twice as fast. Maybe even stop the place from burning down. He tossed his cigarette and rushed outside.

He threw the duffel into his truck before jumping into Vince's Wrangler. The engine roared to life, tires spinning wildly as he careened past the loading docks onto the razor wired lot where the Kenworths were parked. He wedged the Jeep between the tractor-trailers and sprinted back. The clock in his head spurring him on.

Lungs on fire from the exertion as he leaped into his pick-up and started it, he banged his head against the door window as he took a final look behind him. A brilliant white light flickered and sizzled from the third floor.

An instant later, the entire roof caught fire.

Chapter 26
Chatterton County, Virginia

The rain was coming in sideways, pelting everything and everyone without mercy. Pushed by fifty mile an hour gusts, the thunderstorm raised holy hell in Chatterton County and had the Fire Department scrambling to deal with one alarm after another. Patrick and his crew, who had taken an overtime shift at Station 9 to increase manpower for the call volume, scurried madly in the deluge, readying their truck after the incident they had just finished. The squad had spent the last hour and a quarter battling a room and contents fire in a townhouse after the owners' candles had caught the bedroom curtains ablaze. Had they arrived a few minutes later, the whole row of twenty-year-old wood framed homes would have burned to the ground. They were in a hurry; the next emergency was simply a matter of minutes from coming their way.

Patrick was breathing hard. Sweat soaking him beneath his heavy turnout coat, combined with the rain, made him miserable all the way through. The radio hissed, static from the lightning causing it to crackle. A call was about to be dispatched as thunder crashed overhead. Instinctively, Patrick knew it was for his unit.

The voice of the midnight shift supervisor at the Emergency Communications Center boomed over the speaker. She was speaking calmly, but quickly.

"Engine 9, are you cleared from your last incident?"

Patrick flung the section of hose he was carrying from his shoulder onto the tailboard, raced for the cab, and grabbed the dashboard radio handset. "We're ready. Just finished repacking our water supply line. You got us another?"

The crew of firefighters hadn't had a break since coming on duty. Patrick was tired and hungry. They all were, and they weren't the only ones. The entire department was running balls to the wall with emergencies caused by the storm, and that meant the Inspection Division as well. He'd been listening to the radio traffic of all the inspectors. Vince was conspicuously absent. He should have been on the airwaves a long time ago.

The dispatcher's voice interrupted Patrick's worried train of thought. "Captain Meagher, stand by for a call. Engine 9, Engine 16, Truck Company 7, Battalion Chief 5, respond to 415 Commercial Boulevard, Standard Cold Storage building, for a possible lightning strike. Time of dispatch: zero one oh five hours. All units responding, this is a reduced manpower response."

Barely finished repacking the hose line, the crew manning Engine 9 jumped on board and started strapping on fresh air tanks as the driver, Tom Perrent, stomped on the accelerator. Water dripped from Patrick's fingers as he reached for the mic once more to confirm the assignment. He hesitated when he heard Shane's voice coming over the fire channel.

"Chatterton Communication, this is Battalion 5; I am en-route. Reduced manpower; understood, the

163

other units normally assigned for this incident are being held in reserve. Have you got anything else regarding this alarm on Commercial Boulevard?"

The dispatcher's reply sputtered through the speaker. "Battalion 5 and units responding, we received notification from Richmond Fire headquarters; they received a call from a citizen from one of the condominiums nearby. The woman said she thinks lightning may have hit a building on the other side of the highway. She smells a lot of smoke coming from that direction. Richmond is trying to clear a city police cruiser to go and check it out— they're closer, and Chatterton Police have their hands full at the moment."

"Okay," Shane said. "Battalion Chief 5 to Engine 9, what is your location?"

Patrick was ready. "Chief, we were a couple miles away in an apartment complex knocking out a small working fire. We just turned onto Mandarin Turnpike. Stand by." He saw a bright orange halo ahead in stark, foreboding contrast against the dark, wet night. "Chatterton; we have a large glow in the sky. It's a working fire. Upgrade to a full assignment; send the remaining units that would have been alerted originally for this incident."

Tom Perrent slowed after turning Engine 9 onto the service road for the warehouse. A quarter mile off, flames topped the large trees in front of the building. Patrick opened the slide window separating him from the firefighters gearing up behind him in the crew compartment.

"Simons, you grab the five inch supply line off the back and secure it to the hydrant. When Perrent has our hose lines hooked up and flowing water from the Engine to the sprinkler system standpipe connection, he'll hit the air horn twice as a signal. You hear that, you get the hydrant going asap and get your ass back here in a hurry."

"Gotcha, Cap. Just another day in paradise." Simons nodded and screwed the face piece breathing tube into his air pack.

"Horvath," Patrick continued, "pull the deuce and a half attack line to the back door near the stairwell, and wait for Simons. I'll give you the word when to go in."

The big man coolly cinched his helmet securely into place, saying nothing. After twenty-three years, this was just another 'job,' as the veterans called it, and as always, he was ready.

The brake drums squealed as Engine 9 came to a stop at the hydrant four hundred feet away from the burning warehouse. After Patrick saw Simons grab the water supply hose from the hose bed and begin connecting it to the hydrant, the fire truck raced off, the five-inch diameter hose zipping out the back and slapping the ground behind the tailboard.

Once in front of the building, Patrick heard the water gong for the sprinkler system ringing as water spurted from the device to make it chime, confirming it was operating. He took a long look at the two sides of the structure he could see and readied his report to the dispatch center and other apparatus responding to the address. Something wasn't right. There was too much fire considering the sprinkler system was in operation. He stared at the flames as he spoke.

"Engine 9 is on scene at a three story brick warehouse with fire showing through the roof and out the windows of the third floor. Captain Meagher will be in command. I am switching the radio from the dispatch channel to Fire channel D now."

Patrick snapped the last clasp of his turnout coat, slung an air-pack onto his back and grabbed the portable radio. "Tommy, I'm going to do a three-sixty and see what we've got all the way round this thing. Get hooked up to the sprinkler support system as fast as you can."

Perrent released his seat harness and hurried to the back of the Engine. After spinning the coupling of the large diameter hose onto the intake housing, he hustled back to the cab and alerted Simons with the air horn. Along with the mournful wails of other emergency vehicles approaching the warehouse, the two loud blasts added to the thunderous cacophony of the storm.

***

"Battalion 5 is on scene." Pulling up at the warehouse, Shane broadcast his arrival and parked his staff car in front, making sure he would not impede the positioning of the fire trucks that were headed his way. He spotted Patrick approaching from the southeast corner of the structure and waved him over. "What do you have, Captain, and what's your action plan?"

"We rolled up, laid a five inch supply line. There was fire through the roof and on the third floor. Gong was sounding. Engine 9 is supporting the building's sprinkler system and standpipes on each floor. I have my crew establishing a two and a half inch attack line to go up the rear set of steps. I completed a lap. Place looks empty and no cars in sight; not a life safety hazard as far as I can tell. Nothing else to add. Figured when you got here, you'd take command. I'll go and join my crew and await your orders. Something ain't right, Shane."

"Okay. I'll get the pre-plans from your unit and take over from here." Shane watched a tornado shaped funnel of sparks, whipped by the wind, twist high above the burning structure. He removed his turnout gear from the back seat and donned it. Behind him, colored emergency strobe lights bounced in all directions and mixed with the growl of approaching diesel engines. The rest of the first assigned units had arrived.

Shane charged off to retrieve the fire pre-plans for the warehouse, barking orders as he went. "Battalion 5 is assuming command. Truck 7, pull to the rear. Have your driver prepare for ladder pipe master stream operation, should it be needed. The remainder of the crew will provide ventilation of the building with your large exhaust fans, and light up the scene with the truck's onboard generator. Engine 16, you'll support them and give Truck 7 all the water they need. Set your two remaining firefighters in front as a rapid intervention team and safety back-up for all other crews."

Shane yanked Engine 9's door open and snatched the folder for Standard Cold Storage. Once back inside his vehicle, he continued giving fire ground orders while skimming through the essential information contained in the pre-plan. The fire was rapidly consuming the roof and blasting out the top floor like a blowtorch, the wall of rainwater from the storm having no effect. He raced through the comments section listed in the pre-plan.

"Primarily Class A ordinary combustible material; cardboard and burlap packaging materials; separate storage area for five gallon containers of cleaning products." He skipped to the contact information, and after a jolt, reread the last line. ". . . owned and operated by Hassan Muhktar." Without hesitation, he reached for his cell phone and selected the first name on speed dial. "Sorry to wake you, Chief Lowell, this is Shane Meagher. I'm out here in the warehouse district off of . . ."

"Meagher? What the . . . why are you calling me at this hour?"

"Believe me, it's not what I want either. We're on scene at a working fire near Mandarin Turnpike, and there's some . . ."

Shane heard the growl on the other end of the line as Lowell cut him off again. "This better be damn important, Meagher."

Shane bristled. "Look, I'm just letting you know right off the bat. The place is owned by the same guy who owns Criton Chemical, Hassan Muhktar." He thought the line had gone dead for a moment.

"Alright . . . I'll see you there."

***

After a two-hour battle, there was still no sign of Lowell. Shane finally got the report he was waiting

168

for in his earpiece. He tossed what was left of the lukewarm coffee one of the cops had brought him earlier, gave a small sigh of relief and switched the radio selector back to the main dispatch channel. "Chatterton Communications; mark the Commercial Boulevard incident under control."

The dispatcher acknowledged the report. "Attention all personnel, the incident at Commercial Boulevard is under control at zero four ten hours."

Shane's relief was short lived.

"You've got to be kidding me. Meagher, what exactly is going on here?"

Shane turned abruptly. "Chief Lowell, I didn't hear you drive up. What we had was a fire; it's under control. I'm not going to get set up as a fall guy like the incident at Criton, so I called you right away."

"Oh, really?" Lowell snarled sarcastically, making no effort to conceal his irritation. "Just get to the point, Meagher, and tell me what happened."

"We got banged out for the alarm sometime after one in the morning during the height of the storm. The original call came in from Richmond. It was a reduced response. My brother's unit was nearby and got here first, reporting fire through the roof and third story windows. They got on it right away. The caller said it might be a lightning strike, but . . ."

"What do you mean, *might*? Or didn't you or your hotshot brother notice we had a storm blow through? Goddamn power is out all through this half of the county because of lightning strikes. And the water gong, the sprinklers are operating, right? They should have controlled this."

"Because for one thing, we found a gas can." Bruce Simons walked toward the two men answering Lowell's question. "And when we got here, all the windows were open on the third floor in a place meant to be weather tight for storage at all times. Two sure signs it may not be storm related."

"Just what I need." Lowell massaged his temples. "So where is this can and Captain Meagher?"

"I left it at the base of the back stairs, Chief Lowell," Simons said, "behind the door where it was found. Firefighter Horvath is watching it to keep the direct chain of evidence intact as part of standard procedure. And Patrick, I mean Captain Meagher, is still inside directing the other crews."

Shane grabbed his radio. "I'm going to contact Ken Digman. He's our fire investigator for this district." Shane turned to his crew member. "Good job, Simons. The next person who touches that can is Digman, got it? And my cell is on the front seat; toss it to me, will you? I think I better get police forensics started on this now. It's all adding up to being a crime scene."

Lowell slid his hand across his mouth. "Damn it to hell, let me get this over with and call Muhktar." He walked over to his Crown Victoria, sat down with his own cell phone and closed the door.

Shane turned his attention back to the warehouse. "Command to Captain Meagher: give me a report."

"Captain Meagher to Command; no leak to cleaning products, and we're beginning secondary operations to eliminate hot spots. The sprinklers were overwhelmed rapidly. I can't figure out why just yet."

"Okay. Keep your efforts to fire extinguishment only. I'm getting our Fire Inspector and the police forensics squad over to investigate this. I'll notify you when they arrive."

"Ten-four Chief, we'll wait for them. Captain Meagher, out."

Chapter 27
Standard Cold Storage

By seven in the morning, the violent storm had been reduced to a dreary mist. As Patrick and Fire Inspector Ken Digman navigated the fire's aftermath inside the warehouse at Standard Cold Storage, Shane stood at the command post with Lowell and Major Walter Carson of the Chatterton Police Department, who had arrived after his forensic officer was called to the scene. They watched as Hassan Muhktar parked his Lincoln and headed their way. Shane couldn't help but see Lowell's eye begin to twitch as Hassan approached.

"Mr. Muhktar," the Fire Chief said, "it's not a total loss, thanks to the sprinklers." He took a step back and pointed at the warehouse, where tendrils of smoke still rose from the building.

"Tell me again, Chief Lowell," Muhktar said, his voice flat, "as you did on the phone. The storm is not to blame for this; it was a deliberate act?"

"Yes, it looks that way, but it'll take a while to collect and analyze all the information. We're doing all we can to . . ."

"Never mind." Muhktar flicked his hand, cutting him off, sounding thoroughly uninterested. Turning, he directed a smirk, almost a grin, toward Shane.

Shane didn't respond to the strange expression, but the cool, almost bored manner of Hassan's response to Stanley, considering his warehouse was a smoking shell, got all his attention. It didn't add up, especially considering Muhktar's behavior at the Criton fire. Shane made sure to avert his eyes, but kept listening as Hassan went on.

"Before I left, I had my assistant get in touch with our insurance adjuster. Mr. Meninguez will be here soon to begin his damage assessment. He in turn has contacted an arson investigator, someone they use for criminal acts such as this."

Voices coming over the command post speaker interrupted him.

"Fire Inspector Digman to Command; I'm on the first floor. Get in touch with the Division and have Inspector Rigardo bring the chemical analyzer unit to the scene. We need it to determine and record any use and types of accelerants. Also, the police forensic technician, Officer Kenney, is here with me photo-documenting the scene, as you requested."

Hearing the report, Shane turned away from Lowell and Muhktar and nodded at Bruce Simons. "Can you take care of that call to the inspection office for me? Here, use my cell." He tossed the phone as the sound of two car doors closing came from behind. He swiveled, hearing his father's familiar voice.

"Well now." William Meagher pocketed his keys and walked toward the group, accompanied by a shorter man Shane didn't recognize. "Since you're asking for a chemical analyzer, I'm thinking you must be having an idea that this bit of a thunderstorm wasn't the cause of the fire?"

"Dad! What are you doing here?"

Stanley Lowell frowned. "Yes, William, what *are* you doing here?"

The man beside Shane's father stepped forward. "That would be my doing. Caesar Meninguez; Experon Insurance." He began distributing business cards.

"Mr. Meninguez." Hassan pocketed the card without looking. "This is Stanley Lowell, Chief Officer of the Fire Department. He'll cooperate with you fully. And it seems everyone knows you but I—"

William regarded him coolly. "Retired Chief William Meagher, Mr. Muhktar. I now investigate. Caesar has already given me some of the particulars. And hello, Stanley." He cast a sideward glance at the Fire Chief before extending his hand toward the police major. "Walter Carson, always good to see you. Finally got yourself promoted, eh?"

Smiling, Carson grasped William's hand firmly. "Yes, I guess they figured I'd be easier to look after, buried up to my neck in paperwork. Always a pleasure to see you, William. We'll work with you any way we can."

Lowell stiffened. "And this is okay? I mean with you, Mr. Muhktar?"

The warehouse and chemical plant owner looked past the Fire Chief and spoke to the insurance adjustor. "Mr. Meninguez, you may call my office whenever you are ready. Nadia will provide whatever records you need."

"Thank you." Meninguez faced the group. "I'll get started now, and if there's anything I can do for any of you, please, don't hesitate to ask." He opened his clipboard and turned away from the assorted brains trust.

"Major Carson, Mr. Meagher." Muhktar crossed his arms. "This loss is unacceptable, especially after the accident at my chemical plant. My entire enterprise in Chatterton is in jeopardy. I can tell you I don't like being victimized. I won't tolerate it."

"I understand." Carson produced a small notebook. "Is there anyone who may have reason to do this?"

Hassan frowned. "I can't think offhand. I'm sure there are any number of people who'd enjoy ruining me."

"What about the forklift driver from the Criton fire, I understand you let him go?" William said, his head cocked to the side.

Carson followed up on William's question. "Mr. Muhktar, what can you tell me about this?"

"Ebi Rostum, one of the plant workers. I can't tell you much. Criton employs many such workers. He failed to follow explicit operating procedures on the loading dock, and his incompetence started the fire. I dismissed him."

"Rostum, Ebi. Got it." The major picked up his police radio. "We'll have something in minutes. Later today my detectives will get more detailed information from you."

"Like I just told Mr. Meniguez," Hassan Muhktar replied. "You can start by calling my executive assistant, Nadia Nuha, at the office. She handles all my business details. I just want this incident resolved."

"Shane, sorry to interrupt," Simons said as he rejoined the group. "I phoned the Fire Marshal's office. Rigardo hasn't come in and hasn't called. No one knows where he is, but the chemical analyzing unit was there, and I got it on the way."

Shane turned to William. "Dad, have you heard from Vince? We might need him with this investigation, and it's not like him to not report in."

His radio crackled. "Inspector Digman to Command, first floor is taken care of. Plenty of water damage. We're on to the second."

***

Patrick had meticulously scrutinized each of the pallets on the second floor of the warehouse. Fortunately, the liquid ammonia based cleaning products inside them hadn't leaked, and he and his crew could work more closely with Ken Digman as the investigator combed through the rubble.

"Hey, Pat." Digman took a break from probing a small pile of debris. "Go ahead and clean out the remainder of that broken glass from the window on the landing. That'll help Truck 7's ventilation fans clear out the rest of this smoke, and we'll be able to see a whole lot better in here."

Patrick grabbed an axe and slogged through the wet clumps of pink insulation toward the stairway. "So what do you think, Ken, about the cause? This isn't because of lightning, is it?"

"Always have to consider it until it's ruled out, of course, but let's face it, with the open windows and gas can, arson is more than a strong possibility. And since Criton and this place are owned by the same guy, there sure could be a connection. Something doesn't seem right with all of this. Maybe someone's carrying a grudge?" Digman scooped some fire debris into a metal tub to be analyzed. "After Vince gets that chemical identifier up here, we'll know pretty soon. Something overpowered the sprinkler system."

"That thing can give you results that quickly?" Patrick chopped at the wire-reinforced casement window.

"Yes. We got the device after you left the Inspection Division. It provides results in less than two minutes. With its on board spectral library, we'll have a good idea if an accelerant is involved."

Patrick removed the remaining shards of glass and shot a quick glance out into the fenced in lot below. The gravel yard seemed empty except for three Kenworth trucks. He shouldered his axe and grabbed the handrail to follow Digman to the third floor. On the second tread, he stopped.

"Hey, wait a second." Patrick put the pickaxe down and peered more closely at the tractor-trailers. "Let me see your radio a second will you?" He grabbed Digman's Motorola. "Captain Meagher to Command."

"Go ahead."

"Command, send one of the cops into the lot on the north side. Have them check on a green Jeep wedged between two of the semi's."

Looking down from his vantage point, Patrick had a good view of the command post. He watched as Shane motioned Major Carson over. He, in turn, appeared to talk to a uniformed policewoman, who then headed toward the storage lot.

***

On the landing at the top of the steps on the third floor, with the roof completely burned away, the work detail huddled in the dismal morning light as Inspector Digman gave his instructions. "Officer Kenney, take a few pictures of the layout first. Patrick, you and Firefighter Horvath start over by that far corner. Extinguish any hot spots and be alert for anything that seems out of place. Watch out for a heavily charred V-pattern on a wall that might indicate the origin of the fire."

The forensic police technician then began to photo document the scene. Suddenly, his portable radio sputtered to life, picking up an exchange between Carson and the policewoman sent to investigate the Jeep.

"Major, I'm going to run a plate check on a 2008 Jeep Wrangler, P as in Peter, F as in Frank, one, four, three, two. Keys are in the ignition. I'm looking for the registration. And that gate lock? Definitely looks like a bolt cutter got it."

Patrick stepped closer to the radio. "Did she say that plate started with a PF? That stands for Professional Firefighter."

Officer Kenney's police band radio blared once more.

"Police Dispatch to Major Carson, we have that information on Ebi Rostum. Last known address; room 200, Quality Inn at 899 Willas Road. Drives a 2005 brown Dodge Dakota truck. License RXM-287. Motel Clerk hasn't seen him and says Rostum's payment is overdue. The room is empty."

"Oh, Christ," Patrick said, "Vince was telling me and Shane about this guy."

"Hey." Horvath dragged a scorched, soggy section of sheetrock from the middle of the rubbish on the top floor. "We got something—some*body*—here. Maybe we got lucky and the son of a bitch killed his own ass."

Patrick hurried over toward his firefighter.

Digman checked the Fire channel on his portable before speaking. "Chief Meagher; firefighters have found a casualty. Stand by."

"Hey you two." The forensic officer focused his camera. "Move over and let me get some shots, then clear the rest of that crap off his back and turn him over." His police radio hummed. He turned up its volume, and they heard the voice of the policewoman in the storage lot below.

"I got the owner's name from the registration for this Jeep. Prepare to copy."

"Alright." Digman bent over the burned corpse. "Let's roll him onto his back."

Officer Kenney hesitated and lowered his camera as the body was flipped over. "This isn't the arsonist. His wrists are bound together with wire. This is a homicide. Let me get a picture of his hands and wipe off that ring he's wearing. It could help identify him."

Kenney's radio crackled again. Patrick, riveted to the police band as the female officer continued her report, stooped over the charred remains and whisked the ashes from the gold band, exposing its engraving. He fell backward against a beam. His helmet, sent flying by the hard impact, landed next to the body. "Oh God . . . it says 'Firefighter of the Year'!"

Just at that moment, the police radio next to Patrick hissed as the policewoman read the name on the Jeep registration.

"Rigardo,Vincent, Charles."

Chapter 28
The home of William Meagher

The late afternoon clatter of pots and pans on the stove had long since been replaced by a soft silence, the kind a gentle snowfall makes as it covers the ground, allowing only muted echoes to be heard. The dining room table in William and Kathleen Meagher's forty-year-old Cape Cod still bore half-filled glasses and plates of leftovers where family and friends who'd attended Vincent's wake had left them. Hours earlier, a large crowd had packed the house where Vincent Rigardo had spent so much time. Clinking glasses in toast after toast and retelling stories for the umpteenth time, they filled the house with bittersweet tributes. Now, the silence spoke more eloquently.

Sequestered in the den after the long, emotional day, William, Patrick, and Shane stood in the wash of light from a lamp, an opened bottle of Jameson's on the end table. William's voice was low and heavy with grief. "It's surely not your fault, and you can't be blaming yourselves for Vincent's death. There wasn't a thing you could've done that would have made a difference."

"But, Dad." Shane broke away and sank onto the couch. "Vince was trying to tell me about Rostum, and I told him to forget about it. Now he's dead. I should've paid more attention."

"Burned him alive." Patrick spit the words out like they were acid. "Why didn't he just go home after work instead of heading out in that storm? What the hell was he doing at the Standard Cold Storage warehouse in the first place?"

"I know you're angry and hurt; wishing things were different and whoever did it made to pay, but since we're not knowing who did anything, you'd both be wise not to bandy names about or spout any accusations. That being especially so since you're officers in the Fire Department."

"I haven't said a goddamn thing to anyone outside this room." Patrick balled his fists, the former Golden Gloves boxer wanting to beat the living shit out of whoever had brutally murdered Vince. "I just want to catch the scumbag who did this and make him pay in every way possible."

"We all do." William responded quickly. "The police are working hard on it."

"We know that." Shane sank deeper into the cushions. "I just feel helpless. I hope Walter Carson's detectives get a lead soon."

"We can only hope," William said. "But there wasn't much Hassan Muhktar could offer the police beyond hiring and standard identification procedures. Huge facilities like Criton get tons of employees, and the monotony of that kind of work causes a lot of turnover. I do know all police agencies in the state have been contacted, but so far no sign."

"What about prints on the gasoline can, Vincent's Jeep; maybe the guy's done something somewhere else, and they've got him on file out of state?" Shane's index finger traced circles on the arm of the couch.

"They're looking, Shane. So far there's nothing. But loners like Rostum always turn up. It's just more difficult, since the man's been living in a motel, paying for everything with cash. He'd only been on the job a short while."

"And that's it?" A picture frame fell to the floor as Patrick took his frustration out on the wall with his fist. "We just sit around?"

"Patrick, you need to calm that temper of yours. The investigation is being handled properly. On top of that, Marcus is looking into a few things, and I've begun my work for the insurance company as well."

"Well, that's good to hear." Shane stopped his imaginary sketching. "So what's your plan?"

"I've reviewed Inspector Digman's report," William said. "He confirmed a mix of diesel and ammonium nitrate and some type of accelerating agent. He's waiting on final confirmation from the State Police lab. I've also met with the Chatterton police forensics team, and I'm going to head over to Standard Cold Storage to take a look around."

"So that was the flammable mix?" Patrick muttered as he stared out the window. "Any gas station has diesel, and an agricultural supply center will have the nitrates. Simple and effective. Muhktar will be pissed off, probably having his own products used against him. Think you'll find anything at the warehouse they didn't? What else you got up your sleeve?"

"Well, I'm thinking the killer must've been in a hurry to leave that gasoline can by the doorway when he saw Vincent's Jeep. In a storm like that, I'm sure he wasn't expecting to be discovered. Maybe he made another mistake in his haste to get away. I'll be searching to see if that's so. I also contacted Mark Radcliffe, Chatterton Fire Department's public information officer. He arranged a television spot on Channel 8 News, Crime Watch. Maybe someone who won't talk to the police will talk to me?"

"That's a damn good idea." Shane brightened. "Since tips from the public remain anonymous, maybe someone will step forward. Reward money is good motivation, and I'm sure the insurance company isn't too happy having to pay out a big arson claim. They'd be thrilled to pay you a recovery fee and stick it to the son of a bitch who did this."

They heard a man's voice headed down the hall toward the den from the kitchen. Shane pushed up from the sofa just as the door swung inward.

"Whoa! Hey, Marcus, come on in. Grab a seat. Your ears must be burning."

"Sorry, I'm later than I said getting over here." The FBI agent flung his jacket over an armchair. "After the service, I got a priority call from my boss. We have a transport ship full of Marines leaving Iraq soon, and another IED killed a squad of soldiers near the port. I've been ordered to attend a high level meeting."

"I saw it on the news. No need to apologize, Marcus. I fully understand, and by the look on your face, I can tell it's important. Here." William handed him a bottle of Coke.

"I have to be at headquarters in DC tomorrow, but looking into Vincent's murder is a priority too, as far as I'm concerned."

"And we can't thank you enough, Marcus." William pulled up a chair. "Have you got anything?"

"There is something." Marcus took a big swallow and snugged the cap back on top of the plastic bottle. "I just heard from our Baltimore office. I'll be contacting Walter Carson of course, but wanted to tell you first." He put his soda down on the mantel, squaring his broad shoulders as he faced the Meaghers. "We found Rostum's Dodge Dakota."

Shane's jaw dropped. "You're kidding? Where? Please tell me he was with it."

"The truck was discovered at BWI Airport in the long term lot."

Patrick drew in a sharp breath, his hand clenched. "Baltimore? Son of a bitch, then he's gone? Did anyone see him?"

"Parking lot surveillance cameras got a glimpse, but it's a very grainy night shot. Whoever it was had a black hooded sweatshirt cranked down pretty tight. Doesn't do us any good as to who it was, only what he was doing."

"What do you mean?" Patrick said through clenched teeth.

"Guy walks to a trash can, dumps what turns out to be a green Nike Sports bag."

"And?"

"We're running tests now. Got a bloodied shirt, Vincent's Glock and some kind of chemical residue, maybe an accelerant. It's all still being analyzed."

"Well," Patrick slumped into a chair, shaking his head in disgust. "Did anybody see this guy Rostum? Somebody inside the terminal maybe?"

"We canvassed the whole area, talked to all the carriers, agents and handlers," Marcus said. "Showed them Rostum's most recent Criton picture ID. Not a one had seen him, and no ticket was purchased. This figure being at the airport doesn't guarantee he flew anywhere. Using a public transportation terminal is a pretty typical ploy. Whoever is in that photo could have stolen a car, or grabbed a bus out of town."

"My friend." William settled his hand on Marcus shoulder. "We've been knowing each other a long time. I'm thinking you're not finished telling us something here?"

"William, we don't have much. He's living out of a seedy hotel on the Pike, and the locals there are pretty blind and tight lipped. A lot of them have something to hide themselves and avoid talking to law enforcement of any kind, let alone us Feds. We're checking for bank records, credit cards, etcetera, but at this point, Ebi Rostum is a ghost, in more ways than one." The agent's eyes furrowed before continuing. "I contacted Interpol headquarters in Lyons, France. We have so little to go on, and the truck was at the Baltimore airport. It was worth a shot."

"And I'm taking you got a response?"

"Yeah, I got one alright. Ebi Rostum is dead, been that way a while."

Patrick's jaw dropped. "You're telling us Rostum is dead? Then who the hell is the guy from Criton?"

"Slow down a second. I got the name from an Israeli database. Rostum was an Iranian engineer working on the Russian built nuclear power plant in Bushehr, Iran. The one *allegedly* for peacetime purposes only. He died from a leak, which is just about all we can confirm. There isn't much of a record for people working on a military project that supposedly doesn't exist in a country that does all it can to hide everything from us."

Shane threw both hands up. "Who is our guy then?"

Marcus had been pacing the room, and now he stopped to lean against the edge of William's desk. "Let me explain. I was surprised too when I read the report, and we're doing what we can to unravel this, but it's not like Iran will cooperate. We won't be getting shit from them as far as help is concerned, and let's be realistic, it's even easier to steal an identity in a country like that than it is here."

"So what's your theory?" William asked.

"We're working on that. So far, what we've put together indicates that when this engineer died, someone took advantage. Someone who had connections. The engineer wasn't a common laborer. Much like we have stolen identities and social security cards here in the States, same is true there, but much easier to do when technology and record keeping aren't exactly state of the art."

"I'll be damned." Patrick shook his head in disbelief. "So we have no idea who worked at Criton?"

"Not at the moment. Maybe he was just somebody desperate to obtain a work visa or passport any way he could to get out of Iran. A false set of papers to hide his real identity would do that. It sure explains choosing to live in a motel and paying in cash. He

187

wouldn't want to leave much of a trail. We've seen it before."

William had been quietly taking it all in. "So we may be dealing with someone who found his way here and is now carrying a grudge against one of his own countrymen for being fired? This puts a twist on a television appearance I'm going to make. I'll be asking the public to come forward about a man who doesn't exist, don't you think, Marcus?"

"I'll grant you it's a twist, William, but it doesn't change a thing as far as what you're trying to accomplish. Right now any information from any source could give us a lead. Besides, if you do get a response, the caller will be speaking about Ebi Rostum as far as he or she will know."

"That's true enough. I'll go ahead as planned, but surely will not even come *close* to what's been said here tonight. You'll be telling Walter Carson, eh, Marcus?"

"I'll meet the Major in the morning, advise him to share this information strictly on a need to know basis and keep a tight seal on it. He'll know what to do. Then I have to get up to DC and see what my supervisor has regarding our troops leaving Basra. I'll fill you in if I get anything more about this Criton character."

"I can't thank you enough," William said. "We'll talk again after I get over to the warehouse and look around, and of course, if Crime Watch develops something."

Patrick spoke up. "Since you're going to police headquarters tomorrow, could you swing by and give me a ride to pick up Vincent's Jeep? The police are done with it. Then I should finally get over to his cubicle and get his stuff."

"Not a problem." Marcus nodded. "I'll be by somewhere around nine to pick you up."

Chapter 29
Criton Chemical Office

Nadia stuffed Hassan's two daily newspapers, *The Wall Street Journal* and *The Iran Daily News*, deeper into her bag and shifted the strap on her shoulder. She stood waiting in the atrium of Richmond's Warsaw Building for the elevator that would ferry her up to the Criton office suite.

Nadia faked indifference to the mixed chatter around her. Truthfully, she listened intently and automatically, without appearing to do so, and surreptitiously absorbed conversations, loud or hushed, all the while remaining unnoticed. That was easy—other than the traditional garb she wore, her clothes were conservative, off-the-rack styles from JC Penney and not much for garnering attention. As a child in Aliabad, she'd eagerly picked up tidbits of information not meant for her ears, a talent she shared with Farid and one of the reasons he was such a good journalist. The tactic played to her quiet sense of humor as people's interactions exposed bits of their characters, like a mosaic she enjoyed piecing together. She'd been doing it for years as Hassan's wife and executive assistant.

To her left, the two thirty-something ad execs—she'd caught their market schemes before—discussed the hectic schedule of their daughters' soccer team. They no longer complained as they usually did, because a hot divorcee had showed up at the last game.

Nadia rarely offered more than a congenial nod when encountering the same faces each day. Ruth, a senior insurance underwriter at Experon, was her one friend, but she didn't see her all that often, only an occasional lunch at nearby diners, and lately all they exchanged were emails. As for relatives, Farid was her only family, and no one knew they were connected. Worlds away, he worked for an unpopular independent newspaper in Iran, and she missed him terribly. Nadia never considered her husband, Hassan, in the context of family. Their relationship was nothing more than a corporate arrangement.

The elevator pinged and short-circuited her thoughts. The doors opened, and the crush of bodies propelled her into the far corner of the car.

Criton's office clock chimed as Nadia reached her floor. She habitually arrived each morning at eight, taking an hour of quiet to prepare for the start of each day. She brewed three cups worth of Turkish coffee, turned on the TV, and read and prioritized emails for Hassan's review. She booted the office desk computer and opened her own laptop.

As the Dell hummed to life, Nadia glanced over at the plants clustered near the entrance, and smiled. Water sloshed in the can as she flitted between the ornamental fig tree and the bamboo palm, plants Hassan had selected himself. Considering his otherwise chilly demeanor, she found his appreciation for the shrubbery refined, almost gracious.

Plants watered, Nadia stepped into Hassan's office. Her husband was particular about his routine and wanted the shades opened halfway. He expected to find *The Wall Street Journal*, still banded, on the left side of the blotter, and *The Iran Daily News* open at the center of his desk.

As Nadia unfolded the newspaper, she scanned the bold type that headlined a scathing attack on her brother's newspaper, Sharq. The columnist, Anwar Hadid, condemned what he considered the treasonous writing of a Sharq staff reporter, Farid Barmeen, for defaming Abbas Muhktar with an allegation of the sheik's complicity in black market sales in Khorromshahr, Iran.

Dizzy with alarm, Nadia steadied herself, thoughts spinning wildly.

The clock struck the quarter hour. In fifteen minutes, Hassan would walk through the door. His first appointment was soon after; he'd been hounding her about it. A senior executive and lead counsel from DuPont Industries were slated for the final negotiation in their purchase of Hassan's River Road estate for their plant expansion. Nadia had to get the file on his desk and complete her review of the emails before the meeting convened.

Clicking the TV remote, CNN News, the station Hassan specified for the reception area, flashed across the screen. Nadia switched to Channel 8 to catch a few minutes of the local news coverage she favored.

A journalist from Crime Watch stood with two men in front of the burned shell of Standard Cold Storage. Seeing Criton's warehouse, Nadia tapped the volume.

"In conclusion, Mr. Meagher, is there anything you'd like to add regarding your investigation?"

"Well, on behalf of Experon Insurance Company, I request that if any of your viewers have seen this man, they contact me. His name is Ebi Rostum, and he's a person of interest in the arson and murder of a Chatterton firefighter that took place here." He reached for a photo in a manila folder.

"And as always," a second man, outfitted in a Fire Department dress uniform added, "all calls will remain anonymous."

Meagher nodded. "Yes, Chief Radcliffe, thank you. It's important viewers understand that any calls made using this secure number go directly to me." A phone number appeared in a tag line at the bottom of the screen.

Nadia's squinted at the television. Hassan had mentioned William Meagher in a message to the sheik.

Above the number, a photograph of Ebi Rostum filled the screen. Nadia gasped as she recognized the face, even with the scraggly beard. It was Sheik Muhktar's personal attaché, Jalal Hamadi.

The elevator alert tone sounded in the hall. Nadia jabbed the recall button on the remote, and once again CNN's familiar drone filled the room. A United States Naval Captain was discussing preparations underway for the 2nd Marine Division to leave the Persian Gulf. In the background, an American transport ship, the U.S.S. *Defender,* lay at anchor.

The elevator doors had barely slid apart before Hassan stepped out and headed straight for his office. "I want the information from the demolition company I chose to raze the manor house on my desk. And bring me my messages."

Nadia quickly skimmed through the incoming mail. Three messages caught her eye immediately.

One was from Mayor Jackson Stamper about zoning, another from Carter Demolition Company regarding the River Road property, and the third was from Abbas Muhktar referring to a meeting with Jalal Hamadi. About to open them, she was distracted by the vibration of her phone that alerted her to a personal email. Quickly, she typed her password into her own PC and clicked on the message. It was from Farid.

Nadia's already agitated heartbeat accelerated. She tore through her purse, eyes zipping back and forth between the computer screen and the closed door of Hassan's office. Her groping fingers closed around the flash drive on which she stored Farid's photos and letters. Slipping it into the USB port, she transferred his message without reading it and swiftly removed the device. She dropped it into her jacket pocket and shot a tense glance at Hassan's door as she deleted the message and returned her nervous attention to Criton's business emails.

Nadia printed out the proposal from the wrecking company and read Jackson Stamper's message. Hassan had gotten his way. The rezoning had been approved, and the estate property was now considered commercial land. She looked up as the team from DuPont entered the waiting room.

Nadia smiled. "Mr. Goreman, Mr. Avsett, gentlemen, please have a seat," she said. "I'll tell Mr. Muhktar you're here." She collected the printed messages and knocked lightly on Hassan's door.

He looked up from the newspaper as she entered, a smug grin on his face.

She saw the two men into his office and returned to the reception area, listening as the three started to laugh. Like his father, Hassan could be charming. He kept most people, especially those who worked for him, on edge with alternating fits of anger and geniality. Jalal Hamadi, the sheik's right hand man, was the only one who seemed impervious. He treated Hassan with disdain, as he would a spoilt and greedy reprobate who lived off his father and benefited from the work Hamadi himself did at the sheik's behest.

The flash drive with Farid's newly transferred email burned a hole in her jacket pocket. As the banter subsided in Hassan's office, negotiations would begin in earnest. Nadia retrieved her laptop and stepped into her small private office adjacent to the reception area. She kept the door half open, ears on full alert, and slipped the flash drive into the USB port.

Nadia,

I know you're aware of most of the Muhktars' business dealings. You're also familiar with articles I've occasionally written about them and various corporations conducting business in Tehran.

I've always been careful to report the news as truthfully as possible, yet maintain a blurred line, to some degree, for my own safety. Sharq is under scrutiny, and in a bid to shut us down once and for all, the authorities may confiscate our computers and scan our records for anything they consider subversive or contentious. I need to protect some of my research and writing.

This is where you come in. I'm attaching an exposé that I've been working on—it's of a sensitive nature, and I don't want the police to come across it. They've been known to search my apartment, and nothing has ever come of it, but they are thorough, and you're the only person I trust.

Keep it safe for me, and I'll let you know when I'm ready to take it back.

Nadia got up to check the reception area and listened for muffled, ongoing conversation in Hassan's office. Trembling, she returned to her desk and opened Farid's attachment.

A series of photographs filled the screen: one of the *Orient Star* at a dock; another of two men shaking hands over a suitcase full of money; a third of armed guards standing beside sacks emblazoned with the Criton logo. There were others. A video clip, she dared not view it now, would have to wait. Hands shaking, Nadia extracted a pack of gum from her bag and removed several pieces. The flash drive fit perfectly in the wrapping. She folded the foil to secure it and placed the pack in her pocket.

She waited for her nerves to settle before returning to the computer in the reception area. The last message from Abbas Muhktar regarding a meeting with Hamadi had yet to be opened.

Why was Jalal Hamadi masquerading as Ebi Rostum?

196

Head pounding, Nadia read the sheik's encrypted email to his son.

Hassan,

As before, Jalal got back to Iran without incident on our corporate jet. He confirmed that 15,000 tons of nitrate were funneled onto the Orient Star *prior to the fire at Criton. Our official records indicate it was consumed in the blaze. The ship has been sold.*

With the subsequent fire at Standard Cold Storage, all investigative efforts should be concentrating on a search for one Ebi Rostum, a renegade arsonist bent of revenge, as planned. The death at the warehouse was unfortunate as it has drawn more heated focus, but they're looking for a man who doesn't exist, so I'm not overly concerned.

I expect you're close to shutting down our Criton operation. You need to confirm that you've resolved the rezoning and sale of your estate and that a demolition date has been set.

It seems Criton has, shall we say, an image problem with the Iranian media. Jalal will set that right. Once that's sorted out, he'll return one last time to Chatterton to attend to the razing of your estate, necessary to keep the authorities focused on finding an arsonist as you leave the country. Nadia will, of course, join us after her work with the lawyers is complete.

Don't pressure him for details and don't concern yourself with his access to our account.

Have Nadia make the arrangements. Soon we celebrate in Bahrain.

Suddenly, the paneled doors to Hassan's office opened, and her husband stepped out with the DuPont executives. He escorted them out of the reception area and shook hands at the elevator.

He returned with a triumphant look and huge smile. "The property is sold. It's all coming together."

Nadia dropped her eyes.

Chapter 30
Qom, Iran

"Mother, it wasn't the first time government watchdogs have disrupted our work at Sharq." Farid filled a chipped ceramic pot with water and placed it on the stove. "I'm not concerned about what they find. What bits of research I have left allows them to believe they need to be mindful, but nothing more. Think of it as a game we play." He unscrewed the top of a mason jar that stood on the shelf above the table and began measuring the black chai tealeaves she preferred.

On the couch in the living room, Behi smoothed a worn quilt over her legs. "Didn't you mention you had one important article in particular that had to be in before twelve? You should go back to the office, it's already past mid-day."

Farid placed the kettle on the gas burner, struck a match, and adjusted the flame. He stared at the matchstick as it burned down to his fingertips, watching the smoke curl. "What's that, Mother?" He tossed it in the sink, pulled the threadbare curtain aside, and looked pensively down the alley in both directions several times. The sky was a deep gray, the color of slate, and a stiff, unrelenting breeze caused an array of sheets hung on the clotheslines between buildings to flap vigorously.

"Your job," she repeated, "you must go, your deadline."

"I'll go when Lelah gets here." Farid moved to the living room and sat on the edge of the sofa cushion. Tenderly, he felt his mother's forehead. It was hot.

"And what about your colleagues?" Behi wheezed, the cold she suffered from the past week now firmly entrenched in her chest. "Are they not concerned about the police causing trouble at the Newspaper?"

"Colleagues?"

Behi reached for the tissue box on the side table. "The ones who helped me with the groceries. Oh, Farid . . ." She placed her hand over her mouth to stifle a phlegmatic cough. "You have faraway eyes. Don't you remember I told you about your three friends, the ones who carried the bags into our apartment when I'd gone to the butcher?"

Farid turned away. There was no way she could know the deadline she'd alluded to concerned Kazem Al-Unistan's threat, the terrorist demanding a stronger indictment against Abbas Muhktar than Farid's first article regarding Khorromshahr. "You worry too much." He forced a smile and stole a quick glance at the wall clock. Twelve forty five. "What time did Lelah say she would be here?"

A knock on the door answered his question. He ambled over and opened it.

"Farid." The neighbor chortled. "Take this." She thrust her shawl at him and waddled past. "Your mother and I have a game of Pasur to finish, and she has better cards than I. Is that chai I smell?"

"Yes, yes!" Behi chimed in. "Get the tea and let's get back to it!" The two old friends kissed each other on both cheeks before Lelah shuffled into the kitchen.

Farid smiled as he hung Lelah's embroidered wrap on a pegboard. "You're in good hands once more."

"Go on, off with you, and try not to be late coming home."

"Farid, you'll do as your mother says." Lelah nudged aside the curtain separating the two rooms, returning with the steaming ceramic pot in one hand and two earthenware cups in the other.

Farid laughed and pecked his mother on the cheek. "I know better than to argue with you two. It's safer to deal with the Revolutionary Guard!" He stepped past the door onto the landing and listened as he always did for the bolt to slide back into position.

Farid hopped down from step to step. At street level, a strong breeze hit him in the face as he shouldered the door open. He made his way through the market to the alley one hundred meters away, where he'd parked his car the night before. A few shoppers scurried toward their own vehicles as clouds roiled overhead.

"Well, that's good," he murmured as he unlocked the door. "Not much traffic." Maybe he'd make up some time getting to work. He folded into the front seat and cast a curious glance at a faded blue Mercedes that had pulled out and blocked his exit. He felt a twinge of unease as he tapped the horn.

The driver held up his cell phone and met Farid's eyes for a few pointed moments.

Farid's pulse accelerated as he recognized Sheik Abbas Muhktar's thug behind the wheel. Instinctively, he clawed at the door handle, desperate to get out of the car as Jalal Hamadi slowly drove away.

Farid never felt the explosion that catapulted the Toyota into the air, sending metal shards in all directions as a fireball engulfed the car. It landed on its top in the alleyway, crumpled and burning.

Chapter 31
Chatterton Government Complex

Patrick Meagher stood before a fenced in compound behind the Chatterton county jail and stared across the lot at Vincent's Jeep. A rush of grief caught in his throat and burned his eyes. Rage wasn't far behind, and he jabbed the call button at the razor wired gate with unnecessary force. "Patrick Meagher. I'm here to pick up a green 2008 Jeep Wrangler, plate number PF-1432."

The rusted louvered call box on the fencepost crackled, and the voice of Police Lieutenant Kristen Michaels buzzed through the speaker. "Oh, hey Pat, it's me. I'll be right out."

Patrick watched the uniformed figure leave the corrugated tin shed in the center of the lot and walk toward him. He'd run a number of car wrecks on the Pike where the no-nonsense police lieutenant was assigned. "What are you doing here guarding cars?"

"Just making some overtime." She smiled meekly and unlocked the gate. "Wish you were here under better circumstances. Come on."

Wordlessly, the two walked past a wrecked police cruiser and the twisted hulk of a Chevy Silverado crew cab.

"I still can't believe he's gone." The lieutenant touched Pat's forearm gently and stepped back as he opened the door to Vincent's Jeep and sat in the worn driver's seat.

Patrick nodded bleakly, started the engine, and leaned across to check the glove compartment. Too choked up to speak, he waved at the officer and accelerated out of the lot. His head reeled from the Jeep's stark reminders of Vince: a balsam scented pine tree deodorizer hung from the rearview mirror, strategically placed to mask the sweaty smell of hockey gear. Vincent's penknife nestled in the glove compartment amidst a stack of maps for off-road bicycling and a couple of golf score cards, prized trophies for the few times he bested William.

A horn honked behind him. Patrick blinked back the tears that were beginning to trickle from the corners of his eyes, but he had no success clearing the grief that caused them.

***

The secretary behind the desk at the entrance to the Inspection Division stood up as soon as Patrick stepped inside. "It's good to see you, Patrick," she said. "How are you holding up?"

He helped himself to a Snickers Junior from the candy dish on the counter. "What can I say, Esther? Most days all I can think about is how none of this makes any sense. I lie awake trying to figure it out, you know? Other days . . ." He trailed off, helpless to articulate a less emotional response.

Esther studied his face. "You look tired. We're all still in shock."

Patrick nodded. "I've come to collect Vincent's things. Can I use those boxes by the copy machine?"

He read something in Esther's gaze that made him uneasy. "What's wrong?"

The sound of a drawer being closed came from Vince's cubicle. "Somebody in there? Did I come at a bad time?" He popped the chocolate into his mouth and headed down the hallway.

He reached the doorway and caught a uniformed fire officer rummaging through the desk. The hunched figure, absorbed in his work, hadn't heard him approach.

Patrick leaned against the doorframe, arms crossed. "Eddie Tammerlin, just what are you doing?"

The Fire Marshal dropped a ring binder and knocked a framed photograph off the desk. "Uh, Meagher, what brings you here?"

Patrick replaced the photo of Vince crossing the finish line at the Richmond Marathon. "I came to get Vincent's belongings. Look at this mess." Disheveled papers and dog-eared manuals were strewn across the blotter. "I asked you a question, Eddie."

The fire marshal stiffened at the challenge. "Not that it should concern you, but I'm collecting official Fire Department property."

"Collecting? Collecting, my ass." Patrick stepped deeper inside the cube. "It looks more like you're tossing his room as if it were a jail cell."

"Don't you question me." Eddie bumped into the office chair as he retreated. "I'm following orders. That's what we're paid to do."

"Following orders? You're the head honcho down here, so why not get one of your division firefighters to do it?" A light bulb in his head came on. "Chief Lowell's orders?"

Tammerlin's face turned crimson. "All notes relating to any investigations are Fire Department property and none of *your* business. They, uh, they could be crucial for follow up by the next inspector." He shut an opened attaché case lying on top of the filing cabinet and grabbed the handle.

"That's Vincent's." Patrick extended his hand.

Tammerlin whipped it behind his back. "This is Chatterton property, and I'm the Fire Marshal. I'm ordering you to leave, Meagher."

"You don't get to push me around." Patrick inched forward.

Tammerlin lost his balance as he stumbled backwards, swinging the case in front of his chest like it was a shield as he landed against the wall. "I'm warning you, Meagher. I'll tell . . ."

"*Tell,* Eddie?" Patrick snarled, but backed off. "I'll be back later, and Vincent's stuff—all of it—better be here." He picked up a pencil, flung it at the wall, and stormed off.

***

"What did you tell him?" Stanley Lowell stood up and circled the small conference table in his office.

Eddie Tammerlin laid the attaché case on the Chief's desk. "I told him it was Fire Department business and that any notes or papers were Chatterton's property."

"Did you find any of Rigardo's Criton notes?"

Tammerlin shook his head. "I didn't see anything lying around, and I looked through just about everything, except this." Eddie thumbed the clasps of the case, and the lid popped open. "When Patrick Meagher busted into Rigardo's cubicle. I grabbed it, and here I am."

"That was some piss poor timing, him showing up like that, but let's just see if there's anything we need to concern ourselves with in there."

Tammerlin dumped the contents and began sifting through them. "I'm not seeing anything about Criton Chemical in here, just some sketches and notes of the mall project out near the interstate. And here's the NFPA manual I saw him with when I caught him reviewing storage regulations about Hassan's warehouse. That's it."

"Maybe he trashed them after you got on his ass to stop his private search into the Criton investigation after it was over and done with. It won't matter much soon. Muhktar is leaving Chatterton for good anyway."

"He's really closing up Criton Chemical then, huh?" Tammerlin sat down and tossed everything back into the briefcase.

"Yeah, he made his money, now he's selling off his house and property to DuPont. They're thinking of expanding. By the way Eddie, you *did* approve the permit to have that house of his wrecked? We're going to have a fire truck stand by during that operation, right? I don't want something to flare up or go wrong. I've about had enough shit crammed down my throat because of Muhktar."

"Yes. Signed, sealed, and delivered. You don't think he'll, well, you know, make trouble about the warehouse concessions that you told me to approve, considering Rigardo got killed out there?"

"I doubt Muhktar will say or do a thing. At this point, he'll just take his money and leave. Mayor Stamper will be in for a rough ride with all those jobs going away. He'll get blamed. Next election won't be easy, and if he goes, I'm screwed as well. As you know more than anybody, the position of Fire Chief is a political appointment."

Tammerlin sat up straight.

"You'd like that, wouldn't you Eddie, to back your way into this office? It's no secret you've been salivating to get a Chief's job, but every single one of your applications to become a department head somewhere else has been rejected."

Tammerlin sat stone faced, pushing his wire framed glasses against his nose, saying nothing.

"Alright," Lowell scratched the bald crown of his head. "Don't do anything until I order you. I'm going to call the Mayor and fill him in. Now, close the door on your way out."

"What shall I do with Rigardo's papers?"

"Dump them."

Grabbing the attaché, Tammerlin said nothing else and left.

Chapter 32
Halligan Bar and Grill, Richmond, Virginia

"I'm telling you, Dad, Eddie was on a mission. Stuff was scattered everywhere in Vincent's cube. There were pictures knocked over, manuals opened, drawers half empty. I mean, just the way he reacted when I walked in on him said it all. And the Fire Chief is behind it." Patrick's chatter made the traffic he and his father dodged as they stutter-stepped across the street seem slow in comparison. "What did you find out today at Standard Cold Storage?"

William opened the door to the Halligan Bar and Grill. "Something's going on alright. Let's get a seat." It seemed half the city of Richmond had decided this was where they wanted to get an early start on happy hour.

A booth opened up at the far end of the wall. They jostled past a group of cowboy wannabe's who were feeding the Rockola a steady diet of dollar bills, and singing along with Kenney Chesney as he lamented the perils of women and tequila.

Once they were seated and waiting for a server, William palmed the saltshaker and skated it between his hands. "I went over the inside of that room very carefully. It's the only place where primer residue was identified. If the room was wired, if the fire were electronic in nature, I'd have found evidence."

Before he could continue, a waitress came over.

William ordered three Guinness. "Shane's joining us. He got a call from Sandy over at Applebee's

Restaurant to say Vince had forgotten his backpack the night of the storm. She didn't want to bring it to the funeral. He's gone to pick it up."

"Kind of weird that he forgot it. I don't think I ever saw him without it." Patrick said. "Go on."

"What I was saying is that we overlooked the simple while searching for something more complex. It was a cigarette. Smoking's not allowed in a bonded warehouse, or you can't be insured. It shouldn't have been there. This Ebi Rostum impostor was trained as a firefighter at Criton. It had to be intentional."

"Say, what?"

"A foreign brand. Bahman's. Found it under the ashes on the third floor landing near the chemical signature trail. Looked like a small piece of wood wedged in the grating, real easy to miss. I would have too, had I not bent over to re-tie my shoelace. And even before I went upstairs, I saw a cigarette butt by the gas can near the exit, and it got me thinking. A cigarette is a crude, efficient trigger."

"I'll be damned." Patrick's eyes narrowed, his own stint as an arson investigator enabling him to pick up the thread. "So maybe he lighted it, attached it to the primer, and then he only had what, six, seven minutes after that?"

"Six and a half. Timed it with this one." William pulled a butt from a film canister in his pocket. "Vincent got in the way. Wrong time, wrong place."

"So let me get this straight. He kills Vince and leaves in a hurry, not just because of the fire, but to move Vince's Jeep? God damn it!" Patrick raged, guilt welling up. "The mother fucker played me! I was the first one there, and I was thinking slower and

210

safer defensive fire tactics. I thought the goddamned place was an unoccupied, sprinklered structure. If I'd seen the Jeep, I'd have known Vince was inside and maybe could have saved him."

The waitress returned with their stout, and William waited for her to leave. "Don't be hard on yourself, you couldn't have known." He paused before continuing. "I figure he ran out of time, dropped the can and rushed to move the Jeep to get the hell out of there before the roof exploded."

Patrick shook with anger. "So some murdering bastard, using a fake name, got canned from his job and took revenge? It can't be that simple. There has to be more to it. What are we missing?"

Both men looked up, startled, as Shane dropped Vincent's backpack on the table.

He sat down. "I'm pretty sure when we connect the dots, we'll discover that whoever burned Standard Cold Storage and killed Vince may have also torched Criton."

William and Patrick stared at him, waiting for him to explain himself.

"Take a look." Shane unzipped the bag and pulled out a notepad. He opened it to a page covered in Vincent's distinctive scrawl.

Patrick saw his father's eyes tear up when he saw the handwriting. For moments, William was unable to read what the man he'd considered a son had written. Patrick pulled the pad away from him and turned the page, noting the impressions Vince's pen had left on subsequent pages. He'd felt strongly about what he was writing.

William coughed and took it back. He scanned it quickly. "Might this be what Eddie was hunting for, Patrick? Listen to this. 'There is a V-pattern showing the incipient phase of the fire just to the left of center on the loading dock, not where the burned forklift was, several feet away. The hole in its fuel tank was one inch below the level of the grid deck. It could not have been caused from striking the loading dock as stated. Review pics and measurements.'"

Patrick choked his glass with both hands and stretched forward to read across the table along with his father.

William went on. "'The chemical analyzer confirms a mix of diesel and ammonium nitrate inside an open rag canister. Appears it was placed there, and that's where the V-pattern starts.'"

Patrick slapped the table. "So, Criton Chemical *was* a set fire, and both fires have the same accelerants. I knew it."

Shane withdrew a zip lock evidence bag from the backpack. "When Vince was looking into the Criton fire behind Eddie's back, he found and tagged this melted cigarette butt at the fire's point of origin. His note states that its cellulose fibers would withstand the heat of the burning nitrate, which is why it's intact. Rostum made a mistake. He probably thought it would have disintegrated."

Patrick snatched the evidence bag from his brother. "Rostum started the Criton fire. Rostum started the Standard Cold Storage fire. Rostum killed Vince. Who the fuck is Ebi Rostum?"

William grimaced. "And what's the bet a DNA test will show it's a match to the one I got at the warehouse."

"Revenge fire, my ass." Patrick flung the small bag on the table. "This is much bigger than some disgruntled plant worker getting even. It probably involves Muhktar."

Shane shook his head. "But why? The man is worth millions. Why would he risk alerting the FBI over a measly insurance claim?"

"Didn't Muhktar make it clear that tons of material to make ammonium nitrate went up in smoke? The real question is—why would you need to burn up a huge quantity of nitrate?" Patrick said.

William's face was pale. "Maybe it didn't burn up. Maybe it was never there. Maybe it's somewhere else."

The three of them exchanged a silent look of dawning horror.

Chapter 33
Criton Chemical Office

Nadia squeezed her oversized bag between her arm and ribs and stepped into the revolving entry door of the Warsaw Building. She had never liked the thing. Just last week it had snagged the tote, emptied its contents, and jammed the door. Unable to retrieve it, and much to her embarrassment, the maintenance crew had had to come to her aid. Today, she shuffled her feet to match the rapid spin, and popped through to the other side successfully.

Safely inside the large foyer, Nadia hurried over to the wall-mounted mailbox and jabbed the key into the slot, just as the alert tone for the elevator echoed on the other side of the atrium. She was late for work, and it wouldn't matter to Hassan that an accident on the Interstate had caused her delay. Frantic, she tugged at the two newspapers crammed inside the box, and winced as the remainder of Criton's business mail fell to the marble floor.

"Not now!" she groaned, and looked over her shoulder at the assembled crowd that swarmed inside the car, doors closing behind them. She exhaled in dismay and knelt down to stuff the newsprints and fallen envelopes into her bag. Trudging across the lobby, she found an 'Out of Order' sign taped on the doors of the second elevator shaft.

"This is *not* what I need today." She stabbed hopelessly at the call buttons and watched as the lights for each floor kept going up. Exasperated, she took out her iPhone to check the time and day's itinerary. It was 8:17: she'd never be ready in time for Hassan. Nadia tapped the *Notes* icon and pecked at the screen.

Paperwork and notifications re: Criton; furniture removal and storage before demolition; warehouse fire insurance follow up; Hassan's flight itinerary for Bahrain.

At last, the elevator chimed and, jostled by a second crowd of passengers, Nadia stepped in. Arriving at her floor, she squeezed through the doors as they parted and entered the security code to the Criton office. She stopped only long enough to switch on the desk computer in the reception area before making a beeline for Hassan's office with his newspapers. As she opened *The Iran Daily News*, her knees buckled when she caught sight of a headline in the corner on the front page.

Sharq Columnist Victim of Car Bomb. The article was written by Anwar Hadid, the same journalist who'd condemned Farid before for what he considered treasonous reporting.

Farid Barmeen, a prominent journalist for the controversial newspaper, Sharq, was killed this morning, the victim of a car bomb in Qom.

Nadia grabbed for something to hold onto as the room pitched. She screamed, silently, shock robbing her of breath. Her knuckles whitened on the edge of the desk and two of her nails tore. She didn't hear Hassan come in.

"No coffee yet, eh? You must've got caught in the traffic from the accident on the highway. I passed the wrecker on the shoulder." He pulled out a closet hanger for his jacket. "You look a little shaky. Are you ill? I hope not, we've got much to do today. In fact, I'll make my own coffee; you go ahead and get today's emails ready. Then come back in here. I have to call the sheik, and I want you in on it." Whistling lightly, Hassan made his way to the coffee maker.

Fumbling the door closed behind her, Nadia stumbled toward her office and collapsed into the chair. She booted her PC and frantically searched the internet for more details of her brother's death. She was wasting her time—Tehran blocked all foreign news agencies, and Farid's was just one more death in a region beleaguered by terrorism. She turned on CNN News, but the reporters were droning on about the US Navy transport vessel slated to ferry American soldiers home in the next few days.

The intercom crackled, shaking her from her trance. "Are you done?"

"Almost," Nadia said, afraid he'd hear the tremor in her voice. She closed out her search and printed the morning's emails on the office desk computer, then took them into Hassan's office, wordlessly handing him the stack before sitting down across his desk.

Hassan stood by the coffee maker, blew away the steam rising from his cup, and skimmed the notes she'd given him. "Good. A seven million payout for the warehouse fire." He read the proposals from the movers and demolition company. "Perfect. Everything will be out Friday. The place will be torn down the following day, just before I leave. Oh, make a note to contact that bastard, Hamadi. I'm to meet with him—the sheik's orders. For some reason we have to discuss the demolition, now that we have a date."

Nadia barely managed a faint nod.

Hassan's phone shrilled, and he pressed the speaker after the first ring.

It was the sheik. "Hassan, all is well? Nadia is with you?"

Hassan pulled a cigarette from his pack. "Better than well, and yes, she's here." He slid one into his mouth and thumbed the lighter.

"Good. Tell me some good news."

Hassan brought him up to speed regarding the insurance and demolition. "Experon Insurance is cutting a check for us, seven million. It'll be deposited in the business account, not the Swiss account for Khorromshahr. Does Hamadi still have access to the Khorromshahr account?"

"Of course. Are you still on about that?" The sheik's voice snapped with irritation. "Moving on. Make sure he has your password."

"I will," Hassan growled, "and I'll give him the demolition date as you requested. Why is that so important to you?"

"I want the authorities to see we are doing everything correctly, getting the permit and cooperating in every way. But I have a surprise, a little insurance of my own, to keep them occupied as you leave the States. I'm arranging another 'revenge' fire for them to investigate before the construction equipment even arrives. Hamadi has the details. I want you to get in touch with the police through the mayor. Tell them you've received an anonymous threat, that you think it's from Ebi Rostum, and he's still gunning for you."

"Oh?" Hassan took in a lung full of cigarette smoke, a curious look on his face. "And that's all I say?"

"Yes. I want it to be vague. You'll understand after you meet with Hamadi."

Hassan grimaced. "You mentioned an image problem with the news media in Tehran. Is that resolved?"

The sheik began to laugh. "Have you read the newspaper?"

The article about Farid. Nadia froze. She felt as if she was about to collapse.

Hassan spun the paper toward him. "So, Barmeen got what he deserved. Who was it? Al-Unistan?"

"Ask Hamadi when you meet with him."

"Hamadi?"

Their matter-of-fact conversation almost made Nadia retch. She pressed one hand against her stomach.

"It had nothing to do with Al-Unistan," the sheik said.

Hassan's eyes widened as he peered at the article a second time. "It was you who arranged Barmeen's death?"

"And Kazem Al-Unistan will get the credit." The sheik chuckled, and Hassan smiled across his desk at Nadia.

Nadia's thoughts collided at the sheik's revelation. She gasped, and Hassan raised a quizzical eyebrow as he noted her discomfort. Slowly, she met his eyes. In the seconds it took to absorb his spiteful glee, her failed senses rushed back with a clarity she had seldom experienced. She had spent the years of her life afraid, caught in a cage of servitude and apology. Trapped in an empty, barren marriage, tenderness and freedom had receded into the realm of girlish dreams. Of course, it would be Farid who finally opened the door to that cage.

The two men continued to speak, but Nadia heard only the voices of two children playing long ago.

Hassan and Abbas would pay.

Chapter 34
FBI Headquarters, Washington DC

A barrel-chested Marine Sergeant held the door to the main conference room of the FBI's headquarters in DC open for Marcus. Inside, four people milled around a water cooler off to the side. Commonly referred to as the 'War Room' by those who spent long hours strategizing, a meeting there signified high stakes. Marcus had been in it a few times. Recognizing the assembled brains trust, he knew from past experience that, although small, the gathering reached the highest level of government. Even the limited number of participants had significant meaning—time was of the essence. Assembling a large number of bureaucrats and military brass would slow things down.

"Right on time." Arthur Scoffield, Director of Middle Eastern Intelligence and Marcus's boss, gestured for him to take a seat. "I believe you've worked with everyone here?"

"Thank you, Arthur. Yes, it's good to see you again, Madame Secretary." Marcus extended his hand to Delores Estrada, a silver haired Princeton graduate, Rhodes Scholar, and the United States Secretary of Homeland Security.

"Always a pleasure, Agent Delorme,"

Others at the table included Marcus's friend, Admiral Richard 'the Anchor' Pendragon, Chief Officer of Naval Special Operations, and Navy SEAL

Commander, Captain Omar Matari, who had just flown in from the Gulf.

Commander Matari clasped Marcus's shoulder with one hand and extended the other. "Great to see you Marcus. It's been what, a year since we worked together?"

Marcus pumped his hand. "Yes, we busted that weapons cartel working off of the Keys. Your Spanish was a little suspect, as I recall."

"*Perdon? Mi Espanol es magnifico!*" The Saudi Arabian born Matari grinned. "But for this assignment, it will be you who needs to brush up on his language skills. Farsi doesn't get used much beyond the Persian Gulf region, and you might need it."

"Yes, you just may." Director Scoffield took up a position behind the small podium at the end of the polished oak tabletop. "Our intelligence has recorded a spike in violent activity recently in this area." He pressed the keyboard of the laptop to his right, and a satellite image of the Persian Gulf appeared on a large monitor behind him. A sliver of land starting at the mouth of the Shatt al Arab waterway, the outlet between Iran and Iraq, was shaded in. A grainy photograph of a lean, fierce looking man filled a second, smaller screen. "Our analysis indicates one militant group in particular, Asaib Ahl al-Haq, is responsible. Its leader, an Iraqi, is a man by the name of Kazem Al-Unistan."

The Secretary of Homeland Security lifted the beaded lanyard holding her glasses around her neck and slid the frames into place. "Details. What else can you tell us about him: history, ideology?"

"Like Bin Laden, he comes from an extremely wealthy family, and his notoriety is on the rise. Let me play this clip for you that the Mossad in Tel Aviv sent us. Al-Unistan himself posted it recently." Scoffield dimmed the lights and pressed a backlit button on the remote control console by his chair. A large high definition television behind him blinked to life.

Al-Unistan, a red keffiya adorning his head, sat cross legged on an ornate, embroidered carpet, flanked by two masked and hooded disciples, hands clasped in front of them. His intense, glossy black eyes, like those of a Tarantula stalking its prey, commanded attention, but the group's eyes were trained on a printed translation of the speech he made in Arabic.

"The Iranians have a plan for a great empire. It extends from the shores of Sudan to the mountains of Afghanistan in the north. To the south, the strait of Bab Al-Mandab, the entrance to the Red Sea, falls beneath their boots, and to the east, the port of Khasab, Oman on the Persian Gulf, is threatened. They seek to control the great peninsula that Allah ordained for those who follow His word. Unity in the Arab world is threatened by seeds deliberately sown by the Iranian intelligence agencies. They provoke unrest in Yemen, Saudi Arabia, Kuwait, Qatar and even in the kingdom of Jordan. The hated Al-Quds corps ..."

Scoffield paused the tape. "That's the covert action arm of the Iranian Revolutionary Guard."

"... even attacks our homeland in Iraq by confusing the ignorant and poor with their

222

propaganda. Since the revolution of 1979, all Arabs worry that Islamist Iran will become not simply a regional power, but one that dominates the world. Until now, we have been incapable of dealing with the threat. This is about to change."

The FBI Director stopped the video. "Admiral, please go ahead and expand on the conversation you and I had previously."

"Will do."

Marcus swiveled in his seat to listen to Pendragon.

"At the heart of this lies the hatred between Iran and Iraq. In 1982, with the Iranians on Iraqi soil, Saddam Hussein managed to hang on until a stalemate was reached, which most of the countries in the region accepted. Their focus shifted to the Israelis." The career naval officer took a drink of water. "This is a complex problem we're facing. Muslims of all nations rallied against what they perceived to be a common enemy of Islam, and ignored or denied their own internal squabbles. However, this veneer of solidarity in the Arab world has deteriorated rapidly as economic conditions continue to decline."

Delores Estrada folded her glasses and rocked back in her chair. "And a second facet of this—this situation, shall we call it—stems from our intervention in Iraq, which removed a tyrannical regime, but re-ignited long standing hatreds and further fractured already crumbling alliances." She paused and looked at each man in the room. "This fanatic, Al-Unistan, intends to remedy the atrocities he believes have been committed by the Iranians and the United States. Is that what you're telling us?"

Arthur Scoffield nodded. "Commander Matari, since you're detailed there, please share the intelligence our Station Chief in Basra provided."

Matari opened a small case and inserted a flash stick into the laptop in front of him. "If you would each look at the display monitors in front of you." He typed in several characters on the keyboard and brought each of their screens to life. "There was a significant increase in bombings against American and coalition forces immediately following the troop surge initiated in 2007. Analysts agree it was a counter attack of sorts by insurgent groups to re-establish their self-proclaimed authority. The overlay you're looking at shows the locations and nature of the strikes. The color of the asterisk next to each one denotes the different groups responsible, and those are listed at the bottom." Matari gave them a few moments before continuing his presentation. "Please examine the next graph. Other than an occasional upturn, each month, it shows a decrease in attacks in Iraq as the counter-insurgency strategy, COIN, implemented by our government, started taking hold. By establishing relationships with the locals, even hiring some of our adversaries to work with us, bombings dwindled. In fact, some of the groups claiming responsibility completely disappeared."

"Excuse me for interrupting, Omar." Marcus stabbed his pen at the yellow legal pad he was writing on. "What about Kazem Al-Unistan?"

"Our analysts asked that same question. As I mentioned, there was a drop in IED detonations in Iraq until the announcement of the final American troop withdrawal. Search parameters regarding attacks were expanded, and an increase of bombings inside Iran were also identified during the same period, after the announcement of our leaving."

"I'll take it from here, Omar." Scoffield spun in his seat and faced the group. "What's more than curious is the fact that Al-Unistan's band was secretly funded at times by anti-American Iranian clerics, yet we're piecing together evidence that now he's the one master-minding strikes sweeping through Iran as well as Iraq. We first discovered that through agents on the ground in the province of Zahedan, Iran."

"Wait a minute." Estrada wagged her finger. "Al-Unistan, an *Iraqi,* is supported financially by Tehran to attack us, and our assets are now claiming he's turning against his backers?"

"That seems to be the case, Madame Secretary." Scoffield reached for the console. "Let's listen to a bit more of the video."

Al-Unistan's voice picked up where he'd left off. "The time has come to strike at our enemies. Tehran's expansion must be stopped and the American presence eliminated, their war machine exploded to dust and buried at the bottom of the sea. It was revealed to me in a dream, and so it shall come to pass. And I will watch as the two nations—the United States of America and Iran—then consume each other in battle. Such is the will of the Almighty."

Scoffield drummed his fingers on the tabletop as the clip ended. "This is the most dangerous of fanatics. Our psychological profile depicts him as loyal to no one and completely unpredictable. He answers only to himself and his maniacal view of a

Muslim caliphate. He will use any means to bring about a world governed by Sharia Law."

The room was silent.

His brow knotted, Marcus cleared his throat. "With all due respect, Arthur, what am I doing here at this meeting?"

"I'm getting to that. Al-Unistan claimed responsibility for all the most recent bombings in Iraq." The FBI Director nodded at Matari as a new graphic was superimposed over a map of Iraq. "As you see here, the attacks in Iraq have paralleled the Tigris River, occurring in the cities along its banks and in a dated sequence that roughly matches American troop withdrawal from Mosul in the northwest to the most recent explosion in Basra in the southeast."

"Meanwhile," Pendragon added, "bombing incidents in Iran occurred along *its* most significant river, the Karun, which courses from the northeast to southwest. Attacks took place in areas adjacent to Iran's waterway during the approximate same timeframe as the Iraq violence. The incidents have striking similarities, leading us to believe Al-Unistan is responsible for all of them."

Matari spoke next. "We know that because I snuck into an Iranian bombing site a few days after it occurred with one of our forensic experts. The military was long gone, and as we both come from Saudi Arabian family backgrounds, no one suspected we were anything but a couple more curious locals. Except he knew what to look for. He discovered the same bomb pattern, collected evidence and analyzed it. The bomb making material is an exact match with what we have from Iraqi incidents."

Marcus swallowed hard and pushed back against his chair. "Ammonium nitrate."

"Manufactured in *America*." Scoffield tapped the desktop repeatedly. "You're our resident expert in that field. I want you to start digging and see what you can put together. You'll be working, and remaining in close contact, with Omar after he returns to the Gulf later today. We have a credible source there, a dockworker in the rundown port city of Khorromshahr, who hasn't led us astray yet. Something big may be imminent. Perhaps a strike on the main oil depot and main transmission lines, responsible for ninety percent of all distribution."

The Secretary for Homeland Security stood up, her penetrating gaze shifting from one man to the next. "Gentlemen, we will not tolerate another Beirut."

The catastrophic bombing of the Marine Corps barracks that killed hundreds of U.S. servicemen in Lebanon was a gaping wound they all remembered.

"The President is worried that one more attack like that, and the Middle East tinderbox will explode into full scale war." She gathered her papers and packed her briefcase. "I'll leave you to develop your strategy. Director Scoffield, see me later with your brief before I make my report to the Chief of Staff. The last deployment of the remaining men and women of the 2nd Marine Division is scheduled to leave Basra very soon. Let's see to it they get home."

The four men stood at attention as she left the room.

"You heard the lady." Scoffield opened up a dossier. "Let's get to work on this immediately. We don't have a lot of time."

Chapter 35
U.S.S. *Abraham Lincoln. Persian Gulf*

Navy SEAL Commander, Captain Omar Matari, secured the hatch to his quarters aboard the U.S.S. *Abraham Lincoln* as the nuclear powered aircraft carrier left the coast of Kuwait behind and steamed northeasterly. He was tired; the quick return trip hadn't allowed for much sleep. He rubbed his bloodshot eyes and listened to Marcus over the secure satellite phone link.

"You know, Omar, since that meeting we had yesterday in the War Room, my staff has been putting in overtime researching data on bombings using ammonium nitrate in Iraq. We're consolidating reports, residue analysis and such, and will try to trace where it came from. Getting any trustworthy information regarding similar attacks in Iran is really tough. You got anything for me?"

Omar sat down on his aluminum-framed bunk. "Not much I'm afraid, but I sent the analysis of the Iran bombing I spoke of yesterday to your staff. It's difficult enough to acquire reliable data out of Baghdad, let alone Tehran. Their border is as tight as they come. Other than the reports along the Karun River and a few satellite photos from the Air Force's Defense Support Program, we don't have anything new to add at the moment. We're staying on it. In the meantime, let's review what we do have."

"Let's see." Marcus sounded beat as well. "The extremist faction that Al-Unistan leads is currently strongest in the southern provinces where the Tigris and Euphrates Rivers converge. The man hails from right there in Basra. Besides the fact that it's the third largest city, its strategic importance has been crucial throughout the ages. It's the main ocean gateway to the outside world in the Persian Gulf. With all that oil funneling into the port, it's a prime target that would affect everything and everybody."

Springs creaked as Matari stretched out on his mattress. "Add to that the fact that Basra was the initial site of the Shia rebellion following the 1991 Gulf War and has remained a hotbed of unrest ever since, and you have a cauldron on the verge of boiling over at any moment. And now, with what many consider Iran's covert program to develop nuclear bomb making materials in place, the stakes are higher than they've ever been."

"Al-Unistan has no love for the Iranians." Marcus continued, his voice flat. "His hatred of them is surpassed only by his maniacal zeal to completely wipe out the United States presence in the region."

Matari stared at the gunmetal gray ceiling and scratched the stubble on his chin. "And so he bombs both his enemies, but these attacks are localized. Though they strike terror in the population that fears him, and garner him strength from those that share his views, it's not nearly enough to accomplish his goals."

"You're right about that, Omar, so we're focusing on the pattern of the attacks. Much like the Mongol Genghis Khan, and centuries later the Sultans of the Ottoman Empire, Al-Unistan replicates their southward sweep along the great river valleys, symbolically driving his enemies into the sea, just as they did."

"Yeah, I keep going over that threat he made. Something is definitely in the works."

"If we could find the source of his bomb supply," Marcus said, "then we could apply immediate pressure and get some answers. But I'm going through a big list, American and international manufacturers and their distributors, and not making headway nearly as fast as I'd like. I'm planning to re-check a chemical plant in Virginia. The damn place burned down, but I can't seem to get it off my mind. To tell you the truth, my gut feeling is Al-Unistan already has what he needs."

"I'm with you on that."

"Any clue as to where the strike will hit or when?"

Matari walked over to his workstation and booted his laptop. "Negative. Not another word, and just like you guys in Washington, we're on this twenty-four hours a day. With the Iraqis taking over complete control of security and our remaining troops and advisors about to board the last of the transport ships, everyone is on edge. Of course we're watching the governmental centers, but Command is focusing on the pipelines in Basra. So far, they've remained unscathed, but let's face it, a successful terrorist strike to Iraq's enormous worldwide distribution center would have catastrophic consequences."

"Yes," Marcus said, his voice fading as he spoke. "And with the international airport and huge railway system adjacent to the main port so close to Iran, ending up in a war could well happen. What does Admiral Pendragon have in mind?"

"What you probably already suspect. Most all available hands, and I mean all, are descending on the main port of Basra to canvas the area: bomb teams, tightened security, covert inquiries. Even my SEAL team will be getting orders, though we won't be sent there. The Admiral figures I might blend in better with the locals and see or hear something, but he wants to keep me close to this floating tin can."

"Where are you headed, Omar?"

Matari glanced at a map of the Persian Gulf as he stretched his arms. "The Abe Lincoln will be on station just off the coast between Iraq and Iran, at the actual entry to the Shatt al Arab waterway. We're almost there—take a look at your map—the small port of Al-Faw. Positioned there, the carrier will be close enough for any immediate action, if needed. It's also where the navy brass decided to move the transport ship Defender for that last division of Marines and support personnel. It's less congested, a safer distance from Al-Unistan's home turf and closer to international waters. And as far as he and Basra are concerned, the entire area is cordoned off. He couldn't drive a bicycle in there, let alone a truck loaded with explosives."

"I see it," Marcus said. "Al-Faw. Right there on the southeast end of the peninsula, across from Khorromshahr, Iran. Is that where you are?"

"You got it. That's the sector SEAL Team 2 and I are being deployed to."

"Stay sharp, Omar. I have a meeting with my team, and I have a call to make to a friend who's familiar with that fire at the ammonium nitrate plant in Virginia. I better get going."

Omar snapped his head from side to side to loosen the kinks. "I will. You stay in touch and send me anything that catches your attention. I'm relying on that gut instinct of yours." He flicked the off switch for the TS-4 satellite phone. Beyond his port window, the southern coastlines of Iraq and Iran were bathed in brilliant sunlight.

***

"Now that's what I call a pretty sight!" Lance Corporal Terry Newkon tweaked the rangefinder of the tactical binoculars as he stood on the bow of the U.S.S. *Defender.*

"Huh?" Private First Class Cordell Washburn idly readjusted his sweat-stained cap to shield his eyes, his back against the forward bulwark. "What are you talkin' about, man?"

"What I'm talkin' about, Private, is that very big and very American aircraft carrier."

Washburn jerked to full attention. "Damn. Lemme have them glasses, Newk."

"Oh, I can see myself back in Virginia already." Newkon shoved Washburn's extended hand away from the binoculars. "Soon this rust bucket will be loaded and we can wave bye-bye to this place. I promised the wife we'd go on vacation somewhere, but you can guarantee it will be somewhere without one speck of sand. Here."

Washburn slung the strap around his neck and pressed the lens cups to his eyes. "And I'm takin' Tasha and the kids to Disney World, no doubt."

The two enlisted men high-fived each other.

"And just *where* are you two going other than getting back to work?" Master Gunnery Sergeant Brian Kemch scrambled up the port-side stairs two at a time.

"Hey Gunny, c'mere an' check this out." Newkon gestured excitedly. "The Lincoln just showed up."

"Gimme those." Kemch's smile undermined the gruff command. "Well, well. Looks like you lazy grunts will finally get your wish, and I'll be done babysittin' your dumb asses."

"Aww, you're gonna miss us." Washburn slapped Newkon's palm. "C'mon Gunny, admit it."

The veteran shook his head. "Yeah, I'll miss you like I miss a case of the crabs. Now if you two jar heads don't finish the assignment I gave you so we can get everyone on this tub, I'll make sure your kids are grandparents by the time I'm done with you."

"Yes, sir!" The two soldiers saluted, both smiling ear-to-ear, and clambered down the companionway to the lower deck.

Sergeant Kemch raised the high-powered field glasses to his eyes and scanned the placid waters of the Gulf. In the distance, a steady stream of empty northbound freighters navigated past the now fully loaded vessels steaming southward and out onto the international waters of the Persian Gulf. He issued a low whistle. "Two tours over here is plenty. Enough is enough. I'm going home, too."

Chapter 36
Henrico County, Virginia

William Meagher pulled into the parking lot of the Short Pump Mall and looked for a dark green sedan with a woman in the passenger seat. Spotting the number plate Nadia Muhktar had given him, he eased into a space close by, got out and carefully placed a checkered cap on his head. Changing his mind about the headgear, he took it off and tossed it back into the car.

Responding to his innocuous signal, Mrs. Muhktar picked up a copy of People magazine and nervously flipped through the pages. If not for the terrified look on her face and her darting eyes, anyone would think she was waiting for someone who'd slipped into the Macy's store for a quick purchase.

Understandable, William thought. She had to be scared to death, what with the bombshell she was set to unload. Considering the little she'd shared with him, William was cautious and more than a little frightened himself.

Just outside the store's double glass entry doors, he scanned the lot for anything or anyone suspicious. If Hassan Muhktar had even the vaguest notion that his wife had turned on him, he'd have had her followed, or worse. Seeing nothing out of the ordinary, William slipped inside.

He came out five minutes later carrying a plastic shopping bag stuffed with a pair of brightly colored throw pillows. He strolled toward the woman's

235

Passat, tossed the bag into the back, and climbed into the drivers seat.

"Good afternoon, Mrs. Muhktar," he said softly, anxious to avoid intimidating her. "I'm William Meagher." He started the car and reversed out of the space.

The woman sat stock-still, peering at the line of traffic to her right as they exited onto Broad Street, a wad of Kleenex crushed into a tight ball in her hands. He noted the puffy bags below her hazel eyes when she turned to him.

"Please call me Nadia, Mr. Meagher. And I prefer to go by 'Nuha.'"

William nodded. "It's brave of you to come forward. I want to assure you that the Chatterton Police won't know your name, on that I give my solemn oath. I can't begin to tell you what your help means, Ms. Nuha.

The glow from the shopping center lights faded as they drove out past the fields and old farms of Goochland County. The coming darkness and William's reassurance that no one was following them seemed to relieve Nadia's dread.

She relaxed against the seat and released an audible sigh. "Thank you, Mr. Meagher. I need your help, too. But I should explain, in case you think badly of me. You must know that I'm expected to do my husband's bidding, both as his wife and executive assistant. No matter what that entails. I keep my head down and never discuss his business. I never have before, ever." She hesitated. "This has been difficult for me." She turned to look out the window, and William glanced across at her, hoping she wouldn't back out. But he felt her steady gaze as she went on. "Now I'm driven by a stronger obligation. You and I have lost people close to us, and I fear there will be many more." She raised elegant hands and dropped them into her lap in a gesture of indecision. "I don't know where to begin."

"Let's start with Ebi Rostum's true identity."

"Jalal Hamadi." Nadia's knuckles turned white, her fingers crushing the sodden tissues in her hand. "He's an agent of Hassan's father, Sheik Abbas Muhktar. Hassan despises and does not trust him, but the sheik does. Hamadi has been in his employ for many years, does all his dirty work. I believe he was once an agent of the Shu'bat al-Mukhabarat al-'Askariyya, the Syrian Directorate of Military Intelligence. He's a dangerous man, Mr. Meagher. The Criton fire was no accident—Hamadi started it. He also started the fire at the warehouse, and it was he who killed the young fire inspector."

Vincent, beaten and burned alive. William clenched the steering wheel with both hands, fighting the urge to interrupt her.

"One of my tasks is to oversee the payroll. For two, almost three months, paychecks were made out to Ebi Rostum. At the time, it was just a name to me. I rarely meet any plant employees." Nadia shifted in her seat. "I should have known. I should have . . ." She trailed off.

"Known . . . ?" William probed.

"Please understand. I could not go against my husband. But there are many things I did know, many things I was shamefully aware of." She dabbed at her eyes. "The fire at Criton was a cover up. Beforehand, tons of ammonium nitrate were moved to one of our ships. Ebi Rostum oversaw the transfer, and I had to ensure the records reflected the loss in the fire. Soon after, I was instructed to make a huge sum of money available to Jalal Hamadi."

William swallowed hard. His hands felt clammy on the wheel, and he could feel sweat begin to bead his forehead.

"It all fell into place when you held up his picture on TV. I didn't know with certainty at the time where the nitrate went, but the *Orient Star* sailed to the Middle East. Jalal worked as a forklift driver to divert suspicion, under the name Ebi Rostum. The fire at the warehouse? It wasn't a revenge fire as the authorities believe, it was simply to mislead the police and . . ."

"Wait, wait a minute, slow down!" William interrupted as Nadia babbled almost incoherently. His mind raced to keep up, leaping ahead to try and get to grips with the Muhktars' motives.

Nadia began to weep, a soft, mewling sound that distracted him. He slowed the car, intent on pulling over.

The woman peered over her shoulder in a panic. "No, no, don't stop. I'm sorry . . . it's just . . . they've murdered my brother." She shook her head and whimpered, then repeated, "They murdered my brother." She paused, taking a deep breath. "And I believe the ammonium nitrate has been sold to a terrorist organization."

William said nothing. Stunned at her revelation, he accelerated and drove on.

A mile passed before Nadia spoke again, her voice composed and flat, somehow cold. "Pull into that gas station up ahead. I have something to give you."

William's heart pounded like a jackhammer. He coasted into the Wawa Convenience Mart, parking in a slot farthest from the front door and a good distance from the pumps. "This is far beyond what I imagined when we first spoke."

Nadia handed him a large envelope and watched as he unfurled the cord at the top. Leafing through several pages, he found emails sent to and from Hassan Muhktar and the sheik; invoices that had to be fraudulent; bank deposit slips; a list of passwords and secure cabinet combinations.

Aghast, William squinted and looked up from the stack. "Sweet Mary and Joseph! Jackson Stamper and Stanley Lowell are on the take? And you're giving me the passwords to all of the Muhktars' accounts?" He flapped the wad of papers against his open palm. He shook his head. "Ms. Nuha, you have to understand my asking. If this has been going on for some time, as I'm reading it, why then are you risking everything, risking your life, to come forward now?" William felt as if she was looking through and not at him.

The woman didn't blink. "Arranged marriages are commonplace in my culture. It is a wife's duty to faithfully serve the man she has been given to. But these men murdered my brother, and are facilitating the possible slaughter of thousands by selling their ammonium nitrate. My first duty is to God and my brother, and I would never be party to acts of terrorism." She fished in her bag and pulled out a computer flash drive. "You will understand all after you see and listen to this video and study the pictures. You must do it quickly, Mr. Meagher." She laid the device in his hand and curled his fingers around it. "It's getting late. I must be getting back. I'll call again very soon. My husband will have a final meeting with Jalal Hamadi before they both leave the country, and if that happens, it will be too late."

William replaced the material in the envelope, started the car and headed back toward the mall without another word being spoken.

Chapter 37
Chatterton County, Virginia

Seated in the mayor's office, Hassan Muhktar's eyes took a slow trip around the room, one he hoped would be his last, and wondered if Stamper had chosen the colors, a moss green with bold gray trim. Perhaps the man was trying for a mix of calm and authority— ironic, given that the office reeked of corruption and greed.

"What more can we do for you, Hassan?" Jackson Stamper slumped wearily in his chair.

Fire Chief Stanley Lowell stood in the corner, both hands buried in his pockets.

Hassan pressed his hands together. "Why, nothing. I'll be leaving the country this weekend. I'm just sorry you haven't a clue as to the whereabouts of the man who put me out of business, and who sends a threatening message that he is not through."

"So this Rostum character seems to have it in for you." Stamper pushed back from his desk. "But what else do you want from me? You made your money here in Chatterton, and I'm stuck with the complaints and all the bullshit."

"Stop whining, Jackson. You were happy to take my money whenever I approached you for a favor."

"Well, what about the cops, what did they say about this threat you got?" Lowell came to stand beside the mayor's desk. "It was an anonymous note? That right? When did you get it? They wouldn't tell me."

Hassan cast an irritated glance at Stamper before rounding on Lowell. "Don't concern yourself with my dealings with the police. Be more concerned that you profited for circumventing the storage requirements at my warehouse, and they don't know about it, especially with one of your own now dead." He let the rebuke sink in before reaching into his pocket and unfolding a single sheet of paper. "This is from my father. 'Effective immediately, Criton Chemicals is closed. Our lawyers will work on our behalf to conclude any outstanding business relative to Chatterton County. As for the special financial arrangement my son has maintained with both of you; that too, is at an end. Since our investment in the mayoral campaign that propelled your administration into office, we have the necessary documentation to ensure your continued cooperation. Any failure or breach on your part, as we decide, shall be your ruin. I suggest you quietly enjoy your money.'" Hassan paused and flashed the note at his audience. The account numbers, deposits and balances had all been highlighted in yellow. "Gentlemen, I believe our partnership is dissolved to our mutual satisfaction. It's been a pleasure."

Without another word or a backward glance, he got up and left the office, making his way through the lobby out toward his car. When he got to the Lincoln, he mouthed a cigarette and flicked his lighter, then hovered the flame at the corner of the sheik's note. He lit his cigarette and watched the page burn before checking his watch. The jet would have landed, and Hamadi awaited his call at the hotel.

Chapter 38
The Persian Gulf

Kazem Al-Unistan wrapped his fingers around the rusted steel railing that skirted the bridge of the *Orient Star*. The ship lay at anchor, and he gazed at the heavily silted waters of the Shatt al Arab as it coursed south and east past the port of Khorromshahr. Far to the west, only the dimly lit contrails of highflying aircraft caught the last vestiges of rapidly fading daylight. Watching the crew scurry on the quarterdeck, Al-Unistan turned to speak to the man beside him, his voice reverent, as if in prayer. "Soon my friend, the beauty of this most holy land will be restored, as Allah, His name be praised, ordained it." He sniffed at the air, heavy with salt.

Al-Unistan's loyal minion, Abdullah Zafir, bobbed his head and gazed at the lush greenery of the alluvial plain on both sides of the waterway. "It is by your hand that this will come to pass. As you lead, the army of Asaib Ahl al-Haq willingly follows, each man prepared to give his life."

"Your father named you well, for you truly are the servant of God, Abdullah." Al-Unistan slapped the devoted warrior on his back and pointed upstream as a small tugboat chugged by. "See how the dredgers work constantly to keep the channels open? Even that barge being pushed would have trouble negotiating the sand bars without their work. The river bottom is always shifting because of the current, and it is not uncommon to run aground. That is why I have chosen you to pilot this ship."

Abdullah nodded. "I have sailed these waters with our fathers since I was a child. I shall not fail you."

Al-Unistan nodded. "I will have word from your youngest brother, Rashid, before dawn. He carries the confirmation I want before we strike."

"But how will we pass through the Americans' security? They search all the ships sailing north toward Basra. Will we be able to get close enough to the oil depot to destroy it? Our men report that security around the port is as tight as they have ever seen it."

Al-Unistan peered at the thick brown water flowing toward the Persian Gulf. "Don't concern yourself with the Americans and their Iraqi puppets. I hope they concentrate all of their force in Basra; it's how I've set it up. I need your thoughts to be clear."

On the main deck far below, the crew made final preparations, securing the main hatchway. The hundreds of barrels of diesel fuel purchased on the black market earlier in the day at the seedy Iranian port were strategically placed amongst the fifteen thousand tons of ammonium nitrate manufactured by Criton Chemical Company. Along with it, the entire hold was laced with explosive primer cord, just as Jalal Hamadi had instructed on the dock of Khorromshahr when Al-Unistan had taken control of the ship.

Kazem headed for the elevator, clad in a linen kandura that had been one of his father's robes before he met his death, assassinated by the Shah's secret police for organizing protests against Reza

Pahlavi decades ago. He felt it fitting that he should wear it now. He pulled a cell phone, taped and wired to two triple A batteries, from his pocket and showed it to Abdullah.

"Hamadi set this up as the primary detonator, which you'll need to hide personally in the hold. I'll be following you on board another craft with the trigger; a second cell phone. I need only place a call to the one you see here." Al-Unistan studied Abdullah's face for traces of fear or doubt. The man's mission was to blow himself, the ship and his crew to bits, but there was no trace of hesitation in his steady gaze.

"And our course?"

Al-Unistan flared his hand gracefully in a wide arc toward the southwest. "The American forces are concentrated at the depot. That's not where you're headed. You'll follow the line of freighters leaving Basra, since they're not seen to pose any threat to the Americans."

"I don't understand. Away from Basra; the oil lines?"

Al-Unistan let out a guttural laugh. "With our campaign of bombings against both the Americans *and* the Iranians, I intend to set the two at each other's throats." He lifted his arms in a grand gesture. "The *Orient Star* will be flying the Iranian flag. Your task will be to obliterate the American war ship docked at Al-Faw, and annihilate its troops in Iraqi waters. With the light of a new day, Allah will receive you as a martyr, and our two enemies will go to war. I will then unite the region, as Allah commands me."

Abdullah's awe was gratifying. "It is a brilliant plan. They won't anticipate an attack from a vessel heading away from their defenses."

Al-Unistan handed him the wired cell phone and stepped into the ship's elevator. "Go now," he said. "I need to rest."

Chapter 39
Chatterton, Virginia

Patrick closed the door to William's den behind Shane. His father's voice on the phone had alerted him to something ominous at play, and both brothers had dropped what they were doing to meet up at their parents' house. Agitation was unusual for William, a man who'd spent close to forty years in emergency services. Now, seeing how compulsively he raked his fingers through his hair, Patrick's suspicion that something had spooked him was confirmed.

"I can't tell you where this came from, but we've stumbled onto something far bigger than we imagined." William got them each a bottle of spring water.

Shane and Patrick sat down on the sofa and waited for him to go on.

"I met with someone who gave me sensitive, or should I say, explosive information about Criton and the Muhktars. Some of it corroborates Vincent's notes and validates your original skepticism about the Criton fire, Patrick."

"This wasn't some scam, someone after the reward money?" Patrick said.

"Oh, this was the real deal. No doubt." William pulled a chair up toward the coffee table, opposite his sons. "Here, take a look yourselves."

Patrick scooted closer to Shane as William removed several documents from a mustard colored office envelope and laid them on the table.

Seconds after glancing through them, Patrick rocketed from his seat. "Holy Shit! This guy with the beard in the Criton I.D. photo calling himself Ebi Rostum, is the same guy with the bald head in this one, and his real name is Jamal Hamadi? This is the motherfucker who killed Vince at the warehouse?"

Shane continued to rifle through the stack of papers. "Have you told the police, or Marcus? What are we going to do about this?"

"Nothing yet and yes, I called the major, who's on his way back from a police convention in New York. Trust me, I'm calling Marcus in a couple of minutes. But check this out first." William gave Shane a bank statement with some hand written notes in the margin.

"Muhktar bribed Stamper *and* Lowell?" Shane spread the documents across the table, studying them with growing incredulity. "Account numbers. Passwords. Illegal tax credits. Approved storage code violations. If the money is all still in the banks, can it be frozen?"

"The accounts are with a foreign bank, and it would take some doing to freeze these assets, I'm afraid." William threw his head back taking a huge swallow. "Hassan Muhktar is leaving the country in a matter of days."

"We have to talk to Marcus." Patrick sat down again and did his own search through the mess on the table. "Is there *anything* we can do?"

"I don't know. Vincent was definitely on to something, and he was our family." William's voice trailed off, then strengthened. "Look, I want to try and get Marcus again. I *have* to get him down here. I'll be back in a few minutes."

Catching William's inflection and worried look, Patrick cocked his head and studied his father. "Alright, but why are you leaving to call him?"

William ignored him. "Just stay put. I'll be right back." He left the room and closed the door.

Patrick turned to his brother. "There's something more going on. I've never seen him like this. We need to find a way to help him nail these guys and return the insurance money. It's fraud; he can earn quite a fee."

Shane walked over to the mini-fridge under the bar. "You want something else?"

"Grab me a soda instead of this water. " Patrick picked up one of the documents on the coffee table. "Take a look at these notes. Seems Muhktar and this guy Hamadi have dinner meetings to make their plans. Always from six or so until nine, and dig this, the two bastards can't even stand one another."

Shane exchanged a can of Coke for the notes Patrick referred to. "Who would know all this? These are specific, detailed; it has to be someone close to Muhktar."

"Muhktar." Patrick seethed. "God damn it, these pricks have to pay for what they did to Vince. And you know what pisses me off on top of it all? Muhktar lives in Station 14's district. We protect the son of a bitch." Patrick tossed back his drink and slammed the can down on the table. "Who knows, maybe you and I can come up with something to nail him."

William opened the door.

"That was quick," Shane said.

"I caught him in his car. He was off to meet his staff, but he's on the way here instead. Said what I have to say should wait till he gets here. Do you want to stay and eat something before he shows up? I have to talk to him alone."

"No thanks." Patrick stood. "We'll head out to get a sandwich at the *Firehouse Sub Shop*. I'm off tomorrow until nine P.M., and Shane set up a night drill for my crew. I want to hammer out a few things."

"You're off during the day?" William said. "Can you do me a favor? I have several appointments, one is at the state lab for the DNA tests on those cigarette butts. Will you stop by my office in the afternoon and pick up the insurance information on Standard Cold Storage? It's in the file cabinet closest to the door. I need it for a meeting I set up with Stanley Lowell. I want to hear his version of what went on. Then, it's off to see Walter Carson and let his detectives take over from there." William walked his sons to the door. "Call me tomorrow when you have it and we can meet somewhere."

Shane waited until they reached his brother's diesel pick-up. "Pat, you're off until nine? And I sure as hell don't recall my organizing a night drill."

"Murrie is working for me until then. But there's no drill, it was just the first thing I could think of so we could leave." Patrick looked over his shoulder and lowered his voice as they stood by the truck. "Dad's got a lot on his mind. I'm pretty sure he doesn't need to hear all I have to say about Vince's murder and what I got rolling around in my head."

Shane opened the door. "Since when do you keep secrets from the old man?"

"Come on, don't give me that look. Just get your ass in the cab and hear me out. I've got an idea before we go any further with Dad."

Chapter 40
Criton Chemical office

The handset rebounded out of its cradle as Hassan Muhktar pounded the office phone back into place, disconnecting his call with Jalal Hamadi. He was used to giving orders, not taking them, especially from someone he considered hired help. He stormed over to the bar and jerked a bottle of twelve-year-old scotch from the shelf, knocking two crystal flutes from the rack as he did so. Splashing a liberal amount into a tumbler, he chugged the single malt and narrowed his eyes at his wife.

Nadia, seated across his desk, watched him impassively.

"I'd like to kill the son of a bitch." Hassan tugged at the starched collar of his shirt, his face and neck glowing pink. "Telling *me* where we'll meet." He grabbed a box of Bahman's and ripped the last cigarette from the pack. "It's bad enough my father insists I obey his instructions, but now he orders me to make a dinner reservation at a place of his choosing." The cigarette surged brightly.

Nadia clicked her pen. "And where does he want to go?"

"Where does he want to go?" Hassan lowered his head and glared at her.

Jaw set, Nadia said flatly, "Yes. That's what I said. Where, and what time?"

Caught off guard by her response, Hassan mumbled, "Birani's Lobster House. Six o'clock tomorrow. He knows I hate the place." He took one long drag before pulverizing the butt in the ashtray. It teetered for a moment at the edge of his desk and then fell onto the carpet. "And he dares to scold *me* about being prompt as well?"

"I'll call, make the reservation and leave a message at his hotel." Nadia gathered her notes. "Is that all he said?"

Hassan returned to the bar. "Jalal said the sheik wants you to stay at the Sheraton after you've finished up here. And by close of business tomorrow, you're to be out of the house. I think he intends to burn it to the ground, just like the plant, before the demolition."

Nadia's mind raced. "But why, if it's to be demolished?"

"It's obvious. To keep the authorities focused on our Ebi Rostum and his threat."

Nadia nodded, carefully masking her growing anxiety. "The demolition company comes in the following day. I'll plan on staying at the hotel until you send for me from Bahrain. That was the plan, wasn't it?" She stood up without waiting to be dismissed.

"Just do as he says. It's coming from my father. I'm leaving for the day." Hassan took his suit jacket off the back of his chair and headed for the door.

Nadia followed him out of the office and watched as the elevator lights blinked, showing the car's descent. She picked nervously at her nails. Jalal was back, and that meant big trouble was brewing. As much as Hassan hated him, the man terrified her, now more than ever. She thought of Farid and felt suddenly cold, as if someone had walked across her grave. Trembling, she reached for her handbag. William Meagher's business card fell onto the desk as she fumbled it from her purse. Grabbing her cell, Nadia entered the main office number listed below his name and waited as the phone began to ring. Her call went straight to voicemail.

Chapter 41
William Meagher's den

William waited for Marcus in the yard, his usual calm eroding as the implications of Nadia's revelations continued to magnify. He had somehow gone from investigating a fire to becoming a key figure in an international terrorist plot.

Marcus pulled up and leapt out of his car. As they hurried up the driveway toward the house, he shot questions at William, keeping his voice down but making no effort to mask his consternation.

"How the hell did you get a positive ID on this guy posing as Ebi Rostum?" he said. "And you're telling me he's a major player for black market sales of Criton's ammonium nitrate in the Middle East? How is it even possible that you find out something our own intelligence is still working on?"

Inside the house, Marcus slung his sports jacket on the coat rack as he followed William into the den. "I am up to my ass in something regarding national security; only did a detour because you're saying you have critical information regarding a terror strike, of all things."

"Let's start with this." William indicated the pictures of Rostum/Hamadi. "Former Syrian secret police; you may never have found him. Up front, the Criton fire itself *wasn't* an act of terrorism, but the nitrate material didn't burn up—it was already processed and on board one of Muhktar's ships. It's been sold to a terrorist organization. It was a cover up, Marcus, and this man made it happen. It looks like he's the one who murdered Vincent, too. He was under orders from Sheik Abbas Muhktar."

The government agent sat motionless as he read the text beneath the photos. "Abbas Muhktar in Tehran?"

William nodded. "Hamadi's boss. And then there's these." He handed Marcus the notes he and Vincent had put together outlining the fires they'd each investigated separately, complete with matching details as to the materials used, bags of ammonium nitrate and diesel fuel.

Marcus pored over the notes, and William silently waited until he looked up.

"Vincent was in the right place at the worst possible time." He cursed under his breath. "I'm so sorry, William." He rifled through the stack of papers on the table. "No wonder Hassan Muhktar didn't seem concerned about the fires or the insurance claims. I didn't press the right buttons."

"We all could have dug deeper and sooner. Patrick was the only one who smelled a rat from the start. It also appears that the mayor and fire chief were complicit to some extent, although I doubt they had anything to do with the murder. I plan to interview Stanley Lowell tomorrow as part of my insurance investigation and then turn it all over to Major Carson and Chatterton P.D."

Marcus picked up Nadia's envelope, a grave look on his face. "Where did you come across this information and who else knows about it? Patrick and Shane?"

"I showed them the pictures, the evidence against Stamper and Lowell, and how the fires were identical, but I didn't tell them who my source is. They don't know yet how big this is because I wanted to run it by you first. After you and I are done, I know I'll have to divulge it anyway." William opened a drawer and pulled out the flash drive Nadia had given him. "Hassan Muhktar's wife, Nadia Nuha, is also his executive assistant. She knows just about everything there is to know about his business. Hassan and the sheik had a journalist for an Iranian paper murdered because he'd uncovered their deal to sell Criton's nitrates illegally in the Persian Gulf. That correspondent was Nadia Nuha's half brother and her only kin, a fellow named Farid Barmeen. Besides handling the nitrate sale and killing Vincent here, Jalal Hamadi personally eliminated Barmeen with a car bomb."

"So she's angry, angry enough to turn on her husband. Sad about her brother, but lucky for us. Hell, William. As for Stamper and Lowell—County P.D. will take care of them, but we can't touch Muhktar just yet."

"He's leaving the country soon."

"I've got to get back to Washington right away with your information about the nitrate sale. Can I take these?" He stood up, collected the papers and jammed them into the envelope.

"Sit down, Marcus." William half shoved the FBI agent into a chair in front of his desk computer. He plugged Nadia's flash stick into the USB port and slid the mouse over the icon that appeared on the screen. "Your national security issue—does it have anything to do with a man by the name of Kazem Al-Unistan?"

Marcus stared aghast as pictures of Hamadi, Al-Unistan and the *Orient Star*, presumably loaded with ammonium nitrate, appeared in a slideshow on the computer screen.

"How did you get your hands on these?"

"Barmeen sent it to his sister for safe keeping, but wait, we're not through." William clicked on the included attachment.

The two men stared at the monitor as a video downloaded and a discussion between Jalal Hamadi and Kazem Al-Unistan began. William paused it. "Barmeen recorded this on the dock in Khorromshahr, Iran. You'll have to pay close attention. The dialogue gets broken up after a minute or so. The first voice in the exchange belongs to Al-Unistan, the second, Hamadi."

"The voyage went smoothly?"

"Not a single glitch, and right on time, as always. You want to tell me why you're unloading some here and keeping the rest on board?"

"You receive a fortune for your services. Be satisfied with that. You're not paid to ask questions."

William hit 'pause'. "This is where it gets corrupted. Hamadi is up next, then, Al-Unistan again."

"We ... care about what you do ... ship ... only that we ... paid. Will ... keep it ... Khorromshahr?"

"Iraq ... depot ... security ... pipeline ... Basra, not ... explode ... there. The Amer ... ship ... Faw ... blame each oth ... and I will watch ... comp ... annihilation."

258

"That's it." William leaned over to eject the device.

Marcus stayed his hand. "Hold it." He moved the cursor and replayed the last sound byte.

"The Amer ... ship ... Faw ... blame each oth ... and I will watch ... comp ... annihilation."

Marcus vaulted from his seat. "9:45. I can make it in seventy five minutes." He extracted the flash drive, collected the notes and pulled his car keys from his pocket.

"Seventy five minutes? What are you talking about?"

"No time to explain, William." Marcus hustled toward the door. "You take *only* the things you showed me about the fires and the fraud to Major Carson. He'll know what to do about Stamper and Lowell." He then looked squarely into William's eyes. "You don't know a damn thing about what we just looked at, understand?"

William nodded and swallowed hard as Marcus raced past the garage out to his car.

***

Marcus stomped on the accelerator as soon as he cleared the ramp merging northbound on I-95, his phone already on speaker mode as the secure line buzzed.

"Scoffield. What is it Marcus?"

"Arthur, I'm en-route to headquarters and I expect to be there in an hour and fifteen minutes. Establish a Sat-Com link in the War Room to Omar Matari in the Gulf right now."

259

"Done."

"Tell him to prepare his team for immediate deployment to Khorromshahr. He's to track down a vessel now flying an Iranian flag; the *Orient Star.*"

"Delorme, you want a U.S. Navy counter insurgency SEAL team to infiltrate an extremely hostile country right now, at zero five fifty hours Iranian time, and find a vessel flying their colors?"

"Yes sir, that's correct, sir. SEAL 2 is on the *Abe Lincoln,* 35 kilometers away from Khorromshahr. What time does the U.S.S. *Defender* sail from the Iraqi peninsula tomorrow, their time?"

"Twelve noon, Marcus, you know that. You're going to have to give me a reason as to why we're planning to insert an elite military unit inside Iran, of all places, in what amounts to an act of war."

"As of now, we only have about twelve hours to stop a war, Arthur." Marcus zipped between lanes, cutting off cars, oblivious to their blaring horns. "I'll give you a full briefing when I arrive. We anticipated an attack, but we might have guessed wrong. All our security is concentrated on the oil transmission lines and depot in Basra, and traffic headed up the waterway, but we need to focus on Al-Faw. I have intel that Kazem Al-Unistan may be plotting to detonate an entire ship and incinerate two thousand Marines and US government officials instead. If that's the case, the blame will fall directly on the Iranian government." Marcus shot a glance at his speedometer: eighty miles per hour. "Remember, Homeland Defense Secretary Estrada said the administration will not tolerate another Beirut. We have no choice. There are no other assets that can neutralize this threat in time."

"I'm having the link established right now. Marcus, step on it."

The needle on the gauge climbed to ninety.

Chapter 42
William Meagher's Office

Once in his father's office, Patrick flicked the light on, opened the file cabinet standing by the entrance and began searching for the insurance papers he'd been asked to pick up the night before. William's meeting with the Fire Chief would be nothing short of volatile, and Patrick wished he could be there when Lowell was confronted with the newly discovered evidence. The thought of Police Major Walter Carson arresting both Stamper and Lowell afterwards brought him some comfort, but Patrick was far from satisfied. Hassan Muhktar and Jalal Hamadi had to be caught, and soon. Tonight, certainly tomorrow morning at the latest, they would be safely on their way with their black market fortune to a country with no extradition treaty.

Finding the folder, he slammed the drawer shut, wishing it was Muhktar's head. He switched off the overhead lights and took a quick look around the darkened room. It was only then that he noticed a glow emanating from the row of buttons on the desk phone. Seeing it was the main office line and not the private hot line for tips, Patrick grabbed a pen and paper and poked the lighted tab to retrieve the voicemail. He strained to catch the hushed voice of a woman, who spoke as though she feared discovery.

"Mr. Meagher, Hassan has a six o'clock meeting with Hamadi at Birani's Lobster House and won't be home before nine. He alluded to the fact that Jalal intends to burn down the house just like Criton prior to the demolition, which is slated to begin tomorrow. I'm staying at the Sheraton if you need me."

Stunned, Patrick held the phone near his ear for long moments after the message ended. Several more seconds passed before he put the receiver down, and a minute or more before he decided what to do about it. He took out his cell and called Shane.

"Listen, I'm at Dad's office, collecting the insurance information on Standard Cold Storage. I also picked up a voicemail that's got me thinking."

"Okay." Shane drew the word out. "Hope Dad's good with that."

"It wasn't on the tip line and he'll be more than okay with it once he knows what it's about. I don't know who this woman is, but it has to be his deep throat. She said something about a meeting at Birani's tonight at 6.00, and a plan to set fire to Muhktar's house after that just like he did at the chemical company."

"Jesus. That doesn't give us a lot of time. I don't know, Patrick."

"Just keep thinking about what they did to Vince, for Christ's sake!" His brother remained quiet. "Shane?"

"Alright, we'll do it your way." Shane reluctance was palpable. "But you better tell the old man about this business meeting they're having at the restaurant. The police won't get another shot at Jalal Hamadi."

"I will."

"Are you going to be able to get all that shit done that we talked about before you get back on duty?"

263

"I'll get it done. You just make sure you're at the station when I get there." Patrick hung up.

William was next up. "Hey, Patrick. Did you find what I needed?"

"Hi Dad. I got it. Where are you? What time are you meeting Lowell?"

"I'm leaving the forensics lab with the DNA results on the cigarette butts. As for Stanley, he's put me off until 8:45, said he forgot there's a mandatory Board of Supervisors meeting. It's not a big deal. By nine or so, he'll belong to the cops."

"That skinny, beady-eyed bastard. If he only knew." Patrick went on to relay Nadia's message to his father.

"Birani's, on Westmoreland?" William confirmed.

"That's the place. Hamadi and Muhktar together— it's perfect, and I don't think the police will be able to track them after tonight."

"I know. I'll call Walter Carson. For now, what's a good time and place for us to meet?" His father sounded tired, as if he were a thousand miles away. There were far too many moving pieces, and it was all happening fast.

"I need to put some fuel in the truck, do some running around and important business to knock out on my lap top. How about around eight at Southern States Agricultural Supply on the Pike? It's a mile from Station 14, and that will give me enough time to finish what I need to do."

"Eight it is. Please, Patrick, be careful tonight. I've got a bad feeling."

Chapter 43
Birani's Lobster House

Hassan shook his empty glass at the waitress as she whisked by, delivering three steaming red lobsters to the women who were seated in the next booth. Hassan viewed crustaceans as slimy, sinister looking creatures not intended for human consumption. He pretty much viewed Jalal Hamadi in the same disparaging light.

"I'll be with you as soon as I can." The harried food server offered a strained smile before laying the heavily loaded tray on a side table and distributing a platter in front of each of the women. Then she hurried off.

"Make it quick," Hassan called after her, then mumbled, "Pathetic service." He re-checked his watch, his eyes more than a bit bleary from the pair of double bourbons and water he'd already scoffed down in the forty-five minutes he'd been waiting. Irritated, he looked up as a man approached his table.

"I see your manners haven't improved, Hassan." Jalal Hamadi shook his head derisively as he unbuttoned his jacket and settled into an open chair. "Always thinking others owe you something. It's not one of your better qualities." The powerfully built former Syrian agent scooted his seat closer, deliberately invading Hassan's personal space and enjoying his discomfort.

Hassan glowered and moved his chair. "Don't speak to me that way, Jalal, I should . . ."

Hamadi leaned forward and interrupted him. "What you *should* and *will* do is lower your voice and listen."

The waitress returned, handing a fresh Jim Beam to Hassan and looking inquiringly at the bald, clean-shaven Hamadi. "I'll have a bottle of Perrier. Better bring one for my associate as well. Thank you."

"Coming up," the young woman responded buoyantly, seemingly relieved by the courtesy of the new diner.

"It's almost seven," Hassan hissed, inching his seat closer to the table. "You said to be here at six."

"I said nothing about *my* being here at that time. Besides, I also told you to enjoy your evening." Hamadi flicked a few breadcrumbs from the small loaf Hassan had nibbled on across the tabletop. "I see that you are."

His laconic smile set Hassan's teeth on edge. "I didn't come here to be insulted, or treated like a child. You tell me you carry word from my father. What is it? I want to get this over with, you son of a bitch."

Hamadi matter-of-factly crooked his arm over the back of the adjacent chair. "The sheik is a cunning man and unfortunately, as I see it, a doting father. That you are his only son and sole heir, also unfortunate. When I think of the money he's placed at your disposal, money that he entrusted me to make available to you, this elaborate plan to sell the nitrates to Al-Unistan . . . from where I stand, you've never earned a penny." He leaned forward and dropped his voice, spitting words in a staccato snarl. "And please tell me, now that you've drunk yourself into a stupor,

266

that Nadia is out of the house and the office has been wrapped up."

Red faced, Hassan grabbed Hamadi's wrist. "Get out of my face." He tightened his grip. "And just remember, I know that you take more than your share from the Khorromshahr account. I will never understand why my father trusts you. The remainder of the money? Don't touch it. There will be consequences, even for you."

Hamadi peeled Hassan's fingers off his wrist with little effort. "I more than earn my share. I should take extra just for having to work at Criton and putting up with you. And be prepared—I will take more if I like, as soon as I complete the last part of the sheik's plan. You've nothing to say in the matter."

Hassan reached for a napkin and dabbed at the sweat that had formed on his upper lip. He knew what Hamadi was capable of, had even seen him beat a man to death for threatening Abbas. He took a long drink from his cocktail. "What is the last part? I want to be gone from this place as soon as possible."

Hamadi smiled. "Must I lay this out for you?" He chuckled contemptuously. "The threat against your life, the one you were told by your father to report to Stamper and the police? Rostum will strike again, but it's really just another diversion to keep them busy as you leave the country. And as a plus, your house will burn and we'll all make a little more insurance money. It will look just like the arson/revenge fire at the warehouse." Hamadi stopped as the waitress returned.

"Gentlemen, are you ready to order?"

"I'll have your prime rib, if it's edible." Hassan tossed the menu in the woman's direction.

Hamadi picked up Hassan's menu and stacked it on top of his own. He gave them to the young woman, along with a twenty-dollar bill. "Apologies. My friend has enjoyed one too many."

She smiled her thanks and slid the bill into her apron pocket. "What can I bring you?"

"Oh, nothing. I must be going."

The waitress scribbled Hassan's order and retreated to the kitchen.

"You're leaving?" Hassan said. "You tell me to make a dinner reservation here, knowing I despise this place, and then you order nothing after you threaten and insult me?"

Hamadi shook his head as he tugged on his sleeves. "You're drunk, Hassan. And after tonight's work at your place on River Road, I plan never to see your sorry ass again."

"Fuck you, Hamadi."

"A little after seven o'clock; I've got a job to do. Goodbye and good riddance. Enjoy your meal, have another drink or two. That should keep you until nine. Remember, like I told you, those are Daddy's orders."

Chapter 44
Chatterton County

"This is the file you asked me to get for you last night at your house, right?" Patrick tossed the folder containing the information on the Standard Cold Storage fire through the window of his father's car even before it stopped moving. The papers cascaded off the passenger's seat and onto the floorboard.

"Whoa, can't you wait until I park?" William turned off the engine and leaned over to pick them up. "It's barely after eight. You still have an hour before you have to report to the station. What's your hurry?"

"Sorry. Got a lot to do before I go to work." Patrick put his elbows on the car's window frame. "Did you talk to Major Carson about the meeting at Birani's? Did he say what he was going to do? Maybe he picked them up by now?"

"He's on it. Wouldn't go into detail, and I didn't ask. The police department will move only after they talk to the Feds, see what they want to do. It's got to be done right by the numbers. Something is probably in the works though. Hamadi won't get away."

Patrick craned his neck to look at the clock on the dashboard. "But Carson did say he'd join you around nine in Stanley's office, let you get the information regarding the insurance fraud out of the way first? I'm sure he'll have brought the hammer down on Jackson Stamper just before that, right?"

"What's with all the questions?" William said. "Shouldn't you just concern yourself with this night drill that Shane lined up?"

"Thats taken care of. We went over it last night at *Firehouse Subs*. Look, I got to get going. I have to pick up something inside, still a few things to do before I get to work. Good luck with Stanley. I'll be in touch so we can talk more about this." Patrick stepped away from the car as William drove off.

The wind was picking up, making the chill in the air more pronounced. Patrick lifted the top of the toolbox in the bed of his truck and took out a dark blue hoodie. Pulling it on, he closed the lid and trotted into the store as dusk settled in. It would be a tight squeeze to get his work done and be on duty before nine.

Chapter 45
Shatt al Arab Waterway

The rainbow of pastel colors preceding sunrise was gaining strength on the eastern horizon. On his way to the captain's cabin, Kazem Al-Unistan stopped on the main deck of the *Orient Star* to enjoy both the view and the crisp morning air. Even as a boy growing up in Basra along this very river, it had always been his favorite part of the day, a time to reflect on upcoming events. Today, high above the mist hovering over the water, the air was as clear as he could remember. It was as if each day before this was meant to herald this moment.

Reaching the captain's quarters, he knocked lightly.

"Abdullah, it is time." He pushed on the door and poked his head past the riveted bulkhead. "Today, your death will bring the greatest honor, and you will become a martyr for those that will follow in your name."

Working at his chart table, Abdullah ran his pencil against the edge of a ruler, marking the final leg of the ship's course on a map of the river. He circled its termination point, the harbor of Al-Faw. He put the pencil down. "I'm ready, Kazem."

"Come." Al-Unistan stepped aside and held the door open for the man who'd agreed to sacrifice his life by piloting the vessel that would bring death to his unsuspecting crew, and thousands of American soldiers.

271

They strode toward the starboard companionway and ambled down the ramp, where a Boston Whaler, tethered to the side of the freighter, bobbed like a fishing cork in the three-foot chop.

Reaching the skiff, Al-Unistan turned to the captain. "How long will it take before you're in position?"

"Right now we're twenty seven kilometers from Khorromshahr. We'll be in place in approximately two hours. Is there anything else?"

"Yes." Al-Unistan clasped the man on both shoulders. "For whatever reason, if this ship is not blown by twelve o'clock, ignite a flare and toss it in the hold yourself. The American vessel must be destroyed."

The two said their goodbyes, and Al-Unistan stepped over the rail to clamber into his small launch.

***

Dense, early morning mist swirled in the harbor of Khorromshahr, perfect cover for the camouflaged Zodiac being pulled into the underbrush in the shadow of the docks. Omar Matari slipped a tattered, greasy robe over his clothing and reached for the secure TS-4 satellite phone as he stepped on shore. The members of SEAL Team 2 had received their assignment two hours ago. They were to confirm the target, the *Orient Star,* and report back. If the ship was headed to Al-Faw, he was to acquire and neutralize all enemy assets. In military terms that meant only one thing--kill any hostile combatants on sight.

"Eagle One," he murmured into the phone, "there are no ships in port. I'm leaving the Zodiac one and a half kilometers from Pier 6. SEAL Team 2 will stay with it while I mix with the locals and try to acquire some Intel on the *Orient Star*." Omar adjusted the wireless tactical headset and checked the Sigg-Sauer 9 mm he had stashed under his bulky garment. "I'll report back within the hour."

"Eagle One copies," Marcus replied.

Omar thought Marcus sounded apprehensive and edgy, exhausted, too. He flipped the voice-activated communicator into a waterproof sack in the prow of the inflatable. The FBI agent's trepidation was understandable. With the explosive cargo on board the freighter, the power and technology of the American military was utterly useless. There could be no air strike or artillery barrage. The success of the mission would rest solely on the marksmanship of twelve soldiers armed with M107 sniper rifles.

Omar grabbed a pint of Seagram's Seven from a watertight compartment. He took a healthy swig and swished it in his mouth before spitting the alcohol into his hands and smearing it on his outfit. He turned to his second in command. "You know the drill; radio silence. If I'm not back in sixty minutes, you take off, then call command and follow orders." He jumped from the watercraft and disappeared into the bushes.

***

A shabbily dressed man stumbled out of the weeds along the river and past the enormous crane anchored on the edge of Pier 6 in Khorromshahr. He approached a group of workers wrestling with several fifty-five-gallon barrels that had toppled over onto the dock, the pungent sulfur-smell of diesel filling the air. Omar staggered up to the man giving orders.

"Have you any work, *effendi?*" He belched loudly.

"*Effendi?* Your lord and master I'm not, nor am I taking on a drunk." The foreman waved his hand in front of his nose and took a step back. "Who are you and what do you really want?"

"I'm a man without a job, a sad state of affairs." Omar swayed unsteadily and smeared a dirty sleeve across his face. He took a gamble. "My uncle scrapes a living at the fish market, but said I would find a day's wages loading the *Orient Star* this morning."

"The freighter left earlier, probably while you had your head stuck in a bottle. Get out of here. Go find your uncle and guzzle some more whiskey with him." The supervisor raised his fist, feigning to strike Omar.

The dockworkers laughed.

"I can help clean up that diesel spill. Is that what you were loading on the *Star*? Where's it headed?" Omar pressed.

A brawny, sweat covered wharf hand dragged a torn bandana across his brow. "How should we know? Downstream; is that okay with you?"

A second worker pointed at the oil-slicked harbor. "Maybe if you start swimming now, you can find out yourself."

The men laughed again as Omar tripped and fell over an iron cleat welded to the edge of the pier.

Omar got up from all fours, steadied himself and flashed his middle finger at his tormentors. He wove an erratic path away from the crowd toward the alleyway that would lead him back to SEAL Team 2.

Moving more steadily along the river's edge, he pulled his watch from his pocket: 8:15. He started running. With twelve men on board, the top speed of the inflatable boat was about twenty miles an hour. With any luck they would reach Al-Faw in about three hours.

Chapter 46
Chatterton County, Virginia

A light bit of traffic thrummed on the dark and wooded stretch of River Road. Hamadi had counted on that--some random driver would, at some point, pass by and call in the blaze. His low beams illuminated a rutted service road a quarter of a mile ahead of him for the gas transmission lines that paralleled Hassan's property. Downshifting, Hamadi eased onto the gravel track and wound his way through a grove of loblolly pines until he spotted an equipment shack belonging to the utility company. He tucked the pickup behind it.

The truck's door didn't make a sound as he pressed it shut with his hip. He shouldered the Nike bag, identical to the one used at the Standard Cold Storage fire, and hiked back toward the fire hydrant stationed along the roadbed alongside Muhktar's driveway. The bag wouldn't be making the return trip; purposely left as a calling card for the police that Ebi Rostum had deliberately started the fire.

He rummaged through the bag, pulled out a red *Out of Service* hydrant maintenance ring, and secured it to the barrel of the hydrant. Investigators would figure out afterwards that it was another Rostum ploy; identical to what was used at Criton Chemical. He cinched the hood of his sweatshirt tight and moved through the dark patches in the woods toward Hassan's house. A roll of thunder echoed, and a twig snapped under his boot.

276

Creeping behind a hedgerow, he spotted the security alarm, it's light off. The house was in darkness, which made sense--most of the furniture was gone, and the dozers would be here in the early morning. Crouching perfectly still, he listened for any sound and checked the time. The luminescent dial glowed; 8:45. Hassan would still be at Birani's; his wife, at work as ordered. Hamadi cat-walked toward the side door and pried it open with a crowbar, taking a moment to admire his work. The amateurish marks were obvious, sure to get noticed by investigators.

Inside, the garage was pitch black. Kneeling, he trained the beam of his miner's headlamp on the contents of the Nike bag and removed a ten pound bag of diesel-soaked nitrate.

Opening his knife, he sliced along the Criton Chemical label and tore the burlap. Snapping the blade shut and hefting the bag, he walked backwards along the wall for about six feet, trailing the colorless granules before depositing the remainder beneath the wooden steps that led into the house. A familiar sulfur smell filled the garage. He took out a cigarette. Seven minutes after it was lit the fire would start, maybe ten to fifteen more before a passerby would see the first flames and call it in. The fire department would arrive less than five minutes later. A car rumbled past. He froze. It droned on, heading down River Road.

Hamadi lit the cigarette and attached it to a short length of slow burning primer cord. Then he sprinted to his truck and headed back to his hotel.

***

Hassan grudgingly paid his dinner bill and, unsteady on his feet, left Birani's. His voicemail alert sounded as he unlocked the car. He relaxed against the headrest and listened to his father's message.

"Hassan, I hope your dinner meeting with Jalal went well. I spoke to him earlier. He assured me he's on the way to set up and start the arson fire at the estate. He'll make it look like Rostum did it. You'll know by now it's why he told you to remain at the restaurant and why Nadia is to stay at the hotel. We celebrate in Bahrain this weekend."

One clear thought cut through Hassan's foggy mind. He'd forgotten his passport, visa, and laptop at the house . . . and Hamadi was there. The cell phone tumbled to the floorboard. "Come *on!*" Panicked, he juggled the keychain, struggling to get the key in the ignition. He'd never make it. The engine roared to life. Tires spinning, the Lincoln careened out of Birani's parking lot.

Chapter 47
FBI Headquarters, Washington DC

Hearing Omar sign off after another update, Marcus grabbed the percolator from the side table in the War Room and refilled the ceramic mugs for Arthur Scoffield and himself. After racing up from William's house, he'd briefed the FBI director, who in turn passed the information higher up the chain of command. Now, a desperate hunt for Kazem Al-Unistan was underway. Operating under the code name, Eagle One, Marcus was gulping coffee by the pot. Combined with the adrenaline flooding his veins, he was wound up tight as any spring. He handed the cup to his boss.

"So you're telling me, Arthur, there simply wasn't enough time to convince the Pentagon to reprogram any of the satellites to orbit above Khorromshahr to at least take a look and try and find the *Orient Star*?"

"Even if I'd succeeded, the damn things couldn't have their orbits modified quick enough to do any good. Quite a few of the brass think any attack on Al-Faw would be a diversion." Scoffield talked while pacing in front of a wall map of the Persian Gulf. "That distorted video of yours didn't convince enough of them Al-Unistan isn't after the pipelines. It was all I could do to get SEAL Team 2 deployed to Khorromshahr, and that only because Homeland Defense Secretary Estrada stepped in."

Marcus wished he hadn't given up cigarettes. He was desperate for one and would have given a month's pay to renew the habit he'd finally kicked cold turkey three years ago. "And while they debate strategy, we've got Omar Matari dressed up like one of the locals, poking around hours before a fifteen thousand ton bomb obliterates a fully loaded transport vessel. Do they have *any* idea just how big the explosion will be? Fifteen thousand tons is *five* times more than that ship transporting ammonium nitrate in Texas carried years ago. It accidentally blew up, destroyed *half* the port and killed almost a thousand people!" He rubbed the back of his neck. "What time is it over there, Arthur?"

"Eleven thirty five. Matari better be getting something quick."

Marcus picked up the satellite phone as its incoming message light began blinking and strained to hear Omar's report. Between the Zodiac's outboard motor humming at full throttle and the wind rushing over the microphone in the commander's mouthpiece, it took all his concentration to make out what he was saying.

"Eagle...this is Fal... GPS shows SEAL Team 2 is...ninety miles south of the dock at Khorrom..., continuing at max...speed. Estimated arrival at Al-Faw, five to ten min... Still no sign of the *Orient Star.*"

Marcus turned up the satellite phone's volume, but it was no use. He got up and stood in front of the Persian Gulf wall map, trying to imagine the pounding SEAL Team 2 must be taking, bouncing from one wave crest to the next in the windy delta region of the Shatt al Arab. He didn't like the odds, liked his options even less, but there were no other choices. The *Star* had to be found and the threat neutralized. There wasn't much time left before the noon launch of the *Defender* and possible incineration of an entire division of Marines, not to mention the obliteration of a very large piece of the Iraqi city of Al-Faw, and maybe the start of a war between the United States and Iran. Marcus felt a headache steamrolling in around his temples, and it was growing worse by the second.

"Falcon," he said to Matari, "continue on two-seven-five degrees into the harbor. We've calculated that for the bomb to have maximum effect on the port, the *Orient Star* has to be within five hundred yards of our transport ship."

Marcus looked over at Arthur Scoffield pacing off to the side, his forehead a mass of deep wrinkles as he settled the phone he'd been using gently back in its cradle. Scoffield closed his eyes and pinched the bridge of his nose. Marcus heard his sigh halfway across the room.

"That was the Chief of Staff. He said he was releasing some choppers from our naval base in Basra. They're already up, providing air cover to protect the oil depot."

"Jesus Christ! *Now*? And just exactly what are they supposed to do? Fire a missile or two?" Marcus stared at him, aghast. "At most we have fifteen minutes, they won't make it in time to do anything anyway. Did he at least advise the *Defender* to establish a defensive strategy?"

They were both exhausted, nerves shot.

Scoffield scowled at him. "The Iranians claim the river as theirs, and they still trade heavily with the

281

Iraqis at Al-Faw. If a commercial vessel, especially one flying their flag, uses the marked channel and avoids our designated perimeter, well, just what do you suggest other than what we're doing with the SEAL team? We can't board the vessel, and the captain will probably just blow-up the *Star* if we even try. With the power of that bomb, they're already probably close enough to take out our ship."

"For God's sake, it's *not* an Iranian vessel!" Marcus raised his voice, struggling to rein in his frustration. "Can't the brass convince Tehran?"

"They're trying; been at it non stop, but damn it, Marcus, you just brought all this to their attention, and you know full well Iran isn't going to drop everything and cooperate with us. The Iranians don't trust anything we say, and let's face it, we'd feel the same about them."

"In a nutshell," Marcus said quietly, "Seal Team 2 is our only chance. God protect us."

The headset hummed in his ears.

"Eagle One, this is Falcon, we've spotted a ship, Iranian flag on the masthead, relative bearing two-seven-six. She's at the mouth of the harbor right now."

Marcus gestured for Scoffield's attention and hunched over the table. "Falcon, I'm putting you on speaker. Go ahead."

"Rangefinder shows eighteen hundred yards and closing. We're approaching the vessel's stern port quarter. Stand by...we have activity, someone in the pilothouse... I am confirming that...we have acquired a target and will take him out at five hundred yards."

"Negative, negative!" Marcus shouted into the mic. "That is not your target. I say again, that is not going to be Al-Unistan. We must find and take out Al-Unistan! He will detonate from a distance. Are there any small boats near your location?"

The speaker crackled. "Eagle, this is Falcon. We've got two small craft, both about a mile and a half away from the *Star*. I also have a loaded freighter steaming up river behind one of them. It's flying the Union Jack."

Scoffield pointed at the world clock for Baghdad. "It's 11:48, we have to make a choice!"

Marcus clamped his hand on his forehead, his eyes squeezed tightly shut. "Falcon, break off pursuit and proceed in the direction of the those two boats. We'll identify that freighter from here."

Chapter 48
Shatt al Arab Waterway, Persian Gulf

Kazem al-Unistan stood at the bow of the Boston Whaler and adjusted the two-inch viewfinder of the video camera he had trained on the *Orient Star,* now displaying the Iranian flag. He'd prove to the world that Tehran was behind the attack against the Americans. He paused and squinted when he noticed something bobbing in the turbulence behind the *Star.*

Without warning, the shrill burst of a steam-whistle blasted the air directly behind him. Al-Unistan flinched and spun in its direction. An overloaded northbound cargo ship, hundreds of rectangular corrugated freight containers stacked high on its deck, was sailing perilously close by. He braced for the large bow waves heading for him. The Whaler rocked precariously, rollers slamming into it. The murky water of the Shatt al Arab spilled over the sides.

As Al-Unistan held tight to the gunwale, the craft he thought he'd spotted behind the *Orient Star* turned about and hurtled in his direction.

***

"Eagle One!" Omar was practically yelling, trying to overcome the noise of the Zodiac's four-stroke engine. "The *Star* has got to be near the *Defender,* are you sure our target isn't on board?"

Scoffield pinned Marcus's wrist to the tabletop as he reached for the mic. "Are you certain Al-Unistan is not on board, Marcus? How do you know he doesn't want to die with a front row seat?"

"I *don't* know for certain." Marcus could barely get the words out, the distorted conversation he'd heard in the Khorromshahr dock video crashing in his head like a wrecking ball. "But that exchange between Al-Unistan and Hamadi…the maniac doesn't want to die killing our men. He's too ambitious. He's got much bigger plans that no doubt he wants to stick around for." He shook his wrist free. "Falcon, do you have a visual of Kazem Al-Unistan?"

***

The Zodiac pitched wildly. Clenching one of its guy ropes, Omar crawled to the front and scanned the turbulent river basin. "I have two small craft ahead, both dead in the water. Target One, eighteen hundred yards to starboard. Looks like a small fishing boat. Two subjects on board." Omar barked at the six snipers lying prone on the right side. "Safeties off, stand by." He crushed the earpiece against the side of his head, the wind making it almost impossible to hear Marcus's reply.

"Falcon, what about the second target?"

"Eagle, second target is an open skiff, fifteen hundred yards to port. One subject on board." Omar barked at the SEALs on his left. "Murdock, Nollen, Range, Sommers; this one's yours. Get ready!" Omar wiped the spray from his watch face. "Eagle One, we're out of time!"

***

285

Kazem Al-Unistan let go of the gunwale as the cargo vessel's bow waves calmed. He checked the clock on the control panel. 11.55. It was time. He picked up his binoculars. The *Orient Star* had entered the harbor, but something else was in his field of vision. *A boat?* He zoomed in on the craft, and the twelve men on board in camouflaged combat fatigues coming straight at him. *Americans!* Kazem lunged for the stern, and the backpack that held the cell phone detonator.

***

"Eagle One, second target is looking right at us...He's scuffling around in his boat...He's tearing through a backpack." Water sprayed onto the binoculars lenses. Sweat stung Omar's eyes. "I see a red *keffiya* on the console...He's got a phone...*He's gonna blow the* Star*!*"

"Take the shot! *Take the shot!*" Marcus shouted..

"Take him!" Omar shrieked the order. The marksmen fired as one.

Thirteen hundred yards away, a gruesome halo of fine red mist and bone fragments was spewed into the air. It was all that remained of Kazem Al-Unistan's head as his body catapulted over the side of the Boston Whaler and began to sink to the bottom of the Shatt al Arab.

***

Stunned, the captain of the *Orient Star*, Abdullah Zafir, lowered his high-powered field glasses very slowly. Then rage took over. The strap broke as he

286

ripped it from his neck and threw the binoculars. The lenses shattered as they struck the corner of the metal chart table.

With Kazem Al-Unistan assassinated right before his eyes, the mission was in his hands alone. Abdullah jerked the door open for the locker marked *Emergency* and raked a canvas pouch full of flares from the top shelf. Several fell to the floor. He snatched one and stuffed it in his belt beside a deadly Mac-10 machine pistol.

We must not fail.

Kazem's last words fortified Abdullah and fueled the all-consuming hatred roiling in his gut. Setting the throttle to its slowest possible setting, and with the *Orient Star* nearing the buoy-marked perimeter of the American transport, he mouthed a final prayer and tried to calm himself. He opened the door of the pilothouse. Down on the main deck, the tip of the fast-burning primer cord jutted out from the hatch above the cargo hold. Deep in the bowels of the ship, the primer cord's terminal end was attached to fifteen thousand tons of diesel soaked ammonium nitrate, an improvised explosive device of cataclysmic proportions that needed only a spark.

* * *

"Uhh, Newk, what do you make of that ship that's headed toward our port side?" Private First Class Cordell Washburn nudged Corporal Terry Newkon and leveled his M-16 on the bulkhead of the U.S.S. *Defender*.

Newkon swiveled in Washburn's direction, binoculars at the ready. "Dry bulk carrier; twenty five thousand tons, max. She's not carrying a full load; look at the waterline."

"I can see she's light, man, but that's not what I'm talking about. Another hundred yards, she don't make the turn to the pier and ends up in our defensive perimeter. We were put on alert for that, and the *Defender* is a transport ship, it don't have anything in the way of heavy artillery for defense. I'm not liking this at all, Newk." Washburn flipped his weapons switch to full-auto.

"Roger that." Newkon scanned the freighter's pilothouse. "Hey, we got movement on its bridge. Stay sharp, Cordell. I'm gonna radio the Sergeant."

***

The Marines were the first things Abdullah Zafir saw when the elevator doors opened and he stepped out onto the main deck. They were armed, and their weapons were aimed at him. His heart felt as if it was about to tear apart, and his breathing all but stopped. Eyes unblinking, he trudged past his crew as if in a trance, paying no attention to their perplexed looks and evading the wild questions that came from all directions.

"Stop where you are, or you will be shot. There will be no second warning!" The stern, aggressive command coming over the American's bullhorn in Abdullah's native Farsi had the exact opposite effect on the *Star*'s captain. He yanked the flare from his belt and chaffed the abrasive ignition cap across its head. Instantly, a waterfall of brilliant sparks began to cascade onto the steel plated deck. He gripped the incendiary tightly in his left hand and drew the handheld machine gun from his waistband with his right. He fired a lengthy burst at the Marines, red-hot shell casings bouncing at his feet as he made a desperate charge toward the primer cord with the sizzling flare.

***

The barrage of .45 caliber rounds coming from the *Orient Star* slammed into the *Defender*'s port side bulkhead. As Washburn emptied his clip, Newkon dove to the deck, hot metal shards landing on his helmet and back. He pressed his cheek against the M-16's stock. One eye closed, he fixed the other on the gun sight and released his breath. He squeezed the trigger slowly.

Three hundred yards away, a flare flipped into the air and spiraled harmlessly into the muddy harbor. Newkon's target, Abdullah Zafir, blood splattered across his chest, splashed in right behind it.

Chapter 49
Chatterton County, Virginia

Stanley Lowell thumbed through the documents William Meagher had placed on his desk. "Look, I'm tired, Meagher. The meeting with the Board of Supervisors was a long one, and it's after nine. I just want to get out of my office and go home. This shit you're showing me about an illegal overload at Standard Cold Storage, on top of discrepancies Vincent Rigardo allegedly found at Criton; it's all circumstantial."

William replaced the papers Lowell flicked across his desk in the folder. "You okayed it, and a firefighter was killed, in part, because of it." Anger was slow to build in him, but now it rose, close to the surface. "Listen here, you arrogant prick, there's more to this, and don't think Major Carson and his detectives haven't read this stuff."

"Carson." Lowell leaned back, hands laced together behind his head. "All this so-called evidence is worthless. Rigardo is dead. There's no one to support his theory. And you know, Meagher, I'm thinking of running for the Board. First thing I'll do after the election will be to fire Carson. He's become a relic."

"Why don't you tell him that yourself? He's on the way over here now."

As the two men glared at one another, the fire department speaker on Lowell's desk crackled.

"Local alarm for Engine Companies 14, 1, 18, Truck 14 and Battalion Chief 5, respond to 15880 River Road for a structure fire. Time of dispatch is twenty one ten hours."

A knock on the office door came right behind the announcement. William looked up as the Chief's secretary poked her head into the room.

"Sorry to interrupt, Chief, I just got off the phone with our communications center. The dispatcher wanted to make sure you knew this is Mr. Muhktar's residence."

Lowell snapped his head in her direction. "What?" Shooting up, he ripped his uniform jacket from its hook. "This meeting is over, Meagher." Without a backward glance, he raced from the office.

Still fuming, William reached in his pocket and took out his phone. "Walter, it's me. I'm guessing your visit with Mayor Stamper is over?"

"Ex-mayor. Stamper folded like a house of cards after I showed him what we had. I'm in my car headed over to arrest Lowell now. You with him?"

William's shoulders sagged in relief. "Lowell just left. There's a fire at Muhktar's place. How about I step outside, you pick me up and we ride over there together?"

"I'll be there in a couple of minutes. Oh, and by the way, I sent Lieutenant Michaels and one of her men to arrest someone I'm sure you will want to meet personally. She called saying she picked him up at The Marriott and was on the way to the jail for processing. I think I'll call back, tell her to bring him and meet us at Muhktar's instead. It could prove interesting and useful."

291

William reacted to the news as if a crushing weight had been lifted from him. An image of Vincent, a young man he considered a third son, appeared in his mind's eye, smiling. William dropped the phone on the desk and buried his face in his hands, unable to hold back tears any longer.

***

Patrick bolted past Shane as he held the door to the Fire Station open for him, paying little attention as he hustled straight toward the apparatus bay.

"Where the hell have you been?" Shane sounded nervous. "I thought you weren't going to make it. Did you get everything done?"

"Well, I made it. I told you I would. No calls have come in from the Emergency Communications center, have they?" Patrick tossed his turnout gear next to Engine 14. "Have you heard from Dad? His meeting with Lowell was supposed to start around a quarter to nine."

"No. If Stanley was arrested, I'm sure I'd have heard by now. But things are coming to a head; I can feel it."

Patrick grimaced as he rubbed his jaw. "You aren't kidding about that, and in more ways than one."

Just then, the Klaxon horn went off, alerting firefighters at Station 14 that they had a call, Patrick grabbed a fresh battery from the charger in the radio room and ran out into the apparatus bay. As he jumped into his turnout gear and buttoned his coat, he saw the far bay door open. Shane was already in his staff car and on the way as the dispatch assignment came through on the radio.

"Battalion 5, engine companies 14, 1, 18 and Truck 14, we received a call on 9-1-1 from a passing motorist. She said she saw flames starting to come through the roof of an attached garage at this address."

Patrick climbed into the front seat of Engine 14 and latched his seat harness as Shane's voice boomed through the station's wall mounted speaker.

"Battalion 5 is responding. Dispatch, is there any other information?"

"This is Chatterton Dispatch; Chief Meagher and units responding; computer shows a permit issued by the Fire Marshal's office. The building is scheduled for demolition. There are no lights on and no cars in the driveway."

"Ten-four Chatterton. When all Units have marked en-route, switch this incident to Fire Channel Tac-B and clear the main dispatch channel."

Shane sounded uneasy. After the talk they'd had the other night, it was understandable. But having worked with him countless times throughout their careers, and both having known Vincent Rigardo most of his life, Patrick knew exactly how his older brother was going to react. Racing to this call, he was depending on that.

***

Patrick pulled on the cord suspended from the roof of the cab. The air horn for Engine 14 blasted the night air, driving traffic to the sides of the highway as it barreled down the Pike. Along with the Federal-Q siren raising hell, it was difficult for him to hear Shane's report as he arrived at the fire.

Patrick covered one ear and concentrated as Shane spoke up. "Battalion 5 is on scene with a large two story single family dwelling, fire showing through the roof of an attached garage. Battalion 5 will be River Road command. Engine 14, you will be first to arrive, but the hydrant out front is out of service. Leave your five-inch supply line at the end of the drive and proceed up here to me. Engine 1, drop your manpower and have your driver pick up 14's line. Proceed to the next hydrant to establish water supply. Lieutenant Crossbie and Truck 14, provide lighting and stand by as a safety back up until other units arrive."

Seconds later, the communications center answered. "Battalion 5 is River Road command. All responding units switch to Tac-B. Time: 21:20 hours."

Shane's report gave a clear snapshot of what was going on, and hearing it, Patrick knew what to expect. The delay establishing a water supply, along with the empty house being slated for destruction anyway, would keep the firefighters out of danger. They'd fight the blaze from the outside. There would be no need to risk anyone. It was a textbook plan.

Turning onto River Road, a flickering orange glow in the trees pinpointed their destination. Patrick grabbed his mic. "Engine 14 on location; confirming assignment. Hydrant is out of service. Coming up the driveway now."

In the background, the remainder of the assigned apparatus began rumbling into place as Patrick and his crew pulled to a stop in front of the house.

Leaping out and joining his brother, Patrick screwed the breathing tube for his face piece into his air pack. "What do you want us to do, Shane?"

"Set up a portable deck gun with an inch and a quarter tip here in front of the building; Side 'A', and direct it's water stream where the garage and main house intersect. We'll cut the fire off there and prevent its extension into the house."

Patrick acknowledged Shane's directive and walked off, shouting the order to his crew. A sudden squeal of tires from behind made him jump. He leapt out of the way, just missing being struck by a black Lincoln Navigator sliding off the driveway and tearing a four-foot divot in the grass.

Hassan stumbled from his car, leaving the engine running. "I must get in my house!"

Patrick grabbed him. "You can't go in there, Muhktar." The man smelled of alcohol.

"I've got to get my passport! I can't leave the country without it, and I left my laptop in the safe along with a great deal of cash. I have to have it all so I can go!"

About to respond, Patrick paused when another voice, a familiar one, sidetracked him.

Stanley Lowell stomped toward them as a pair of firefighters aimed a set of bright halogen lights at the burning garage. "What's going on here?"

Shane joined the group. "Garage fire, Chief. We're working to getting a handle on it."

"Lowell." Hassan elbowed past Patrick. "Tell your men I need my passport and PC. Now."

Lowell couldn't miss the menace in Muhktar's voice any more than the alcohol on his breath. And though he was Chief of Department, his rank meant nothing when on the fire ground. The rules were rock solid in the field of emergency services; unless the Chief assumed command, Shane, as incident commander, gave all the orders.

Lowell made his decision and laid a shaky hand on Shane's forearm to get his attention. "Uh, Meagher, this isn't an unusual request. We've gotten plenty of things for citizens during fire ground operations. How about it?"

"Chief." Shane removed Stanley's hand and took a step back. "I'm not sending anyone in there until it's completely safe. It won't be long. We contained it to just the garage because the Fire Station is so close; it didn't have much time to spread."

Behind them, a cloud of steam, water from the deck gun gouging at the seat of the fire, was spreading. It was a sure sign of a successful fire attack. Though loud, the hiss it made didn't keep Patrick from hearing a car door close. He spun to see his father and Walter Carson get out of a squad car.

"Dad, Major Carson, what are you doing here?"

Carson answered. "We have business to take care of, but it can wait. A couple of my officers are coming, and they're bringing someone you might know, Mr. Muhktar." He turned to Shane. "Let me know when this incident is under control, will you?"

Shane observed the few flames remaining. "Will do; it won't be long."

"Well, then, you can get my passport and laptop." Hassan weaved unsteadily toward his house, pointing at one of the first floor windows. "They're in there, in my safe. Here's the combination." He pulled out a scrap of paper, scribbled a series of numbers on it, and handed it to Patrick.

"You don't seem too upset with your house having caught fire, Mr. Muhktar. Any reason for that?" Carson didn't wait for an answer, instead turning in the direction of the piercing blue strobe lights bouncing up the driveway. He watched as Lieutenant Kristen Michaels got out of the squad car and approached them. He held up his hand at the second officer standing by the cruiser. "Vitton, you stay there and keep an eye on our guest."

The young officer signaled his compliance before leaning over and rapping on the rear window of the police car. "Hey pal, looks like you're stuck with me a little while longer. You okay back there?"

The manacled figure sat back against the seat saying nothing, the dome light in the roof of the caged interior shining off the top of his smooth head.

Chapter 50
Chatterton County, Virginia

With the fire extinguished, the house and surroundings were enveloped in a thick haze of smoke that made everyone at the scene resemble ghosts moving in a bluish-gray cloud. The crews had transitioned from fighting the blaze to salvage and overhaul operations, prioritizing the prevention of possible rekindling of what appeared to be a fire of suspicious origin.

As he sprayed water on smoldering hot spots, Patrick caught the restive look Walter Carson gave Stanley Lowell. In turn, the Fire Chief cut nervous glances at the Major, avoiding direct eye contact and inching closer to his car.

As Carson moved toward Shane, Patrick strained to listen in on their conversation.

"I take it the incident is under control?"

"I was about to announce it. Something I can do for you, Major?"

Carson shook his head, a dour look on his face, and motioned for Lieutenant Michaels to join him as he made his way over to where the Fire Chief was repeatedly toeing at some gravel.

"Stanley Lowell." Carson grimly shook his head. "You are an utter disgrace. It gives me great pleasure to place you under arrest and have you join Jackson Stamper in his cell. Lieutenant, get this piece of garbage out of my sight."

Hearing the mayor had been nabbed, Lowell offered no argument, backing away instead. The bumper of his car stopped his retreat as he spun away from the approaching policewoman. His outstretched hands landed on the fender near the door.

"Why, thank you for the cooperation." Michaels jammed her knee between his legs, kicked at his ankles and bent him over the car. "Keep them spread, Stan. You're under arrest." She started to pat him down.

"Hey!" He tried to turn around.

She shoved him, and his head bounced against the roof. "Be quiet, Stanley." The cuffs snapped into place. "You might as well get used to this position. It's a jail favorite. Let's go."

Patrick did a double take as his father blocked their path. He had seldom seen William so angry. "You'll have plenty of time now to think about Vincent Rigardo, you twisted son of a bitch."

Watching Stanley being led away, Patrick handed the hose line to one of his firefighters and walked toward Shane. On the way, he observed the inebriated and visibly agitated Muhktar, whose attention had turned from the house and was now focused on Lowell's arrest.

"I'll go in now for Muhktar's laptop and passport," Patrick said.

Shane nodded his approval.

Patrick secured his helmet's chinstrap and approached Hassan. "I'll need your keys."

Muhktar handed them over, then turned and made for the two squad cars. Lieutenant Michaels, on her way back to the house, stepped in front of him, extended her arm, and planted the palm of one hand firmly against his chest. The other she rested on the top of her holster. "You need to stay right here."

Patrick trotted off, entered the house and found a staircase, noting where smoke had banked halfway down the walls. He located the secured cabinet with ease, and once he'd retrieved the laptop and passport, took a few moments to look around. Although plush white carpeting had turned sooty-gray, the ceiling fan blades had not drooped, so smoke, but not heat, had extended into that part of the house.

He stepped outside and saw Hassan Muhktar heading his way. Wordlessly the man snatched and pocketed his passport, wrenched the laptop away and moved toward his Navigator.

Patrick, Shane, and Carson watched him hunch over the keyboard of his PC.

The brothers exchanged a tense look.

Without warning, Hassan thrust the laptop aside and leapt from the car. "It's gone...the account...the money...it's all gone!" he cried, moving toward Lieutenant Michaels once more. "Everything! There's nothing left." Intent on passing her to get to Hamadi in the back of the squad car, he ignored her warning to stay where he was.

Carson stepped forward. "Michaels, make sure he doesn't go anywhere."

Furious, Hassan protested as the policewoman drew him back to the Navigator.

"What are you going on about?" Carson said. "What money is gone?"

Hassan was too incensed to be evasive. "The Khorromshahr account!"

"Say what?"

Quickly, Patrick reached into the car for the laptop and scanned the screen. "There are two bank accounts listed here, Major; that's it. One for Criton Chemical and this one says Insurance Claims. There's a tidy sum in both. What is it that's missing, Muhktar?"

Wild eyed and railing incoherently, Hassan dodged Michaels and moved quickly toward Hamadi. He crashed full force into the policeman standing guard at the squad car. The collision sent Vitton sprawling against the side window, giving Hassan an opportunity to yank the Glock from his holster. As the cop pushed away from the car, Hassan hit him with the butt of the pistol and screamed at the passenger in the back seat, "You stole my money. Where is it, you..." he switched to Arabic, and Hamadi reared against the window, yelling back.

"*Gun!*" Carson shouted, and Michaels wheeled instinctively, pulling her own side arm.

Something Hamadi said must have pushed an already crazed Muhktar over the edge. He fired three shots from the semi-automatic into Hamadi's heart, shoulder and right eye. Then he turned and leveled the .40 caliber weapon at Carson.

At ten yards, four hollow point rounds from Michaels' gun slammed into Hassan Muhktar, killing him instantly.

EPILOGUE

Lips pursed above the rim of his *Worlds Greatest Golfer* mug, legs fully extended on the desk, William was startled by the phone's ring. Hot coffee spilled and soaked the box score of the Yankees latest win over the Sox, after half the cup ended up on his shirt. He jerked his loafers from the desktop and reached for the phone, knocking several files onto the floor.

"Son of a, uhh, Meagher and Son Investigative Services."

"I see your phone manners haven't improved. Maybe now that Patrick has retired and come on board, you should let him answer your business line?"

"Marcus." William pushed another pile of folders to the middle of the desk. "It's about time you called back. Tee time at Kingsmill tomorrow is at eight, and bring your wallet. Unless you're calling to bail out with some lame excuse?"

"Don't worry, I'll be there; your ass is mine. But you know, William, since you're the one who got that humongous insurance fraud recovery fee, you should be paying for my round."

William opened the humidor on his desk and plucked a plump Rafael Gonzalez from the stack. "Come, come, m'boy." He clipped the tip off the cigar and slid it under his nose. "I just read that article in the Post. You're the one who got promoted, and I'm sure it came with a raise." He thumbed the lighter and eased back.

302

Marcus laughed. "Speaking of money, even though Muhktar's accounts were frozen, I heard Nadia got all the proceeds from the sale of the estate. Hassan put it in her name to improve his tax situation. Funny how that worked out so well. What did she get—two million?"

"Two and change."

"Poetic justice. What's the latest with the trial? I've been too busy with the new job to follow it as I'd like."

"Stamper got his plea bargain, but he'll still end up with four to six at Greenville. It's pretty much the same for Lowell, and for good measure the judge hit him with a contempt citation also. He wasn't at all pleased with Stanley's perpetual whining that he was only following orders." William blew a series of perfect smoke rings.

"Did they indict Edward Tammerlin?"

William chuckled. "No, the Grand Jury figured it's not a crime to be sloppy and dull witted. If so, Eddie would be serving life without parole. He did give up Lowell, but Rob Dawbins, Chatterton's new Chief, fired him right off the bat. Speaking of pairs and justice—Hassan Muhktar and Jalal Hamadi—the government's book on them is as dead as they are?"

"Yes," Marcus said, "and everyone in law enforcement all the way down the line is glad of that. Rarely do we get such a tidy and well-deserved ending. Case closed."

"It's a shame the mastermind gets away scot free. I'm guessing the long arm of the law can't be reaching into Iran."

"That's not what I'm hearing. I have a feeling some news will be breaking on the internet just about the time we tee off."

William's feet landed on the floor. "About Abbas Muhktar?"

"Hey, Iraq and Iran trade more than goods, you know. The sheik was stopped at the airport in Tehran. It seems someone leaked the news, with evidence, to the Revolutionary Guard that he sold Criton products to the enemy to blow up his fellow citizens for profit. I wouldn't give two cents for his life."

"Someone, eh? And I'm sure you and the FBI wouldn't know a thing about that?"

"Hey, don't look at me. Simply a bunch of thieves getting their just reward." Marcus laughed softly. "How are Patrick and Shane?"

"They're SCUBA diving in the Cayman's."

"You know my friend, that was beyond generous, your splitting that recovery fee with them."

William flicked cigar ash into the tray. "What else would I do with $900,000? You'd have done the same."

***

"Grab me another Corona while you're up will you, Pat?" Shane stood on the dive platform on the rear deck of the *Devious Doins*, rinsing off their SCUBA gear. The chartered boat lay at anchor near Snipe Point off Little Cayman Island.

Patrick flipped a bottle at his brother and plopped onto a reclining lounger. "What time did you tell Maggie we'd be back at the resort?"

Shane caught the beer and snapped the cap off. "I said around seven, but with her taking Shannon and Colleen shopping with Colin, I don't think we have to worry about being very prompt."

"Man, can you believe this?" Patrick sighed. "I mean look at this view. That water is seventy feet deep; it looks like ten."

"No kidding." Shane's lime wedge fell to the deck as their bottles clinked together. "Sure is nice going first class all the way without worrying about money ever again."

"Nadia made it all possible, and of course, Vince." Patricks voice faded as he stared at several birds diving into the warm, turquoise water.

"I'm glad she got that estate money." Shane agreed. "She told Dad she wanted to take care of Farid Barmeen's mother financially. Apparently they had a rough time of it, even before he was murdered. It couldn't have worked out better. Well, you know what I mean. She gets a good chunk of change and we divvy up and anonymously donate the cash from Hassan's Khorromshahr account to all those charities for wounded vets and such."

Patrick continued to gaze wistfully as soft white puffs of clouds skimmed along the horizon. "Yeah, I suppose so, but it can never replace losing Vince."

Shane could read his brothers turbulent thoughts. He'd had to work through many of his own. "We did the right thing, Pat. Hassan was killing our soldiers and we may never have discovered any of this if it hadn't been for Vince, and he murdered him, too. Those G.I.s deserve the cash and no one will ever know it was us. And as far as I'm concerned, though we only planned to steal Hassan's money, he and that son of a bitch Hamadi got what was coming to them in the end. Let it go."

The boat caught a sudden swell and the scent of cinnamon and roses drifted on a shifting wind as Shane's words mixed with the familiar fragrance. Sniffing at the air, Patrick abruptly lifted his head at the striking serendipity of the moment. Abbey, he thought ... she approved as well.

ACKNOWLEDGEMENTS

Books are difficult enough to write, this one especially so as it is dedicated to my late son, Matthew, who passed away while it was being written. The novel could not have been completed without the loving support of Matt's sister, my daughter, Kristen. What greater acknowledgement could there be than the love of our children?

A huge thank you to my brothers and sisters in the Fire and Emergency Services everywhere and, closest to home, the Chesterfield Fire & EMS Department. Everything we did, everything you still do, remains a source of inspiration. I must also mention Fire Chief Robert L. Eanes, my department's original Commander and the man who hired me. It remains my honor to have served.

A special shout-out goes to my good friend and canoe-paddling sidekick, Division Chief Mike Pennino, a great sounding board and devil's advocate around many a campfire. Fire Thieves came to life thanks to friends like Mike, and my long suffering golf partner and chipping instructor, Lieutenant Bruce Simmons.

Thank you also to Mary Rosenblum of New Writers Interface for her guidance and critique. More than instrumental, her belief in this project was the original wellspring of my enthusiasm.

But the biggest thank you is unquestioningly reserved for my superb editor, herself an award-winning writer, Jennifer Skutelsky. Her knowledge, skill and experience in every facet of the production of this novel, were far and away the reason it even exists.

My final acknowledgement is for each of you who read *Fire Thieves*. It would be little more than words on a page without your support; it's just that simple.